Jaylin:
A Naughty Aftermath

Naughty Series

Jaylin:
A Naughty Aftermath

Naughty Series

Brenda Hampton

www.urbanbooks.net

Urban Books, LLC
300 Farmingdale Road, NY-Route 109
Farmingdale, NY 11735

Jaylin: A Naughty Aftermath Naughty Series
Copyright © 2019 Brenda Hampton

ISBN 13: 978-1-62286-219-1
ISBN 10: 1-62286-219-8

First Mass Market Printing December 2019
First Trade Paperback Printing February 2019
Printed in the United States of America

10 9 8 7 6 5 4 3 2 1

This is a work of fiction. Any references or similarities to actual events, real people, living or dead, or to real locales are intended to give the novel a sense of reality. Any similarity in other names, characters, places, and incidents is entirely coincidental.

Distributed by Kensington Publishing Corp.
Submit Orders to:
Customer Service
400 Hahn Road
Westminster, MD 21157-4627
Phone: 1-800-733-3000
Fax: 1-800-659-2436

Chapter 1

Jaylin

The word was change. Everybody wanted me to be a changed man, but when all was said and done, fuck what anyone else wanted. What mattered in my life was what I wanted, what my heart desired, and as of today, my heart was still where it had always been. That was with Nokea. Unfortunately, though, her heart wasn't with me. It was on another journey, had taken a different path. Per my own request, she had taken the steering wheel away from me and started to drive her own life. During that time, she met a man, Dr. Travis L. Cooper, who somehow or someway managed to sweep her off her feet. There was no question that Nokea had been swept off her feet before, but this time was different. This time, she wasn't in a relationship to seek revenge against me. She wasn't doing this to hurt me or make me jealous. She genuinely loved Travis, and to be more honest than I had ever been before, her love for him was a serious blow to me.

For the past few years, I'd had my ups and downs. I witnessed Nokea fall in love with another man right before my own eyes. She had changed in so many ways. The way she lit up when he came around spoke volumes. Their affection for each other was on display every time I was in their presence. He respected her, and she respected him. In the beginning of their relationship, I'd made a few attempts to keep our family together. I put up a fight, but eventually, I lost the battle. Nokea made it clear that she would never live under the same roof with me again, and as for sex, she'd made a decision to give herself to one man and one man only. That man was Travis. I was shut out and had been out for a very long time.

The bright side was we remained close friends. We put our children first, and that was important to me. Our tedious arguments about where they would live, who was responsible for this or that, everything was all settled. For the majority of the time all four kids were with me and Nanny B. My oceanfront estate in Florida was spacious enough for everybody. The children made a choice to be there, probably because I spoiled the shit out of them. There was never a dull moment in my house. I wouldn't have it any other way. Nokea came by often during the week, and on many weekends they stayed with her. The same routine applied to Scorpio, who was the mother of Justin and Mackenzie. Scorpio came by to spend time with the kids during the week as well. On opposite weekends as Nokea, the kids were with her. So, in a nutshell, the situation with our children worked out for everybody. My only problem was Travis. I had to admit that there was a tinge of jealousy inside of me. But unlike I'd done in the past when things didn't go according to my plans, I refused to interfere. I didn't want to tell Nokea how I truly felt inside. As long as she was happy, I guess, so was I.

With soft jazz music thumping in the background, I cruised down the street in my half-roof Maybach. It was white and loaded with luxury accessories that cost me a fortune. More than anything, it was a custom-made gift I had purchased for myself. I'd been working my ass off. Investing in real estate was the best thing I could have ever done. I owned property in almost every major city. Houses and condos from Miami to the Cayman Islands. I even built a new home around the outskirts of St. Louis, the place where I was born and half-assed raised. As of yet, nobody hadn't officially moved into the house, but it was fully furnished. Nokea's parents had parties there occasionally, and whenever I visited that was where I stayed. The kids loved it there, and Nanny B utilized the place when she went to St. Louis to chill with her sister. Owning property and land had become my priority. As a black man, I intended to leave my mark and have as much property and land as I could, for many generations to come. Therefore, whenever I was dead and gone, my family would be riding high. All of those houses and acres of land would be put to good use, thanks to me. I finally woke the fuck up. So did my right-hand man, Shane Alexander. In actuality, he was the one who moved to Florida and helped me kick this shit off. I'd made him a very wealthy man. He was probably the only person on this earth who I trusted with my life.

As I waited for the red light to change, a tall, slender, prissy woman paraded across the street with her poodle. He looked to be every bit the show dog, and his head was held up damn near as high as hers. Swaying palm trees shaded most of the street, and taking advantage of the eighty-five-degree weather, fit joggers got in their daily exercise. Many paused to take a glimpse at my ride, and behind the lightly tinted sunglasses I wore, I peeped my surroundings. From the rear-view mirror, I saw a woman who was swerving in and out of lanes in a Porsche pull up closely behind me. Since the right lane was clear, she veered over next to me. I hastily shifted my head, only because she was inches from tagging the back of my car. She lowered her window. A bright smile was on her freckled face.

"Nice car," she said, chewing gum and showing every bit of her pearly whites. "I was enjoying the scenery, if that's okay."

My eyes narrowed behind the sunglasses that shielded my steel gray eyes. My fingertips brushed against my trimmed goatee. I moistened my bottom lip with the tip of my tongue. If only she knew what I was thinking. I didn't appreciate how close her car was to mine, so it was in my best interest to say what troubled my mind.

"Look all you want, but if you hit this mutha-fucka, there won't be a damn thing for you to smile about. Pull your steering wheel to the right and keep it moving."

Her eyes bugged, and her mouth dropped wide open. Before she could say anything, I pressed on the accelerator, speeding away. I hated to be an asshole, but even though therapy had helped me calm down a little, I was still being me. Arrogant? No. Confident? Hell yes. Out of control? Never. Well, maybe sometimes.

A cool breeze stirred in my car, and as the sun peeked through the palm trees, it caramelized my light skin even more. I was ready to get to my destination, but right as I approached the next light, the call light came on. I hit the button to answer the phone.

"Jaylin Rogers."

"Where are you?" Nokea inquired in a panicky voice. "I thought you would be here by now."

"I'm on my way. I should be there in about ten or fifteen minutes. You told me the fashion show didn't start until six. It's only four, so what's the rush?"

"I also told you I needed some help. It's crazy around here. It seems as if everybody is in a mood to be late."

"I'm not late at all. Besides, you already know from experience what happens prior to these shows. It always seems hectic, but after things get started everything falls into place. Calm down, all right? I'll be there in a minute to help you with whatever you need help with."

"Thank you. I'll see you soon. Come to the penthouse suite first. That's where I'll probably be."

Nokea was always on edge the day of her fashion shows. All week, she'd had me putting my business on hold just to help her. This was the third fashion show she'd had. Each time, they got better and better. She turned her business into an empire. In less than two years it was already worth millions. She had a good start, thanks to me. But I couldn't take credit for all of the hard work she'd done. She, along with her team of designers, was off the chain.

I reached the overcrowded, plush hotel almost twenty minutes later. As soon as I stepped out of the car, my polished, two-tone, full-grain leather shoes hit the pavement. My gray, cuffed Canali slacks hung over my shoes, and with a black, crisp linen shirt on, richness defined me. I tossed my keys to the valet guy, who seemed real nervous.

"Just bring it back to me in the same condition I'm giving it to you," I said, referring to my car.

"Will do, sir. Definitely will do."

With a smooth and confident stride, I went inside, looking around at the busy hotel where Nokea decided to have her fashion show. People in business suits breezed by me, and there was a long line of individuals waiting in reservations. The smell of cigar smoke permeated the air, and with so many noisy kids running around, it could've been a daycare. The fashion show, however, was being set up in a private area, and before I went to the elevator, I took a quick detour to go look at the exquisite room that was almost complete.

The runway was blue and silver with what looked to be tiny diamonds embedded in it. Several rows of wingback chairs surrounded it, and the walls were mostly covered with silky, ceiling-to-floor drapes. Crystal chandeliers lit up the whole room, including Nokea's name, which was scripted on a wave wall with columns on each side. Blue laser lights also zoomed in on her name, and right at the entry was a circular bar for everyone's drinking pleasures. Nokea had mentioned something about confetti raining down after the show was over. But when I looked up, I didn't see anything. I was quite impressed by how everything came together. There was no one, not one person, prouder of her than me.

I headed to the elevator with many eyes traveling with me. My Rolex with a big face filled with glistening diamonds was visible, and my custom attire was always tailored to fit my tall, muscular frame. I entered the elevator, immediately infusing it with musky cologne. The two women to my left were all stares, and a hating-ass white man to my right had the audacity to cut his eyes at me. I chuckled a bit as he gave the evil eye to the women who didn't dare look in his direction.

He was so pissed that, as soon as the elevator opened, he made a speedy exit.

"What was his problem?" one of the women said. "Weird, man, really weird."

I didn't respond. I never did respond, because I had experienced hate at a level that not too many people had ever seen. Over time, the hate grew to new heights. I, however, became motivated by individuals who wished like hell they could be me: the one, the only, Jaylin Jerome Rogers.

The elevator opened at the top floor. The second I made my exit, I could see things were chaotic. Numerous slim and voluptuous models crowded the hallways, gossiping. There were so many cameras flashing that my head started to spin. The one thing I didn't like was too much attention. I hated for people to halt my steps and ask me questions. I was a very private man, and some of these functions Nokea conducted opened the door for too many people to be in our business. I tried my best to make it to the penthouse suite without being questioned. But after a few bold steps in that direction, a reporter who was there to cover the event stopped me.

"Hello, Mr. Rogers," she said with her face too close to mine. "Have you had the pleasure of seeing any of the attire your wife will showcase this evening? Or are you in the dark like the rest of us are?"

One of the models who knew that Nokea and I were no longer married replied to the reporter's dumb-ass question. "Nokea is not his wife, and I'm sure he's in the dark like we all are."

She'd answered for me, so I proceeded toward the door to the penthouse. The reporter also knew Nokea wasn't my wife. She just figured that her question would get a response from me. It almost did. I didn't think she would've appreciated my answer.

I managed to work my way through the crowd, but was stopped numerous times to take pictures.

"Over here, Jaylin," Jazz said. She was one of Nokea's top designers. "We need you over here with the ladies. This photo is for the magazine. Pleeeease."

I was a little moody, but only for Nokea was I willing to do this. I stood in the center, while several of the giddy models surrounded me. The cameras started to flash, but Jazz waved her hands in the air, telling the photographers to pause.

"Wait one minute, okay?" She rushed up to me, removing my sunglasses. "If you don't mind, I want those alluring eyes in the picture too. Smile, Jaylin. With all of these lovely women surrounding you, you need to smile."

Many of the models laughed, and just for the hell of it, I smiled. Jazz blew me a kiss, and after the picture-taking festivities were done, she gave my sunglasses back and thanked me.

"No problem," I said. "Where's Nokea?"

"She's upstairs in the penthouse. I think she's been looking for you."

I had been trying to get there, but that was a difficult task. When I had finally made my way inside, the penthouse was jam-packed with many professional-looking people I had never seen. I heard Nokea call my name, so I swung around with my hands dipped into my pockets. She was standing on the upper level, looking down from the glass balcony.

"Can you please come up here and help me?" she asked. "I really need you, now."

I spoke to a few people who said hello to me, and I tackled the circular staircase that led to numerous rooms. On my way up, I heard the whispers, saw the stares. But the only one I wanted to take notice was Nokea. She stood in front of two models, nibbling at her nails. All she had on was a soft cotton robe that cut above her knees. Her hair was in an asymmetrical bob that was long, feathered, and flipped on one side, short on the other. The minimal makeup she wore was on like artwork, and her long lashes made her look even prettier. Every time I saw her, my heart pounded just a little bit faster. Thoughts of our long lives together were always fresh in my mind. I would never settle for anything less. She would always be Mrs. Rogers in my book.

My somber mood changed fast, especially when Nokea turned her head, smiling at me.

"Look at you." Her eyes scanned me from head to toe. "Come over here and give me a hug before I put you to work."

I removed my hands from my pockets to give her a hug. Her petite frame close to my towering frame felt perfect. "What's up, boss lady? What do you need me to do?"

She backed away from me, releasing a deep sigh. "First of all, I'm so worried about my baby, Jaylene. I wanted to go to her gymnastics competition, and I'm so mad that they scheduled it on the same day as this. Do you think she's upset with me?"

"No. She's not upset with me either, and it's the first time we've missed her competition. Nanny B is there with her. So is your mother. They're going to record the entire thing so you won't miss a minute. Now, what's next?"

"I need you to make a few phone calls for me. The last time I checked, the people who were supposed to do those confetti drops hadn't shown up. I also need it to be much brighter in that room, so I need to get some extra lighting set up quickly. Lastly, the waiting room for the models is too small. If you could find the manager and ask if he could open up another room for us, that would be great. Other than that, I still need to get dressed, I still have to get all of those outfits over there on those racks downstairs, and I haven't even heard from your son. I know he's with Kyle and his parents at the amusement park, but why isn't he answering his phone? Have you spoken to him?"

"Yes. He dropped his phone in some water. It's not working anymore. He's spending the night at his friend's house, and you need to stop all of this unnecessary worrying. Give me the number to the people who are supposed to hook up the confetti. I'll go talk to the manager about the lights and using an additional room. As for those clothes, with all these people in here, you need to tell them to cease all this yakking and start moving some of this shit downstairs. I didn't . . ."

I paused as Nokea peeked over my shoulder, showing her dimples. When I turned my head, the good ol' doctor was coming up from behind, dressed in a casual blazer and slacks. He said a quick, "What's up," to me before reaching out to embrace Nokea.

"Sorry I'm late," Travis said with a wide smile. His dark chocolate skin, meticulously cut, short afro, and light brown eyes turned many heads too. With those big, white teeth, though, one would assume he was a dentist instead of a doctor. He continued to explain his tardiness to Nokea. "Late because I got tied up on an important phone call at home."

Nokea laughed. "I guess that means you were talking to your mother."

"Yes, for almost a whole thirty minutes, nonstop. She told me to tell you good luck tonight. She also wants you to call her when you get a moment."

"Will do. I think I already know what she wants."

Travis leaned in to kiss Nokea. This time, it was his tall frame instead of mine against her. They indulged as if I weren't even standing there. When he lowered his hand to take a light squeeze of her ass, I swear I wanted to grab his damn hand and break it. Nokea backed away from him, then wiped his lips to remove the lip gloss she'd put on them.

"Sorry about that." She pecked his lips again. "I don't want you around here looking like one of the models. But with that being said, I need your help too."

Travis rubbed his hands together. "Use me, baby. Whatever you need me to do, I'm here."

I had to intervene. "The number, if you don't mind. Give me the number so I can call about the confetti."

That fast, Nokea had changed her mind. "I'll get Travis to call, but please go see about the lights and talk to the manager for me. Thanks, Jaylin. I owe you one, okay?"

She owed me a lot, but now wasn't the time for me to go there. I walked away, and within the hour, the room had been brightened, and another room had been unlocked for the models to use. Several people started to bring down numerous racks of clothing, and when I saw Travis pulling one of the racks toward the room, I turned to look away. He came right up to me, patting me on the back.

"Jaylin, I didn't get a chance to say much earlier, but I hope all is well. Nokea has been so excited about this day, and to be honest, I'll be glad when it's over so she can finally get some much-needed rest. I don't think she's had any sleep for the past two days. I keep telling her that's not good, but you know how ambitious women are."

"I do know how ambitious some women are, but I know more about how determined *and* ambitious Nokea is. I'm sure she appreciates you helping out. It appears that she needs all the help she can get."

"I agree," Travis said, nodding. "Because there are definitely some lazy people around here. My patience is running thin with all of this gossiping. If the ladies would come out of that room, maybe they could get something done."

I certainly agreed with Travis's assessment. There were plenty of slackers lurking around. Too many pictures were being taken, and in my opinion, it was time to get this show on the road.

Travis walked away, and just like me, he got busy helping Nokea make this a memorable and successful event. I was finally able to take a seat, and with a glass of Rémy in my hand, I looked up and saw Mackenzie enter the room. Scorpio was with her. As soon as they spotted me, they headed my way. I put the glass on a round table beside me before standing to greet them.

"Hi, Daddy," Mackenzie said, wrapping her arms around my waist.

I kissed her forehead, hugging her back. Every time I saw her, I couldn't believe she was already twelve. "Hi, sweetheart. Nokea is waiting for you. She's in the room over there, so go see if she needs your help with anything. I'll save you a seat next to me."

Mackenzie darted off to go find Nokea. Scorpio stood with her arms crossed. She rocked a pair of hip-hugging, tight jeans that could barely contain her shapely, meaty ass. The strapless top she wore showed her toned midriff, and with stiletto pumps on, she was nearly eye level with me. Her wavy hair was parted down the middle and brushed into a thick ponytail in the back. Nude gloss made her lips shine, her brows were arched perfectly, and like Nokea, Scorpio's long lashes added beauty.

"You know I'm not staying," she said. "I have a lot to do before my big day, and I need to get back home before Justin wakes up."

"I take it Loretta is there with him, right?"

"Yes, and so is Mario. I hope you still plan to come see the new house with us on Friday. If you're unable to make it, please let me know now."

"I will be at your penthouse bright and early Friday morning. And when you get home, tell Loretta not to give Justin any more damn soda. I know she's giving it to him, because that's the first thing he asks for when he comes to my house."

"I told her about that soda. But he persuades her to give him whatever he wants. One can only wonder where he gets that from."

I had no comment. All of my kids were the product of me.

"It looks spectacular in here." Scorpio examined the room. "Nokea has really outdone herself. Tell her I said congrats and let her know that when I get a chance, I'll stop by her shop to see what's new."

I wasn't sure why Scorpio wanted me to tell Nokea, especially since they conversed a lot. It wasn't as if they were best friends or anything close to it, but for the sake of the kids, they got along well. They stayed committed to their weekends with the kids, and whenever one of them had something important to do, they made plans to work things out. I appreciated their efforts. It damn sure made my life a whole lot easier to have my children's mothers getting along.

Travis came in, strolling alongside another rack of clothes to the room where the models were. He waved and smiled at Scorpio. She waved back.

"Every time I see him, he reminds me of Lamman Rucker. He got that lean and tight upper body. And his smile is very charming. What do you think? Do you think he looks like Lamman too?"

"I don't know nor do I give a damn who he looks like. I do know that he may need some Valvoline motor oil to tackle those dry-ass lips he got."

Scorpio laughed and threw her hand back at me. "Ooooh, you need to stop hating, Jaylin. I can't believe you're hating on that man like that. And, uh, those lips would be considered thick and juicy to me."

"I don't hate, baby. I only speak the truth. Besides, why do you care who he looks like? All you need to be concerned about is Mr. Rico Suave, Mario, and your wedding. Are you almost done with everything?"

Scorpio sighed. "Yeah, right. I have so much to do. That's why I can't stay, so have fun and don't forget to tell Nokea what I said. By the way, and before I forget"—she moved closer and whispered softly in my ear—"Travis is fine, but he doesn't have anything, not one single thing on you. I would take a handsome man like you with money and a big . . . well, don't let me go there today. And don't get happy about my opinion, because when it comes to my man, the Latin lover, you and Travis fall waaaay short."

I cocked my head back with a smirk on my face. "When you're ready to come fully correct, let me know. Until then, you'd better tell Nokea yourself about visiting her shop. Knowing me, I'll forget."

Scorpio laughed while swaying her hips from side to side as she sauntered away. I didn't think it was possible, but she had gotten even sexier. It was confirmed by the heads of many men turning, hypnotized, as she walked by them. I guessed her twenty-carat diamond ring was being ignored. Mario had spent a fortune on that ring. I predicted it cost way more than the one I had given to her years ago when I'd proposed.

It was funny how things didn't work out for us, but they had come together for her and Mario. From what I could see, things had been looking up for Miss Valentino. She was getting married, again, next weekend. I'd had some issues with her man, but unlike Mackenzie's biological father, Bruce, who Scorpio was once married to, Mario seemed much better. My concerns revolved around my kids. I had to be sure that Mario was good people. After a while, he started to prove himself to be just that. I couldn't say I considered him a friend or anything like that, but he and Scorpio had my blessings. Yet again, she had hooked up with a wealthy man.

He was deeply in love with Scorpio, but I wasn't so sure about her. She said she loved him, but from my perspective, I thought she loved his money. Mario was sitting on more paper than me. That in itself made her wake up and rethink some things, like who she wanted to be with in the future. We still had a connection, but sex between us wasn't happening either. It had been years since I'd hit that, but make no mistake about it, I hadn't shut down my sex game completely. Every now and then, I tampered with females I'd met here or there. Nothing ever serious, just something to satisfy my sexual needs.

Right after I took a seat again, Mackenzie exited the room where Nokea was. She complained about being tired, so she sat next to me with her head resting on my arm. As we waited for the show to start, I kept thinking about how protective I was of my kids. LJ, my nine-year-old son, was lucky that I let him spend the night over at his friend's house. His friend's parents were cool. I cleared them through an extensive background check, as I had done with Nokea's man Travis, as well as Mario.

Travis had a clean record. His goody-two-shoes ass had only gotten a speeding ticket in his early twenties. As for Mario, he loved to box yet never made it to the big leagues. His family ran a successful Italian restaurant business, but whenever a substantial amount of money was involved, there was always some kind of crooked shit going on behind the scenes. Most of it was dealing with Mario's father. He was into some Mafia shit that made me kind of leery of everything. Mario and I talked about it one day, and after our conversation, I knew that family was important to him, including Scorpio and our kids. To sum it up, business was business, and Mario couldn't do a damn thing about the things his family was involved with. All he did was reap the benefits. Whenever his father died, Mario would inherit billions.

I called Nanny B to see what Jaylene was up to, but I got no answer. I left a message, and finally, the fashion show got underway. The cameras started flashing again, and as the models made their appearances, there was a bunch of thunderous applause, oohs, and aahs. Several celebrities were in the room, but I was never the kind of person to make a big deal over anyone. That was for the media to do, and there were plenty of them on hand to report on the success of Nokea's show.

Everybody was tuned in, and as I looked over at Travis and his brother, Greg, they kept whispering at each other and shifting their eyes in my direction. I wasn't sure what that was about, but I was surprised to see Greg there because Nokea said he and Travis didn't really get along. If Shane were here, I was sure he would've confronted them. He didn't like mess, nor did he appreciate hating-ass black men. He and his wife, Tiffanie, were on a long-needed vacation in Paris. They'd been having some martial problems ever since their son had died suddenly from a heart defect. They were devastated. But instead of coming together, they drifted apart. I wanted them to get back on track, so I purchased the tickets for them just so they could get away from all that was transpiring around them and spend some quality time together. They weren't expected home until next week, and for Shane's sake, I hoped he managed to work things out.

The fashion show went on for almost a half hour. Yet again, I was impressed by the unique pieces Nokea and her designers had put together. It was clothing I had never seen before. Real colorful and very shimmery. The models were on point. They were very professional and sexy, too. Especially the ones with curves. Nokea's place had been a hit because she focused on creating clothing for women in all sizes, not just a few. The crowd couldn't get enough.

Finally, the confetti started to rain on everybody, and it was a wrap. Presenting nothing but classiness, Nokea sashayed down the runway in glittery peep-toe heels and a sapphire blue silk dress that melted on every single curve on her body. The dress cut right above her knees, her back was completely out, and as she turned around and waved, all I wanted to do was massage her P-shaped, ample ass that was perfect. She used her finger to move her hair away from her doe-shaped eyes that were filled with joyful tears.

"Thanks, everyone," she kept saying. "Thank you all so much."

The crowd stood, and the room erupted with applause. Mackenzie was next to me, whistling. She and the young lady sitting next to her kept talking the whole time. It was all about fashion. It was no secret that Nokea had inspired her.

"Sit down, please," Nokea said. "Everyone sit down so I can take a few minutes to thank certain people for helping me pull this off."

The crowd calmed, and we all took our seats. Nokea started to thank everyone, including her models, the designers, the photographers, Mackenzie, she went on and on. Then she got to her special thanks. If it had not been for "him," she couldn't have pulled this off.

She looked at Travis. "Sweetheart, come up here, please."

Travis stood, buttoned his blazer, and smiled as many people applauded. When he stepped on the runway, he eased his arm around Nokea's waist, and she locked hers around his.

"I just have to say this," Nokea said, continuing her praises. "I have been a total wreck for the past several weeks leading up to this. But Travis has been there with me every step of the way. He's encouraged me so much, and his prayers are exactly what I needed. So from the bottom of my heart," she said, gazing into his eyes and expressing her love, "thank you. I love you, and I thank you for always being there for me."

I couldn't even explain what I was feeling right now. Did she really have to go there? Where in the fuck were my thanks? I guessed I wasn't going to get it, because after Travis pecked her lips and everyone applauded again, the show was over. Done. I didn't bother to hang around. Since Mackenzie said she was tired, we left.

Within the hour, we were home. The house was quiet because Mackenzie and I were the only ones there. Jaylene and Nanny B wouldn't be back until tomorrow, the same for LJ. Needing some fresh air, I pushed a button that slid the glass doors aside in the living room. The infinity pool with crystal-clear blue water extending into the horizon was in my view. I gazed outside for a minute before pouring a glass of Rémy, which often calmed me. I took a sip then plopped on the sofa with disgust etched on my face. I had a lot of shit pent up inside of me, and for quite some time, I'd kept it all in. In the past, Nokea always accused me of meddling in her relationships. Claimed her life would've been different if I'd stayed out of her affairs. Said I griped too much about this or that, so I learned to keep my mouth shut and just go with the flow. That was hard for me to do. I could feel it was just a matter of time before I exploded.

Even while we were in the car, Mackenzie questioned my silence. She knew me all too well, and when she inquired about my thoughts pertaining to the show, I simply said I'd had a good time and the show was outstanding.

I looked at her as she was on her way upstairs. "If you're bored, do you want to go to the theater room and watch a movie with me?" I asked.

"Not really, Daddy. We stayed up late last night helping Mommy with some stuff for the wedding. I just want to go finish the book I was reading and then go to sleep."

"All right. Come give me a hug before you go. And don't forget to say your prayers."

Mackenzie came over to the sofa, giving me a hug. After she headed upstairs, I chilled on the sofa for about forty-five minutes or so, finishing my drink. I then tackled the stairs to my bedroom, which took up nearly 2,000 square feet on the second floor. Many renovations had been done, and the huge windows surrounding my bedroom provided a clear view of the sandy beaches and the murmuring Atlantic Ocean's hypnotic waves, which helped me sleep. I walked past my California-king bed that had a tufted headboard and was dressed with black-and-white satin sheets. The French doors to the balcony were cracked, so I opened them wide, hearing a whooshing sound from the ocean hitting the sand. Seagulls squawking could be heard from afar.

It was time to relax, so I stripped naked and closed the draperies to give myself some privacy. I plopped on the bed, lying flat on my back. My arm rested across my forehead as I gazed at the high ceiling, which viewed the dark sky. I didn't want Nokea to be on my mind, but she definitely was. There was no woman, none whatsoever, who could help me shake my feelings for her. I'd tried but had been very unsuccessful. And the thing that bothered me the most was that I feared she had fallen out of love with me.

I sat up and reached for my phone. Business calls were booming, but I wasn't about to deal with any business tonight. Instead, I turned on the TV, delving into one of my favorite shows, *Power*. Minutes later, my cell phone rang. I looked to see who it was. It was a young lady I'd met nearly a month ago. Her name was Kenyatta. I'd only spoken to her twice since we'd had sex after a business function one day. She'd called several times, but I had been so busy that I just didn't have time to hook up with her again. I sighed before tapping the TALK button on my phone.

"Jaylin Rogers."

"You are the most difficult person ever to get in touch with. Is that on purpose?"

I lifted my dick, examining it and thinking about how well she had polished it with her mouth that night. Sex wasn't necessarily on my mind tonight, with the exception of it being with Nokea.

"Not on purpose," I said. "I'm just busy. You already know how I do it."

"I do, and I'm glad I caught up with you tonight. I was trying to find out if or when we're going to schedule some more time to see each other again."

As I was getting ready to answer her question, the doorbell rang. "We can schedule some time, but can I hit you back later tonight or tomorrow?"

"Sure, Jaylin. Don't forget."

I laid my phone on the bed then picked up the remote to switch the TV to the outdoor security cameras. I saw Nokea and Travis standing outside. Not wanting the doorbell to wake Mackenzie, I rushed down the stairs to open the doors. When I pulled them open, almost immediately Nokea's and Travis's eyes dropped below my tight abs to the goodness down below. Nokea quickly pivoted to face Travis. His eyes traveled to my face. I could tell from his blank expression that he wasn't happy about me boldly exposing my nakedness in front of his woman. But she knew better than to turn away from me. Shame on her.

"Don't insult me," I said to Nokea. "It ain't nothing you haven't felt, touched, licked, or tasted before, so stop pretending."

Nokea slowly turned around, shocked and seething as she stared at me in awe with her mouth open. Travis, on the other hand, took two steps back, maybe three.

"No, don't insult me," he barked. "It would be nice if you would have the decency to put on some clothes before we enter your house."

I nodded. "You're right. This is my house, and I haven't invited anyone to come inside. If either of you have a problem with the skin I'm in, that's too fucking bad. Good night, and come back tomorrow when I may be fully dressed."

I pushed on the doors, closing them abruptly. The doorbell rang again, but when I opened the doors, Travis stormed away like a punk. It was no secret that I didn't like his ass, and even though Nokea pretended as if things were all good, she knew I didn't go around being fake with people. She stood defensively with her arms folded, eyes shooting daggers that fired at me from every angle.

"Is Jaylene here?" Her tone was sharp. "I hope not, since you're walking around the house like that."

"My body looks pathetic, I know. So does your face, especially when you come here acting as if the sight of me sickens you. But to answer your question, Jaylene is not here. She'll be home tomorrow. All you had to do was call your mother or Nanny B to find that out." I leaned against the door, posing as I crossed my arms. "Now, is there anything else, and do you still want to come inside?"

"Nokea," Travis yelled. "Come on! I'm ready to go."

A smirk was on my face. I was so sure he was ready. He wouldn't dare allow Nokea to stay much longer. She ignored Travis while struggling to keep her eyes focused on my face.

"Maybe I should have called my mother, but oh, well. I wanted to stop by and thank you, again, for all of your help with the fashion show. You left before I could say thanks."

"You had plenty of time to thank me, but I assume you didn't want anybody's feelings to get hurt by mentioning me. Travis wouldn't approve, but it's all good, baby. You're welcome, and before you get yelled at again, allow me to return to my bedroom and encourage you to have a good night."

This time when I closed the doors, Nokea walked away. My only thought was, *fuck her and that sorry-ass thanks*. It had come too late. I no longer needed it.

Chapter 2

Scorpio

I was too smart. Too beautiful. Too sexy. Too creative in the bedroom. Too caring, and too in love with myself, and with my children, for me to accept a man who wasn't worth millions. In return, I gave that man all of me and then some. Jay Baby could vouch for that. Lord knows I'd been down with him for a very long time. I had his back, and he had mine. While we decided a few years ago to cut the sex, we still managed to have a respectful relationship, especially for the sake of our children.

Without sex, I found myself loving him even more. I looked forward to our family days together, and most of the time, Jaylin was a joy to be around. He was still overly confident, still in control of what he was allowed to control, still a bit demanding when it came to our kids, but I could deal with that. I could deal with his mood swings, too, and at the end of the day, there was no question in my mind that Jaylin Rogers loved me as best he could.

But this was a new day. His love wasn't good enough. I needed more. I needed a man to hold me at night and make me feel safe and secure, and yes, I needed a wealthy man who could take good care of me. I needed to know that I was his number one. Jaylin could never offer me that, and I would be a damn fool if I opted to be with another man who wasn't on the same level as him. There was too much power in this V for me to settle for anything less. Thankfully, I met a man who offered me nearly everything my heart desired.

Mario S. Pezzano was my new man and soon-to-be husband. Tomorrow was our big day. My wedding planner was the absolute best. Her services had cost a pretty penny, but her price was so worth it. My sister, Leslie, and her kids were on their way to Florida. So were a few of my other friends from St. Louis who were only coming to my wedding to be nosy. Jaylin, Nokea, Nanny B, Jackson, my uncle, and the kids would be there. So would my housemaid, Loretta, and a few other ladies we hung out with from time to time. The other guests were all on Mario's side of the family. We were expecting over 400 people tomorrow. I was getting a little nervous, but

I hoped that my bachelorette party this evening would help put me at ease.

Until then, Mario and I made plans to show Jaylin the mansion we would soon call home. He'd made a big fuss about where the kids would live. We didn't mind giving him a tour, not one bit. Besides, I couldn't wait to give him the keys back to the penthouse he'd purchased for me years ago. He said he was going to put it up for sale. Hopefully, he'd get most of his money back. I predicted that he would.

Our new place was only fifteen minutes away from Jaylin's house. It was nearly 21,000 square feet, had six bedrooms, seven and a half baths, and two kitchens that would be utilized more by Loretta than by me. The moment I saw the place, I had to have it. I was sold on the grand staircase that traveled from the basement to the upper level. The marble floors throughout made the place look fit for a king and queen. The master suite was to die for, and the kids' rooms were even more spacious than the ones they'd had at Jaylin's house. Mario wanted me to have whatever I wanted. My happiness was important to him. He also had me spoiled rotten. When it came to proving his love for me, he had gone above and beyond my requirements. In addition to that, we had a fun and exciting relationship. I

loved his family, and most of them, not all, loved
me too. Maybe because I had Italian blood running through my veins. I was sure that was why
many of them approved.

I was standing in the kitchen, drinking cranberry juice when Jaylin came in. A big problem I always had with him was that he never
knocked, just came right in. Mario had a problem with that as well. That was why after we got
married he wanted us to have our own place
where only he and I had keys.

I put the glass on the counter, looking at Jaylin as he stood casually dressed in jeans and a
silver, soft, cotton shirt that rested on the muscles on his carved chest and biceps. His healthy,
curly hair was sharply lined, his sexy goatee
suited his chin to perfection, and his soft-to-the-
touch lips were made for sucking. His attitude,
though, sucked.

"We need to hurry this up because I have somewhere else I need to be by noon," he said. "Where
is Mario?"

"He said we could meet him at the house. I
tried to call you, but you didn't answer your
phone."

"Too late. I'm here now, so let's go."

"Can't you wait until I go put on my shoes and
get my purse?"

"I guess I don't have a choice, do I?"

I walked off to my bedroom, wearing a pair of white, wide-legged, linen pants with a matching crisscross top that showed much of my butter-scotch skin tone. My hair was down and full of loose, wavy curls that flowed many inches past my shoulders. It had grown so long that I wasn't even sure what I was going to do with it tomor-row. I sat on the edge of my bed, slipping into my strappy sandals that showed my perfect ped-icure. My nails had just been done, too. It was one less thing I had to do tomorrow before my wedding. I sprayed on a dash of sweet-smelling perfume, grabbed my purse, and then headed back to the kitchen where Jaylin stood looking at the TV mounted above the fireplace. His eyes shifted to me. He studied me with those mes-merizing eyes.

"Are you ready?" he asked.

"Yes, I am. Are we going in my car or yours? Before you answer, what's up with your funky attitude? Who done pissed you off or how much money did you lose this week?"

"To answer your ridiculous questions, there is no way in hell I'm riding with you because you can't drive. My life is too valuable. I have an attitude because I don't like when people change plans at the last minute. Pertaining to my money, I never lose. Now, go get your panty-less self in my car and let's go."

I happily paraded in front of Jaylin, just to confirm that I wasn't wearing any panties. It didn't surprise me one bit that he had noticed.

I hadn't had the pleasure of riding in his Maybach, but the kids told me all about it. The second I got in and opened my compact mirror to put on some ruby red lipstick, he started complaining.

"Really, Scorpio? You gon' do that shit in here with my white leather seats? You should have put that on while you were upstairs."

"I would have, had you not rushed me out of there. So be quiet and chill. You're starting to irritate me. Besides, why would you purchase a car like this, knowing that the kids are going to mess this up? I can see Justin's chocolate hands all over these seats. Are you going to fuss at him when he touches them?"

"Nope. Never."

"Then why are you fussing at me over lipstick? I guess I don't get a pass, huh?"

"As a matter of fact, you don't. So put the lipstick away and sit quiet like a good girl."

Just to piss him off, I kept the lipstick tube in my hand, pretending to scribble on the dash with it. He attempted to snatch it, but when he grabbed it, the tube dropped on the white carpet, leaving a mark. I covered my mouth, and my eyes grew wide. Jaylin's brows scrunched inward.

"See, this is exactly what the fuck I was talking about. Damn, Scorpio. You be tripping!"

I couldn't believe how mad he was. Displaying a frown, he sped to the nearest gas station so he could tend to the red, tiny stain that really wasn't that big of a deal. I messed with him as he used a rag and stain remover to take care of the mark.

"Looking good," I teased. "Get that spot. Get it good, baby, and don't hurt yourself down there."

Jaylin cut his eyes at me and continued to doctor the stain. I kept bugging him.

"By any chance do you think you could close the top before you drive off? My hair is blowing all over my head, and it's really getting messed up."

He ignored my request. After he removed the stain, he drove off with all of the windows lowered so my hair could blow even more. I provoked him, again, by pulling out another tube of lipstick. That made him swerve the car over to the curb.

"Call Mario to come pick you up right now. I refuse to ride in this car with a messy-ass woman."

"I'm not calling Mario to tell him anything. Drive and stop being so ridiculous. You just want me to get out of here so you can flirt with that chick behind us. She's been following us for a while. I assume you must know her."

Jaylin snatched his sunglasses away from his eyes, squinting while looking in the rearview mirror. When the light changed, the woman in the car drove by us. She smiled and waved at Jaylin. He nudged his head, saying that it was someone he'd known from somewhere, but he couldn't put his finger on it.

I laughed and shook my head. "And here I was thinking that you couldn't even get that thing up anymore. I guess you got it up for her, because she's been following us for a loooong time."

"No, she hasn't. She was only behind me for two minutes. As for getting it up, I just can't get it up for you. It can get up real high if I want it to. Trust me."

We'd had this little debate plenty of times before. Honestly, I did not know who Jaylin had been having sex with. Whoever it was, he kept her/them a secret. I knew for sure it wasn't Nokea, and the kids never mentioned seeing anyone with Jaylin. I popped up at his house quite often. No one was ever there. There had to be somebody, probably women who lived in other cities. It was impossible for Jaylin to go months and months without having sex.

"If you say you can still get it up, cool, I believe you. But since you're not getting it up for me or Nokea, who are you getting it up for?"

Jaylin pressed on the accelerator and drove off. "None of your damn business. I don't know why you're so concerned about me. Aren't you getting married tomorrow? I'm sure Mario wouldn't approve of the questions you're asking me. He may think you're trying to get some."

"Why settle for some when I can have plenty from a man who gives me every single thing I want? That wouldn't be the reason why you're so bitter today, would it?"

Jaylin pressed on the brakes at the red light, looking at me with seriousness in his eyes. "I assure you that I am in no way bitter about you getting married tomorrow. I am so glad to finally get rid of you for good, and I can't wait to throw you out of my penthouse so I can sell it. Mario can have you. He is a much better man than I, and to be frank, your ass has gotten too expensive to be in my circle."

I laughed then reached over to touch the soft curls in his trimmed, coal black hair. "Baby, as hard as you may try, and as happy as you may be tomorrow at my wedding, you need to know one thing: you'll never be able to get rid of me. I'll be yours forever."

"Very few things last forever, and that would not be related to us. And if I have to walk you down that aisle myself just to get you out of my circle, I promise you I will."

"Thanks, but I'll walk myself. I wouldn't miss it for the world, as I wouldn't miss telling you that this car is so Jaylin Rogers. You look good in it, and if I were still in your circle, I would have me one just like it."

All Jaylin did was laugh. I knew I could get him to perk up, even if it was just a little. I didn't think he was jealous or bitter about the wedding. I already knew how he'd felt about us. That was why Mario was now my number one. I had a real connection with him, too.

As soon as we arrived at the house and entered through the front doors, Mario was coming down the staircase with a sexy smile etched on his clean-shaven face. His sleek hair always appeared wet and was neatly slicked back to the top of his shoulders. The peach shirt he wore was unbuttoned at the top, displaying minimal fine hair on his chest. His white, straight-legged pants tightened on his legs. His slender build was packed with tight muscles. Looking polished and handsome as ever, he made me feel proud to soon call him my husband.

"There she goes," he said, admiring me with his deep-set green eyes. "The love of my wonderful life."

Glee was in my eyes as I stood waiting for him to join us in the foyer. Jaylin was next to me, looking up at the high cathedral ceiling and expensive crystal chandelier that hung from it. He had to remove his sunglasses to get a better view of things. As he examined his surroundings, Mario eased his arm around my waist, pulling me closer to him. He rubbed his pointed nose against mine, smiled, and then assaulted my lips with his. I loved how his attention was always focused on me. The way he searched my eyes clearly showed how he felt about me. If Jaylin weren't there, we definitely would have been doing something more than just tasting each other's lips.

Mario backed away from me and reached out to give Jaylin dap. "Come on, man," Mario said. "Let me show you around. It's laid out. The whole place is sick, and we got it all hooked up for the kids."

Jaylin seemed to be in a better mood. "I'm sure y'all do, but the only things I'm really interested in seeing are the kids' rooms. Are they upstairs?"

"Yes," Mario replied politely. He reached out to hold my hand. "Follow us."

While he continued to hold my hand, we all made our way up the grand staircase that had a black, twisted rail. A gold-colored, plush carpet was on the stairs. Our feet sank into it with each step. Jaylin was behind us. I couldn't help but wonder what he was thinking about all of this. The first room we entered was down a long hallway, right by the elevator.

"I think we're going to make this Mackenzie's room, right, babe?" Mario said, looking at me for confirmation.

I nodded and agreed. "I believe so."

"She's the oldest," Mario added, "so she needs the biggest room."

Jaylin looked around at the spacious room, which had its own bathroom. It was perfect. There was nothing to complain about. He walked over to the curved windows that provided nearly the same view of the breathtaking ocean as his bedroom did. And after he nodded, we went to LJ's, Jaylene's, and Justin's rooms. They were just as awesome, only smaller.

"The decorators will be here all next week," Mario boasted. "We asked them to tackle the kids' rooms first. The furniture has already been ordered, we're just waiting for it to be delivered."

Jaylin appeared pleased. He reached out to shake Mario's hand. "This is nice. Real nice, and I think our kids are going to love it here. Thank you. I appreciate all that you've done and what you will continue to do. I'll see you and Scorpio tomorrow."

"Don't you want to see the rest of the house?" I asked.

"Not really. I already saw what I needed to see."

Jaylin turned to leave, and after he was gone, Mario and I went to our master suite on the main level. We embraced each other while discussing our big day tomorrow.

"I hope you get some rest, babe, because you know me and my relatives love to party hard," he said.

"Trust me, I know. My bachelorette party will probably be boring as heck. I'm sure I'll be in bed by ten. What are your plans for the evening?"

"I can't tell. It's a secret," he joked and ground against me as he continued to hold me in his arms. "Probably a lot of naked women and a whole lot of booze. Who knows? No matter what, I'll see you tomorrow. Three o'clock, my queen. Don't you dare be late."

"Never."

We kissed, and after Mario made a quick phone call, we left. He dropped me off at home,

and by seven o'clock that night, I was hyped
and ready to get my party started. Looking sexy
as ever, I rocked a metallic, see-through mini-
dress with a plunging V-neck. Unfortunately for
me, though, during my party, my mind started
drifting elsewhere. The two half-naked men
dancing around couldn't hold my attention. Neither could all the laughter, music, and drinking
we'd been doing. I appreciated Leslie for throwing this party, but I just couldn't get into it. Leslie could sense that I wasn't being my usual
self, and when we stood outside near the pool
area, she inquired about my demeanor. I tossed
back a shot of vodka and cranberry juice before
answering.

"I'm fine. It's just that I'm a little nervous
about living up to Mario's expectations of me.
He's so sweet, and I love him so much. I just
don't want to disappoint him."

"Disappoint him how? I'm not sure what you
mean by that."

I released a deep breath, finally telling someone what I'd been feeling inside. "Don't take
this the wrong way, because when all is said
and done, I'm happier than I have ever been in
my entire life. The problem is I still have some
really deep feelings for Jaylin. I know for a fact
that we will never, ever be a couple again, but

that doesn't make my feelings go away. On the other hand, there's Mario. He is my everything, but if I don't release what I'm feeling inside for Jaylin, I think it's going to hurt my marriage down the road."

Leslie stood in front of me, teasing my hair with her fingers. "Look, nobody ever said you should ignore your feelings for Jaylin. But don't allow those feelings to fuck up everything good you have going on. Girl, many women would love to be in your shoes. And I'm not just talking about Mario's money. He is sweet and loves you to death, and the kids couldn't ask for a nicer stepfather. I understand how you feel, but over time all of those feelings for Jaylin will dissipate. Now, changing the subject. I love your hair. It's beautiful, but what are you going to do with it tomorrow?"

"I don't want to be standing at the altar look- ing like Diana Ross, so I need to cut it. My hair isn't as long and wild as hers, but if I keep letting it grow, I'm headed in that direction. I may see if my beautician can straighten it for me. Maybe tie it up in the back and let a few curls dangle here and there."

"You mean, wear it how Jaylin likes it?"

I laughed. "No, wear it how I like it sometimes. And forgive me but . . . but if I could just have one night with him again, just one, maybe I'll be able to release some of this buildup inside of me. I can't believe how long we've gone without having sex. Only I know how difficult that's been."

"Well, that one night you're talking about can only occur tonight. After you're married, I wouldn't necessarily go there if I were you."

"Unfortunately, I have a roomful of guests, and I can't go anywhere tonight. But if I could, you know I would."

Leslie removed the glass from my hand. "Go," she said with a straight face. "I'll cover for you and tell everyone something came up. Have your last night with Jaylin. After that, Scorpio, be done and lock in the happiness you deserve."

I stood for a few minutes, thinking about this. I wasn't even sure if Jaylin was at home, but since the kids were with Nokea, maybe this was a good time to go see him.

"Okay," I said. "I'm leaving, and please come up with a good lie about where I went. Also, go inside and get me a bottle of Rémy. I have a feeling that I'm going to need it."

Leslie knew that Rémy was Jaylin's favorite drink. She laughed and went inside to get a bottle. After she gave it to me, we hugged, and I left. I was a nervous wreck while driving, and when I parked my car in Jaylin's driveway, my heart started racing. I'd never been afraid to approach him about anything. But lately he'd been acting real strange. If he rejected me tonight, that would bruise my feelings. Still, I had to do this before my big day tomorrow.

With the bottle of Rémy in my hand, I rang the doorbell. Minutes later, Nanny B came to the door. I was sure she thought nothing of my visit. The smile on her face said so.

"Come on in." With a soft blue robe on, she widened the door. Her gray hair was wrapped in a messy bun. It looked as if I had awakened her.

I gave her a hug. "I'm sorry if I woke you up, but I thought Jaylin would get the door. Is he here?"

"I think so. He's in his office or in his bedroom. Then again, he could be downstairs playing basketball. Check his office first. That's where he was before I headed to my bedroom."

"Will do. Go back to sleep and get some rest."

"Chile, you don't have to tell me twice. I am tired, tired, tired."

We both laughed as she went one way and I veered the other way toward Jaylin's office. I knocked on the door, but there was no answer. When I opened it, I didn't see him. All I saw was his extensive wooden desk with a wall-to-wall, built-in bookshelf beside it. Awards were propped on the shelves, and pictures of our children were here and there. Hanging from the vaulted ceiling were two glass raindrop chandeliers that gave the humongous space all the lighting it needed. The floor was black marble with what looked like tiny diamond specks embedded in it. Jaylin spent a substantial amount of time in his office. I often caught him sleeping on the leather sofas. Sometimes I thought he slept in his office more than he did his own bed.

Since he wasn't in his office, I headed upstairs to his bedroom. I teased my hair with my fingers before taking a deep breath. I knocked on the door, but yet again there was no answer. I waited a few moments before opening the door and entering his room. I didn't see him anywhere. The bed was empty, and the whole room was neat as a pin. I couldn't stand all the black and white. If it were my room, this place would be a mess. Not only that, but it smelled good, too. His musky cologne permeated the air, and the masculine smell drew me right in. The silk curtains were closed on one side, but the doors to the balcony were wide open. The TV brought in some light, as did the recessed lighting, which was very dim. I heard his voice coming from outside, so I tiptoed toward the balcony, hoping he wouldn't know I was there. The closer I got to the doors, I heard laughter. I couldn't help but eavesdrop on his conversation.

"You got jokes, but I'll be in Detroit next week. We'll see what's up then." He paused, I guessed, to listen to the other person speak. It wasn't long before he resumed speaking. "Like I said, we'll see. In the meantime, I gotta go. There's an intruder in my house."

I figured he had seen me on the cameras, so trying not to appear too suspicious, I stepped on the balcony with him. With no shirt on, he was chilling back on a round, lounging chaise, surrounded by numerous cream-colored pillows. His feet were propped on some of the pillows, and his arms were locked across his chest, confirming that his workout regime was successful. His abs were super tight. He had on black silk pajama pants, and I could clearly see a thick print of what I hoped would wet me real soon. He looked up at me with curiosity in his eyes.

"Damn, the party over with already?"

"No, actually, the party is just getting started." I reached out my hand to give him the bottle of Rémy. "Would you like to celebrate with me?"

He hesitated before taking the bottle from my hand. Instead of opening it, he placed it right next to him. I sat on the chaise, facing him.

From the way he stared at me, I knew he could already tell something was on my mind.

"Why do you want to celebrate with me?" he asked. "This is supposed to be a night for you and your girlfriends to enjoy."

"I know, but I wasn't really feeling it. I had other things on my mind."

"Other things like what?"

Instead of saying what was on my mind, I leaned in, placing my lips on his. I sucked in his bottom lip before assaulting the top lip, which I soaked with my tongue. I was so sure that he would back away, but when he didn't, I forced my tongue in his mouth, making it dance with mine. The kiss was wet. Slow. Longer than expected and juicy as ever. I decided to back away when I felt a rushing throb in my pussy.

"Does that answer your question?" I asked.

"Yes, it did, but here's what's up." He sat up, looking at me with seriousness in his eyes. "I don't know what kind of celebration you have in mind tonight, but you and I, meaning us, we ain't gon' start fucking again. I've been content with the way things are. I thought you were too. Not to mention that you're getting married tomorrow to a man who loves you very much. I like Mario, and I prefer not to come between y'all."

His words were disappointing, but they weren't firm enough for me to give up. "You're absolutely correct about his love for me, and just to confirm, I have no intention of changing my mind about tomorrow. I just have this urge, Jaylin. A serious urge to make love to you. To be honest, I . . ." I paused as Jaylin sat there, penetrating me like I was crazy. "What is it?" I said. "Why are you looking at me like that?"

"I'm not looking at you. I'm looking through you. Trying to get into your head and understand why you think making love to me the night before your wedding is the right thing to do. Besides that, we've been here before, Scorpio. You came to me before with this 'just one more time' shit. I may have come to you with it too, but what is one night with me going to do for you?"

I didn't hesitate to answer. "A whooole lot, and if you could only feel how moist the crotch of my panties is right now . . . Besides, it's going to do you some good as well. You'll see, just trust me on this. I know it's not right, but being right has never been affiliated with us or our relationship. You weren't right when you came to me when I was about to marry Bruce. Remember your dream that led you to me that day?"

Jaylin sucked in his bottom lip and nodded. "I remember well. How can I forget? That's the night Justin was conceived. I really don't want to put us in a predicament like that again, even though I love the hell out of my son."

"I get that, but this is simply about my 'in the moment' needs, Jaylin. We . . ." I paused because he appeared disinterested and somewhat reluctant. I started to rethink my approach. "If you're not too busy, can we go for a walk on the beach? It's a beautiful night, and I really need to get more of what I'm feeling off my chest."

Jaylin sighed and sat for a moment as if he was in deep thought. His eyes locked with mine, and then he glanced at my breasts, which were sitting firm, with my hard nipples visible. Probably trying to clear his thoughts, he wiped down his face, placed his cell phone on a small table next to him, and then cleared his throat.

"Come on," he said, stretching his arms. "Let's walk."

I removed my high heels and led the way. As we made our way to the beach, waves hammered the ocean and pushed sudsy water right at our feet. We walked hand in hand in the sand, thinking, contemplating, and moving in silence. The humid breeze was soothing, as were the bright stars and half-moon in the night sky. I was sure that a romantic outing wasn't on Jaylin's mind, so I spoke up to break the silence.

"I guess I don't have to ask how often you're out here at night," I said.

"Often enough, especially when I exercise. But you didn't invite me on this walk to talk about exercising. Other than sex, what's on your mind, Scorpio? You've never been afraid to talk to me before. There's no reason for you to start now."

"I know, but you've been acting real crabby lately. I don't know why, but I sense something different with you. I thought it had something to do with me, but then I figured it was something with Nokea. She and I talked, and she has the same feelings I do. It's like you're here, but then again you're somewhere else."

"Somewhere else like focusing on my business and my kids. Is that what you mean? I'm here. I'm just trying not to get involved in what you and Nokea have going on. I am happy for you, very happy, and I want you to move on with a man who has nothing but the best to offer you. I'm sorry if you feel as if my actions mean I don't care. I do care. Maybe too much sometimes."

"Sooo, if Nokea and Travis were getting married, would you be happy for them?"

Jaylin released my hand. He cracked his knuckles then straightened his goatee with the tips of his fingers. "To be truthful, no. No, I wouldn't be, but if that's what she wants, I'm not in a position to do anything about it."

His words stung a little, but in no way was I in denial. I already knew how he felt about Nokea. "Thanks for speaking your truth, but here's mine." I moved in front of him to halt his steps. While face-to-face with him, I placed my arms on his shoulders. "I'm glad that you're happy for me, but if you are the least bit interested in making me even happier, make love to me tonight. The urge I spoke about earlier is real. I'm afraid that if I don't satisfy it now, I'm going to want to satisfy it later, after I'm married. I have every intention of honoring my vows, but this is so deep for me, Jaylin. Real deep, and I want you to have the pleasure of feeling how deep."

Without a blink, he searched my eyes, breaking me down even more with a sedative gaze that provided no answer. My chest rose against his. He could feel my heart palpitating. Finally, he blinked, removed my arms from his shoulders, and turned around. I watched him walk away.

"So, you're not going to answer me?" I shouted. "It's like that? You can't even say one thing?"

"Congratulations," he shouted back. "You're going to make a beautiful bride tomorrow. Even more than that, you're on your way to peace and prosperity."

I ran up from behind, jumping on his back. His legs weakened a little, but he straightened them and carried me while using much strength.

"Peace and prosperity my ass," I said. "Why are you giving me such a hard time? Is it that hard for you to give me what I want?"

"I'm not interested in what you want anymore. Your wants and needs are Mario's concern. Therefore, thanks for the conversation tonight. I will see you tomorrow afternoon at your wedding."

I pouted as Jaylin hiked the stairs with me on his back. When we reached his balcony, he put me down. My dress was up, so I stretched it over my heart-shaped ass he once admired so much. I stood with anticipation, waiting for him to make the next move. That was when he picked up the bottle of Rémy, handing it to me.

"You can take this with you. I already have plenty. Thanks, though. Your thoughtfulness is always appreciated."

I couldn't believe how serious he was. Disappointment was written all over my face. I knew he could see it.

"Just add it to your collection. And one more thing: thanks for your time, Jaylin. Sorry I wasted it."

He didn't respond. I snatched up my shoes and made my way inside. Just as I reached the door, opening it to exit, he rushed up from behind, slamming the door shut. His body was pressed against mine as we both faced the door. My head was turned to the side, eyes shut tight. I felt his hardness threatening to break loose, and when he lifted my dress, yanking my nude panties to my ankles, I didn't dare move. He cupped his hand over my humming pussy, witnessing firsthand a sticky buildup that had been brewing because of him. His middle finger slipped right in, and his lips brushed against the tip of my earlobe.

"The problem is," he whispered, "you asked the wrong damn question. You asked me to make love to you, and that I cannot do. Would you like to rephrase the question?"

As my chest heaved in and out, I was blunt with my response. "Fuck me then. Will you fuck me like only you can do?"

His response was blunt too. He lowered his pajama pants to the floor and unleashed the beast. My mouth watered as I turned around to look at it. Nine-plus inches my ass! Had to be more. Somebody's calculations were off. There was no time to debate it, because Jaylin had stripped me of my dress and we both stood naked while turning up the bottle of Rémy. He wiped across his mouth as the brown liquid dripped from his lips.

"You're going to enjoy this celebration tonight," he said.

I swallowed the alcohol in my mouth before returning the half-empty bottle to him. "Talk is cheap. Hurry up and get on it."

He laughed and chugged down the remaining liquid in the bottle. His abs contracted as he swallowed, and after I pecked them, I lifted his muscle to play with it.

"You'd better stop," he said, tossing the empty bottle in a chair. "You may hurt yourself messing with that."

I laughed while feeling woozy from the alcohol. So was he as he moved me closer to the bed. The second he hit the floor, lying on his back, I knew he was ready to taste me. He tapped his bottom lip then swiped across it with his tongue. I happily kneeled over his handsome, chiseled face with my body facing the bed. I was bent slightly over, my hands clenched together as if I were praying. I definitely needed to do something, because as soon as the tip of his tongue swirled around my pearl, I nearly lost it. I grabbed the sheet, holding it tight with my balled fists. My breathing became shaky, and my whole body melted. I was trying to hold on, but with his tongue traveling deep, and his fingers tampering too, I was slowly but surely slipping away.

Tears were at the rims of my eyes, and my head was spinning. I started grinding my hips on his lips, but his tongue was too dangerous. I felt all of it, especially the tip, which tickled the shit out of my hotspot. It wasn't long before my juices began to leak into his mouth. My loud grunts echoed in the room. I had to let go, so I squirted him with everything I had. His mouth moved fast. He spot-cleaned my pussy, and as I gasped for my next breath, trembling all over, he scooted from underneath me.

He wiped across his shiny lips, hungry for much more as he stood tall and sexy as hell behind me. His hands roamed my curves, particularly my ass, which he smacked then rubbed. We both laughed again, feeling the effects of the alcohol even more. Jaylin stumbled as he positioned my cheeks right where I could feel his steel about to break in. I was in dire need of it, so I hurried on the bed, kneeled, and bent over. I reached back to navigate his muscle toward the crevasse of my pussy. But halting my efforts to take it all in, Jaylin teased me with his thick head and made me drip all over again.

"Give it to me, baby, pleeeease," I slurred in drunken bliss. I was drunk off of him and the alcohol. "I want all of it in there, every daaaaamn inch of it."

Be careful what you wish for, because all it took was for him to hit me with one deep, long stroke before I reneged. My body jerked forward, and my eyes grew wide. He gripped my hips, pulling me back in his direction.

"Don't run from it," he advised and slapped my ass again. "Work that pussy, baby. You know how you do it."

I tried, but as his deep thrusts knocked hard at my hotspots, all I could do was bite my lips to muffle my ongoing moans and groans. I was surprised by how silent he was, especially as I gained some momentum and started throwing my pussy back to him fast, forcing him to catch it every time. His hands guided my hips. Sweat beads formed on our bodies, and neither of us could catch our breath. There was no stopping, no pausing along the way. I was getting the fuck I wanted, and every time his thighs slapped against my ass, it sounded off in the room. Loudly. So did my tearful voice.

"Shit, Jaylin, daaamn!" I cried out with tears welling in my eyes. I loved his ass, and as he put a hurting on me, I kept having flashbacks of our past relationship. In so many ways it was good. He had been so good to me, but he also delivered a lot of pain. Joy and pain that made tears drip from my eyes. Joy that I just didn't want to be without, no matter who got hurt. Pain that I'd inflicted upon myself, as well as upon Nokea. I had to, because I didn't want to be without him. I feared being without him, without his love, without moments like this, until now.

I couldn't stop myself from being so emotional. We had definitely been through a lot. But now this was it. This would finally put the nail in the coffin. My gut told me this was our last hurrah. I did my best to express every ounce of what I was feeling inside. He, however, remained real silent. I wanted him to say something, but as we changed positions, all he did was stare at me as I sat back on my elbows, facing him with my legs wide open. Sex like this meant Jaylin was mad. He was always at his best when something was troubling him.

"Come here and tell me why you're mad." I spoke in a whisper while opening and closing my legs, teasing him. "Say something, and let me help you put your mind at ease."

Jaylin ignored me. He crawled between my legs and locked my hands together above my head. His face was directly in front of mine. Our lips almost touched. We were so close that we sucked in the same air. He witnessed my tears up close.

"Dry your eyes and save the tears for tomorrow. I'm not exactly sure what you want me to say."

I pecked his lips twice. "Anything. I want to know what you're thinking. Tell me what you're feeling. I need to know what you're feeling inside."

"It's your job to make me talk. You haven't done that yet. Either go for it or continue to be defeated."

I guessed I needed to fight back then, because thus far his dick had won the gold. But Jaylin wouldn't dare let me have control tonight. He steered his muscle back in, and while he continued to hold my hands above my head, our bodies rocked fiercely in sync. The arch in my back grew to new heights. My breasts wobbled, and my pussy throbbed and leaked sweet juices all over the silky sheets. The aroma of our sex filled the air. There was no question that we both were hyped.

In a very bold and surprising move, he lifted me from the bed and pinned me on the floor. Every muscle in his body was in use. My legs were wide, and while they were pressed close to my chest by his strong hands, he pounded, ground, drilled his dick into me, and actually fucked me into my wedding day. I was in so much good pain. Pain that made me reminisce about all the sex we'd had. All the times he wanted to experiment with new positions. The multiple orgasms that got more powerful over time. My mind was flooded with thoughts from our past. And when I thought about the day he'd proposed to me, tears rushed to my eyes again. I couldn't force them back. Several slipped from the corners of my eyes. I had become too emotional to continue, and as I started to breathe heavier, Jaylin released the pressure from my legs. His strokes halted, and that was when he leaned in to kiss a falling tear.

"Relax," he suggested while planting a trail of kisses along the side of my neck. "Clear your mind and let's do this shit, all right?"

I slowly nodded, and minutes after we resumed, we crooned in ecstasy together. Shouted the other's name at the same time.

"Daaaamn, Jaaaylin, fuuuuck meeee!"

"I am, baby, I aaaaam. This pussy isssss what's up, Scorpioooo, umph! But who does it belong to? Say that shit loud and clear and let the whole muthafucking world know!"

After another slap on my ass, I happily responded. "You, damn it! Yo' big-dick ass can have it all, baby. It's yours! Fuck Mario. He ain't shit!"

"You damn well better know it, and don't you ever forget it!"

We grabbed each other in a tight embrace and kissed feverishly. I tightened my arms around his neck, trying my best to hang on to the moment for as long as I could. No one, not one single person on this earth understood the love I had for Jay Baby. He was so easy to love. After all he had done for me and for our kids, it was difficult for me to release him. The hard part was I had to. It was time. I knew it, and he knew it too.

As he backed away from our intense kiss, I held his face in my hands, forcing him to look at me.

"Tell me," I whispered. "What's on your mind and why are you so angry?"

His gray, beautiful eyes narrowed to slits. "I'm mad because I want you to get your mojo back and pull an all-nighter with me. You remember how we used to get down, don't you? Mario been sleeping on this pussy. It's too damn good for that."

Jaylin was right on the money. Mario may have been considered a Latin lover, but there was no way in hell he could deliver like this. My body was so tired, but I refused to disappoint Jaylin. I got some of my mojo back when we took a hot and steamy shower together. His dick was curved far down my throat, and for the first time tonight, he was now in my danger zone. While on my knees, I had the pleasure of watching his eyelids flutter and his six-pack contract as he stood in all of his sexiness with water raining down his rock-solid frame. By now it was nearly three o'clock in the morning, my wedding day for sure. I couldn't help but to think what a damn good day it was.

Chapter 3

Nokea

I was so glad the fashion show was over, but now we had to fill plenty of orders. It had been one busy week. I was looking forward to attending Scorpio's wedding, just to be able to relax and have some real fun that wasn't pertaining to business. Don't get me wrong, I loved my occupation. But at times it was very challenging. I had been stretching myself real thin. Too much time away from my children didn't make me feel good. I hated that I missed Jaylene's gymnastics competition. When I spoke to her about it, she seemed okay. She was happy to get second place, and when she showed me her trophy, I was so thrilled for her. Even when she was a baby, she loved to jump around and turn flips. We knew right away that fashion wasn't going to be her thing. LJ was into the golf thing with Jaylin, and every time he hit the green, LJ joined him. I was glad that the kids were tapping into some of their gifts early on. I was grateful to Jaylin for making sure they explored everything. He was the best father ever. Unfortunately, he wasn't the best husband. For a while, I had been bitter about our divorce. There were plenty of days and nights when I cried my heart out about how things had turned out. The "relationship" I carried on with Jaylin after our divorce wasn't satisfying to me. I wanted more, but he had proven to me time and time again that he wasn't ready to be the man I needed him to be.

Therefore, I struggled with my decision to stay intimate with him. And everything changed when I met Travis. He came into my shop by accident one day, and to make a long story short, he invited me to have dinner with him. We instantly connected. Before I knew it, one date turned into two. I started enjoying his company, and I kept having an urge to spend more time with him. After a while, I wanted to be with him more than I wanted to be with Jaylin. I finally made a decision to choose. Jaylin wasn't happy about it, but he said he understood. Whether it was the truth or not, my relationship with Travis was something Jaylin had to accept.

I was up at five o'clock in the morning getting my exercise in. The kids were still asleep, with the exception of Justin who was in the workout room with me, playing with a big red ball. He was busy to be four and so adorable. Years ago, if anyone had told me that I would love him just as much as I loved my own children, I never would have believed them. The same applied to Mackenzie. She was definitely into the fashion thing. Therefore, we spent an enormous amount of time together. She helped out at the shop, but that was only on the weekends. During the week she was in a private school. She was smart as a whip, and reading books was her favorite hobby. She wouldn't be caught without one in her hand, and when she was punished, it consisted of taking her books away from her. That always got her back on the right track.

I finished my vigorous workout, which kept my body toned and healthy. Now, I was in the kitchen putting cereal and milk on the table, with Justin trying to help. He had milk in a cup but kept throwing it on the floor, pointing to the refrigerator.

"I want soda," he whined. "Pleeease."

"No, no soda. You have to drink milk so your bones can be strong, okay?"

He nodded, and as I prepared a new cup for him, Jaylene and LJ came rushing into the kitchen. I gave them morning kisses and told them to get their things ready for the wedding so we wouldn't be late. They both said some of their things were still at Jaylin's house. I hadn't planned on going over there this early, but after breakfast, we all piled in my Range Rover and left. The kids yakked all the way there, and when my cell phone rang, I could barely hear Travis on the other end. He had done an all-nighter at the hospital and sounded real tired.

"I'm finally on my way home," he said softly. "Lord knows my bed is calling me."

"I'm sure it is. Get some rest, sweetheart, okay? I'll probably be at the wedding all day. No matter what time I get in, I'll be sure to call you."

"Sounds good. Have fun and tell Scorpio and Mario I said congrats. Tell the kids I said hello and be sure to take plenty of pictures and send them to me."

"I will do that. These kids are more excited about getting dressed up than they are about being in the wedding. And from what I've heard, it's a wedding that you don't want to miss."

"Well, sorry I'm missing it. I wasn't invited either, but no hard feelings."

"If I was invited, so were you. But if rest is what you need, hurry up and jump on it."

He laughed. "Will do, beautiful. Don't forget to call me later, and as you already know, I love you."

"Love you too. Bye."

Right after I ended the call, the kids started teasing me. Particularly LJ, who was the only one who didn't really connect with Travis as much.

"Mmmmm, I love you," LJ said, mocking me. "You do love Daddy too, don't you?"

Before I spoke up, Jaylene did. "Yeah, Mommy. You do love Daddy because he said so. Nanna said it also, but then he told her to mind her business. Why does she have to mind her business if he loves you?"

"That's a stupid question," LJ snapped. He was too much like Jaylin. I had to put him in his place time and time again.

"Watch your mouth, LJ. No question is stupid, and you will not speak to your sister like that. Do you understand?"

He shrugged his shoulders. "I guess."

I stopped the car just to turn around and shoot him a mean motherly mug. "I said, do you understand?"

"Yes, I understand. Sorry."

"Apology accepted. Now be nice." I drove off and answered their question. "Yes, your father is right and so is Nanna. I do love him. Always."

Jaylene always had to push. "Then why aren't you living with him? Why aren't we all together and you're always with Travis?"

We explained this to all of the kids before. I thought Jaylene understood, but I had to remind her that, even though we loved each other, it didn't mean we were in love with each other and wanted to be together. She nodded as if she understood.

When we arrived at Jaylin's house, I was surprised to see Scorpio's car in the driveway at seven o'clock in the morning. Maybe she had to stop by to get something. Mackenzie said so too.

"I bet she's picking up her jewelry from Nanna. Did you see what she bought Mommy for her wedding present?"

"No, I didn't, but I bet it's something real nice. Now, I need everybody to get their things out of the truck. We can get dressed here and head to the wedding together."

I removed Justin from his car seat, and then we all made our way to the door. LJ had a key to open the door, and as soon as we walked inside, they rushed off to the kitchen and to their rooms. Nanny B was in the kitchen, cooking breakfast.

"Good morning," I said, giving her a hug. "The kids already ate breakfast, but with the way those blueberry pancakes are looking and smelling they may want to eat again. I may have to grab me a bite to eat as well."

"Help yourself. There's plenty for everybody."

"Thanks. Is Jaylin in his office?"

"I haven't seen him this morning yet. He may still be in bed."

What she'd said sparked my curiosity. "I don't think so, because Scorpio's car is outside. Is she here?"

Nanny B scratched her head. "She stopped by last night, but I thought she left. I'm not really sure. Check his office. They may be in there."

I went to Jaylin's office, but no one was there. I then walked to the other side of the house so I could go up the stairs without Nanny B seeing me. Jaylin's bedroom was all the way down the hall, and when I reached the door, I started to knock. Unfortunately, I didn't. I turned the knob, slightly cracking the door. I immediately saw Jaylin and Scorpio sleeping comfortably in his messy bed. She was lying on his chest with her hair fanned out all over it. His arms were wrapped around her, and with sheets barely covering them, I could see that they were naked.

To say I was shocked would be an understatement. Not only was this Scorpio's wedding day, but Jaylin had told me that he and Scorpio didn't indulge themselves sexually anymore. She had told me the same thing. I felt so foolish for believing them. I wondered how long this had been going on. Then I realized that it wasn't even my business anymore. I had no reason to care, no reason to be upset. If they were still having sex, so what? Mario was the one who had to deal with this, not me.

Just as I got ready to close the door, I saw Scorpio's head pop up. Her nipples touched Jaylin's chest. She shook his shoulder to wake him.

"Oh, my God! Jaylin, wake up! What time is it?"

I hurried to close the door and go back downstairs as if I hadn't been upstairs at all. I walked in the kitchen where Nanny B was now setting the table for breakfast.

"I didn't see Jaylin in his office, but I just got an important phone call from Travis. He needs me to pick him up at the airport. I'll be back to help the kids get ready for the wedding. So tell Jaylin I'll see him later."

"Okay. Tell Travis I said hello and be careful at the airport."

I got out of there as quickly as I could. The last thing I wanted to do was see Scorpio. I didn't want to see Jaylin either. I was sure he would have felt a need to explain. I didn't need an explanation, but I had to admit that seeing them together was disappointing.

I drove home, thinking about the past few years Jaylin and I had spent, basically, apart from each other. It surely opened my eyes to many things. While I had noticed numerous changes in Jaylin, today was a setback. I thought that he and Mario were like friends. Why would he even go there with Scorpio? Moreover, how could she lie there with Jaylin on her wedding day, and then go marry another man? It was so messy to me, real messy, and only because my children would be there today did I keep my promise to go. If they weren't in the wedding, I surely would have stayed home.

In a somber mood, I walked into my condo and immediately started to clean up the tremendous mess the kids had made. My housekeeper wasn't coming until Monday, but with all the toys, games, and sleeping bags around, I couldn't wait until then. Just as I'd put LJ's sleeping bag in his closet, my cell phone rang. I looked to see who it was. It was Jaylin.

"Hello," I said.

"Good morning. What's up?"

"Nothing much. Just trying to clean up a little."

"Nanny B said you were here earlier. Why didn't you stay?"

I knew he was fishing, trying to see if I'd seen him and Scorpio together. I played clueless. "Because I had to come home and clean up."

"Nanny B said you went to the airport."

"Yeah, that too."

He paused and cleared his throat. "Are you coming back?"

"Yes, I'll be there a few hours before the wedding to help the kids get dressed. Do you need me for something else?"

"No, I was just asking. You sound kind of strange. Is everything okay?"

I rolled my eyes. "Everything is fine, Jaylin. But if you don't mind, I'd like to get finished cleaning up."

"All right. I'll see you in a bit."

I hung up and sighed. There were so many other things on my mind . . . now this.

Scorpio's wedding had to be the most exquisite and well-put-together wedding I had ever attended. Whoever was responsible for this, they had done an amazing job. It had to cost a fortune, and the flowers alone probably cost in the millions. The wedding was outside, but there were high walls of flowers built to section off the area where the wedding took place. A glass stage-like platform was up front, and behind it was a man-made waterfall with palm trees lined up in front of it. Rows of silver chairs with white silk cushions traveled all the way to the back.

Turquoise was Scorpio's favorite color. It was very much on display. From the flowers to the dresses, everything was so beautiful. The guests couldn't stop talking about how lovely things were. Everybody was looking around, pointing at the candle-lit columns and the wide walkway where Scorpio would soon make her appearance.

Jaylin sat next to me, looking unfazed by it all. Actually, he had been on his cell phone, talking to Shane. Something was going on businesswise. He wasn't too happy about it, and as the pitch of his voice went up a notch, he got up and walked away. From a distance, I saw him standing by the door with a custom-tailored charcoal suit on. The jacket was unbuttoned, his white shirt was crisp and clean, and the silk tie was one I'd purchased for him years ago.

I guessed his conversation had gotten better, because he looked at me and smiled. A wink followed, causing me to turn my head and look in another direction. I was still kind of salty about seeing him with Scorpio. As much as I'd repeated to myself that it wasn't my business and to get over it, I couldn't. It just bothered me. I couldn't explain why, but it did.

I crossed my legs, looking at the yellow, black, and white heels I wore. My dress was gold. It had ruffles in the front and a triangular cutout in the back. The bottom hugged my hips. I was pleased when one of my designers made it for me to wear today.

"Sorry about that," Jaylin said, returning to his seat. "Shane told me to tell you hello. He and Tiffanie just got back. We needed to clear up a few things."

"Did they manage to work things out?"

"Based on what he said, I'm sure they will. Marriages take work. Couples who are willing to put forth the effort, they'll survive."

I guessed since our marriage had failed, he was implying that I wasn't willing to put forth the effort. I could've let him have it right then and there. I also could've given him a million and one reasons why ours didn't survive. That fast, a frown appeared on my face. I wasn't sure if he saw me cut my eyes at him, but it wasn't long before he attempted to clean up his words.

"Then again, you can still give it your all, and if it's not meant to be, you move on. Move on to bigger and better things that bring you the happiness your heart has always desired."

Jaylin wanted me to respond, but I didn't. Especially since the wedding had started. I was eager to see our kids, as well as Scorpio, make their appearance.

Jaylin was to my left, so I had a chance to examine his reaction to everything. When Mario and his groomsmen entered looking handsome as ever, Jaylin was texting. As the bridesmaids entered, he glanced at each one of them, then turned his head in another direction. His first smile came when he saw Mackenzie come in. She waved at us, and when Jaylin took a picture of her with his phone, she kept it moving down the aisle. Jaylene and Justin were next. They were too cute. Many of the guests, including us, stood to take pictures. When they reached the row where we sat, Jaylene blew us kisses. Justin, however, was done. He walked up to Jaylin and sat on his lap. Everyone laughed.

"Man, you have to finish what you started," Jaylin said, trying to put him down. "Go take Mario the ring. He needs the ring that's on your pillow."

Justin slid off Jaylin's lap, but before he walked away, Jaylin straightened his black suit jacket and bowtie. Justin put the pillow on top of his head, messing up the lovely curls in his hair. He put on quite a show, causing everybody to laugh and focus their attention on him. When he reached the front, Mario reached down and picked him up. Surprisingly, Jaylin still had a smile.

"Here Comes the Bride" played on a piano, and a few moments later, Scorpio appeared in front of the double doors. Her uncle was there to walk her down the aisle. I had to admit that everything about her look was breathtaking. The top part of the dress was lace, and with a plunging V-neck and a bottom half made of silk, sexy was written all over it. There was a flowing train that connected to the back of the dress, and her wedding veil was attached to the beautiful bun on top of her head. Tiny diamonds were attached to the veil, and with a few strands of hair dangling along the sides of her face, I had to give her props. Jaylin looked at her for what may have been a split second. Then his eyes shifted to LJ, who was one of the ushers. Even when Scorpio promenaded down the aisle, Jaylin looked, but not for long. I would have given anything to know what he was thinking. When she walked by us, his glance was brief, and her focus was straight ahead. Obviously, there were no plans for her to drop the bouquet on the ground, as I had done years ago because of my feelings for Jaylin. Just thinking about my mistakes with his cousin, Stephon, made me reflect on my past with Jaylin and more so on our marriage and divorce, which I wanted to erase from my memory.

As Scorpio proceeded down the aisle, many cameras and phones flashed. The back of her dress was as gorgeous as the front. Her hourglass figure was what made the dress a perfect ten. This was the best I had ever seen her look.

As she stood up front with Mario, everyone took a seat. That was, with the exception of Justin who was now next to Scorpio, wrapping himself with her train.

"Maybe I should go up front to get him," Jaylin whispered while leaning in close to me.

"No, he'll be okay. He's going to steal the show. Just wait and see."

As the ceremony got underway, I started feeling slightly better. It was too touching for me to be upset right now, and as Scorpio and Mario expressed their love for one another, my thoughts reverted to Travis. I loved him so much, but I would never want a wedding this big. To be honest, I really wasn't interested in having a wedding at all. I loved the way Jaylin and I had tied the knot, which was on the beach with very few friends and family. This, however, was too much. Mario and Scorpio had gone all out. He certainly had the money for this. Scorpio had hit the jackpot. Apparently, his money wasn't good enough for her, especially if Jaylin was still in the picture.

I listened to the words she spoke to Mario, somewhat unmoved because of what I'd seen this morning. And when Jaylin stood and straightened his suit jacket, I damn near fell out of my seat. He wasn't going to make an attempt to stop the wedding, was he? I wasn't sure, but when he stepped in the aisle, I quickly reached for his arm.

"What?" he whispered while leaning in closer to me.

"Please don't," I said. "Let it go, Jaylin, and—"

His face twisted, and he quickly cut me off. "Don't what? I'm going to the restroom. Need to take a leak. Would you like to come watch?"

I sighed from relief and rolled my eyes at him again. "No. Not interested."

He shrugged and walked away.

Jaylin returned a few minutes later. By this time, Justin was laying his head on the silk pillow and pretending to be asleep. Everyone laughed, and Scorpio told him to go play with Jaylin. He sprinted down the aisle, sitting with us for a while. In the meantime, Scorpio and Mario stood holding hands. They were done expressing kind words to each other and were ready to recite their vows. Jaylin seemed tuned in for a minute, and as Scorpio started to speak again, he released a soft snicker, rubbed the hair on his chin, and shook his head. A smirk was on his face, and it wasn't long before he started texting again. His thoughts stayed on my mind. I intended to ask him, sooner or later, how he really felt in this moment. It was strange seeing the two of them in bed and now, during the wedding, pretending as if they hadn't had sex. All night at that, because Nanny B said Scorpio had come over that night. I tried not to think about it, but Jaylin's actions were killing me. He was now playing with Justin, basically ignoring the ceremony completely.

I looked up front again. Scorpio was in tears. Mario reached out to wipe them. They both appeared a bit nervous, but when all was said and done, Mario was told to kiss his new bride. Everyone started to clap, even Jaylin and Justin, who clapped together.

"Ladies and gentlemen, may I present to you for the first time Mr. and Mrs. Mario S. Pezzano."

Cheers and applause followed. Scorpio and Mario looked extremely happy as they made their way down the center aisle, smiling and waving at guests. Yet again, when they passed by us, Scorpio and Jaylin barely looked at each other. She barely looked at me.

The only time I got up close and personal with her was at the reception, where people stood in line to greet the bride and groom. Just like the wedding, the reception was off the chain. Turquoise and white drapes surrounded the spacious room, and the white canopy above was filled with bright white lights that looked like stars in the sky. The wedding cake towered eight tiers, and hundreds of silk-like flowers covered the whole thing. So much food was being served. From lobster to mini-hamburgers for the kids, they had it all. I stood in front of Mario first, congratulating him and wishing them well. He reached out to hug me.

"Thank you, Nokea," he said. He was gorgeous, and every time I saw him, I couldn't help but think about Halle Berry's ex-husband, Olivier Martinez. Sexiness was in the eyes for sure. "Thank you very much. When you get time, you and Travis should come by to see the house."

"You know we will," I said. "The kids can't stop talking about it."

Jaylin was behind me. He shook Mario's hand while I reached out to give Scorpio a hug.

"Outstanding," I said. "You really outdid yourself with this one, and your dress is killing it."

"Thank you. I tried," she said, laughing. "Thanks for coming, and please do come by the house soon. We're not going on a honeymoon yet, so we'll be at the house all weekend."

"Okay. I'll see what Travis is up to tomorrow and let you know."

Scorpio nodded. Her eyes shifted to Jaylin. He leaned in to give her a hug before kissing her cheek.

"I must say, you look beautiful. Congrats and stay sweet."

"You know I will."

She winked at Jaylin, and that was it. We took plenty of pictures, danced with the kids, and ate our hearts out. Jaylin and I sat at a table, not really saying much to each other.

"Why are you so quiet?" he asked.

I shrugged and fidgeted with a napkin in front of me. "No reason. Just getting a little tired, that's all."

"Would you like to dance?"

"Not really."

He placed his hand on top of mine, lightly squeezing it. "I'm getting ready to go. Stop by my house tomorrow morning if you get a chance. We need to talk."

He stood, and not even waiting for a response, he left.

Chapter 4

Jaylin

Nokea didn't have to say one word. I knew she was upset with me about Scorpio. It was obvious that she'd seen us in bed together, and that was confirmed when I saw her on the cameras I viewed after Nanny B said she was there. The truth was, I didn't owe Nokea or anyone else an explanation. Scorpio wanted to have sex, so we had sex. I too was in the mood to have sex, and even though we hadn't gone there in a long time, I was glad we did. I enjoyed my time with her. She made me feel relaxed. She always made me feel appreciated. That's what I loved about her. She cared about my feelings, and she didn't mind telling me how she truly felt. I was well aware that she still loved me, but we both knew that it was time for her to pivot from all of this.

The wedding was beautiful, so was she, and there you have it. There wasn't really much else I wanted to say, except that men like Mario didn't come around every day. What I meant by that was obscenely wealthy men who didn't even push for a prenuptial agreement. If things didn't work out, he was fucked. I knew the kind of woman Scorpio was. She would milk him for every dime. She would demand more than he was willing to give, and she would walk away from that marriage being even wealthier than me. I had to give her credit. She was a master at getting what she wanted.

On the other hand, Nokea was getting what she wanted too. That was Travis. Even though I didn't owe her an explanation, I at least wanted to talk to her about the situation just so she would understand where I was coming from. She seemed real angry with me about something. I wanted to give her an opportunity to get off her chest whatever was troubling her.

At seven o'clock in the morning, Shane and I sat in my office, discussing a few things. I was leaned back in my chair. He was sitting on the sofa. His hands were behind his head, and he was casually dressed in dark jeans and a Plan of Action T-shirt. His locs had grown to dreads, which were in a ponytail, and according to many women, his physique was much tighter than mine. I guessed it was a matter of opinion. I told him how wrong he'd been for ignoring Tiffanie when she'd called him. He refused to see things my way.

"All I'm saying is, as my wife, Tiffanie harasses me. I can't go anywhere without her calling and bugging. If I go sit in another room, there has to be a reason for that. If I go for a walk, I'm walking to get away from her. The only time she doesn't bug me is when I'm sleeping. Then again, I take that back, because she's always waking me up, asking me dumb shit about where I put this or that." Shane was clearly frustrated.

"Look, it's called being married. Maybe you just weren't ready. I've spoken to Tiffanie, and she says the problem is you don't feel obligated to answer her questions or answer your phone. You are obligated, whether you like it or not. I thought the trip to Paris would help. I guess not."

"I said it helped, but we'll be good for a few weeks or so, and then she'll be back at it again. I just need my space sometimes. When I'm not allowed my space, that's a big problem."

"I feel you, but try to shake some of that shit off and show me some of these properties you think we should look into."

Shane came over to my desk, handing me a thick stack of papers with property listings. As we started to inspect them, there was a knock at my door. We looked up. Nokea came in. She looked tired. Puffiness was visible underneath her eyes. The ripped jeans and off-the-shoulder shirt she had on were simple, but her high heels added much sexiness.

"What's up, Nokea?" Shane asked.

"Hi, Shane." She walked in and laid her purse on the sofa. "Am I interrupting you two?"

"Not really," I replied then looked at Shane. "Let's continue this later. Meanwhile, please return Tiffanie's call or go home to see what she wants. You know I don't beg that often."

He walked away from my desk without a response and said goodbye to Nokea before he left my office.

She sat on the sofa, crossing her legs and yawning. "Wha . . . What did you want to talk to me about?" Her little attitude was still on full display.

"I'm sensing something with you. I'm quite surprised, because I thought we cleared the air a long time ago and put certain things behind us. Now I'm not so sure."

"I thought we put certain things behind us too. Obviously not."

"You must be talking about me and Scorpio having sex. Yes, we did, but—"

She raised her hand to cut me off. "Save it. I don't care about you and Scorpio anymore. Who you screw is none of my business."

"No, it's not, but for the record, I've only been with three women since our divorce. That includes Scorpio, who I haven't had sex with in a long time."

Nokea sighed. "Who cares, Jaylin? Do you want a medal or something? I guess three women may not seem like a lot to you, especially since it used to be what . . . three hundred? As for Scorpio, please. All she has to do is cock her legs open, and you'll be there to dive right in. Headfirst, I assume."

I nodded, trying to bite my tongue while listening to her insults. "Three hundred, five hundred, or maybe a thousand. Who knows? Don't hate because I'm an irresistible, handsome muthafucka with the stellar credentials that are required by the majority of brilliant women. Expect that number to keep growing as long as I don't have a wife. After you get done acting ugly, and you're ready to face reality, there was only one woman who caused me to make some serious mistakes during our marriage. But please don't forget that I had been faithful to you for years. Our marriage was good, and you can't deny that. As for your little funky attitude, it started way before you saw Scorpio and me in bed. It's been going on for the past few months or so."

She winced and kept repeating herself. "Again, I really don't care who you have sex with. For you to sit there and talk about my attitude, please. You're the one with an attitude. You're always moody. The only time you're happy is if it revolves around money or the kids. I can't get no love, Nanny B can't, Scorpio can't get . . . well, actually, she did get it. A whole lot, I assume."

I fired back by standing up and touching my manhood. "Hell, you can get some too if you ask for it. Is that why you're mad? 'Cause it was her instead of you?"

If she wasn't mad before, she definitely was now. The frown on her face deepened. She darted her finger at me. "She can have all of you, Jaylin. I do not care. Besides, I wouldn't dare allow you to stick that infested penis of yours in me ever again."

I cocked my head back, kind of surprised by where she was going with this. For the time being, my voice calmed because I didn't want to argue with her.

"If all you came over here to do is insult me, you can get your ass up and leave. I don't know what kind of love you're interested in getting from me.

All of this is coming from out of nowhere. But since you're trying to call me out on some things, I need to call you out too. When did you think it was okay not to thank me for all the help I put forth pertaining to your show? That shit was personal."

"I did thank you. I thanked you several times."

"That thanks was too late. I preferred a special thanks."

"I don't care what you preferred. I preferred to have a husband who was faithful, who put me first, who understood my needs, and who respected me to the fullest. I didn't get that, did I?"

Her ongoing attacks about our marriage were starting to make my blood boil. I walked around my desk, sitting against it. "Women. I tell you, y'all are something else. I can't believe you're still hanging on to that shit. I guess you want me to spend the rest of my life apologizing to you. Is that it?"

"I don't need an apology. What I wanted was for you to take your vows seriously. It was as simple as that. Hebrews 13: 'Let marriage be held in honor among all, and let the marriage bed be undefiled.'"

Now she really had my attention. My face was tight, and my brows shot up. "Let me go get you a choir robe, just in case you want to start singing hallelujah. What nerve do you have coming in here, quoting the Bible, especially with a track record like yours? I've always taken responsibility for what I did, and you damn sure wasn't no saint. If you must take me to Sunday school, you need to get it right because that same verse says, 'God will judge the sexually immoral and adulterous,' not you." I walked over to my bookshelf, removing my Bible. I laid it on the table in front of her. "It also says, in Psalms 118, to trust in the Lord, not put confidence in man. Since you're living by the Word these days, show me where it says to put all of your trust in Jaylin Rogers. That I'm perfect and I will not make any mistakes. Come on, baby. Get the fuck out of here with that shit you talking."

Nokea took a hard swallow. "So, are you saying that I was wrong for trusting you? That as your wife, I shouldn't have trusted you?"

"What I'm saying is this: nobody should be trusted. However, many of us do trust people. Promises get made, vows are taken, people fall deeply in love, but we are all human, and unfortunately, shit happens. I asked for your forgiveness. I thought you gave it. So if you want to keep being bitter about the shit, fine. But I will not ever say I'm sorry to you again for my past indiscretions. I have other things to do than spend my life begging for your fucking forgiveness."

Now I was mad. I waited for her to respond, but she sat silently while gazing at the floor. There was more to her attitude. I could sense it.

"I have forgiven you, but I . . . I'm just going through something right now. Something that I wasn't prepared for, and I don't know what to do."

Thankfully, her voice had softened. I sat next to her on the sofa, trying to find out what was up. "What are you going through, Nokea? Just tell me so I can understand what's been up with you."

She released a deep breath before turning her head to look at me. "You know how much I love Travis, but I'm afraid to tell him that I . . . I'm pregnant. I really don't want any more children, but . . ."

My blank expression caused her to pause. The floor felt as if it had dropped from underneath me, and my heart fell with it. My eyes were without a blink. My mouth was dry as hell. I tried to stay calm, but there was a tiny button inside of me that was dangerous to push. She'd hit it.

"I hope like hell that I didn't hear what you just said. Repeat that, but skip over all that bullshit about how much you love Travis."

Nokea stood and reached for her purse. "I knew I shouldn't have said anything to you about this. As if you would really understand what I'm going through."

I quickly stood and finally let her ass have it. "You damn right you shouldn't have said shit like that to me. You can't talk to me about your love for another man, Nokea! I'm not trying to hear that shit! And if you are telling the truth about being pregnant, you already know what you need to do. You will not have another child unless it is by me!"

I was too close, so she stepped back with her mouth wide open. "What?" she shouted. "Have you lost your freaking mind? Are you telling me to have an abortion because this baby is not yours?"

My head was spinning so fast. I had to step away from her before I did something I would regret. I couldn't believe this shit. I hoped like hell she was trying to get me back for having sex with Scorpio. Maybe that was it. Thinking that it was, I looked at her and lowered my voice.

"Tell me this is a joke. Don't mess with me like this, baby. Please tell me you are not pregnant by another man. If you are, as much as I am against abortions, you know what you need to do."

Nokea looked at me with a straight face, her arms crossed in front of her. "I don't understand how you can stand there and make this all about you. About what you want, Jaylin, and nothing else really matters. This is no joke, and I will not adhere to your ridiculous recommendation. Travis and I—"

The second his name left her mouth, I reached for a thick book that was on my desk and pitched it directly at her. She ducked and dropped back on the sofa in disbelief. Her eyes were bugged and had gotten even wider when I bent over, caging her in so she couldn't move. My face was directly in front of hers as I spoke through gritted teeth.

"Years ago, you had no problem marching your happy-go-lucky ass to the doctor's office to kill my child. My miracle baby could be in this world right now had you not made a reckless decision like the one you're attempting to make now. So don't you dare tell me how ridiculous my recommendation is. What's ridiculous is you not taking the necessary measures to make sure this bullshit didn't happen!"

Hurt traveled deep in Nokea's watery eyes. I knew that mentioning our child would cause her to react, but I was caught off guard when she reached out and slapped the hell out of me.

Not only that, but she lifted her foot, punting her pointed-toe heel right between my legs. This time, my mouth opened wide, as a shockwave bolted through my private parts. I dropped to my knees, cupped my package with both hands, and squeezed my eyes together. My sacks stung. Maybe they were bleeding. My dick had been chopped down by an inch or two and felt like it had been struck by electricity. I was in so much pain that I couldn't even speak. My eyes watered. I blinked fast to clear them.

Nokea moved away from me and stood closer by the door. "Now that I have your attention," she said, "don't you ever again attempt to make me relive one of the worst days of my life. You already know why I did what I did, and had you not been screwing that whore, who you just screwed the other day, we wouldn't even be here."

I was in too much pain to argue with her. I couldn't even move, and when I tried, all I could do was fall forward and rest my forehead on the floor.

"Get out," I groaned in a whisper. "Leave, Nokea, before I . . ." I paused when I felt another painful throb, which made me rock back and forth. I silently prayed for the pain to cease, and after I heard the door close, I rolled flat on my back, swaying from side to side. I took deep breaths while looking at the ceiling. Tears dripped from the corners of my eyes.

I was so upset with Nokea. How dare she expect me to be happy for her? I was reliving the past all over again with her. That shit she'd done with Stephon was fresh in my mind, and now she was pregnant by Travis. This time, there were no questions about the baby not being his. It couldn't be disputed. It damn sure wasn't mine. I meant what I'd said about her only having my children. Selfish or not, that was the way I felt.

I also felt as if I needed a damn doctor. If not that, I needed a highly skilled woman who could nurse my dick orally and help bring it back to life. Surely, I could find someone. I actually had someone in mind.

Later that day, I had gone to the "doctor" and was feeling slightly better. After I left there, I met Shane for dinner at a seafood restaurant. This time, he sat across the table from me, cracking crab legs and telling me I was wrong. He also couldn't stop laughing about Nokea bringing me to my knees earlier.

"I don't see a damn thing funny. She could have damaged me for life. I chilled in the tub for damn near two hours, trying to soothe my dick and sore nuts. I promise you that she's going to pay for that shit."

"Trust me, I know how painful that feels. My ex, Sam, did that to me one day. Her kick was powerful, and she had on heels. I didn't think I would be able to ever have sex again."

"I was thinking the same thing. Nokea was pissed. I didn't know she was that strong."

"Well, now you know. And I know how you feel about her, man, but she has been with Travis for quite some time now. You should've prepared yourself for something like this. Next time, she may be talking marriage. You see how quickly Scorpio made her move, don't you?"

I couldn't wait to swallow my food so I could respond. "She made a move all right. A move right into my bedroom, on her wedding day, getting the shit fucked out of her."

Shane cocked his head back in awe. "What? Y'all still fucking?"

"Not really. She just came by and told me she had a serious itch that needed to be scratched, and we indulged ourselves. Nokea came by that morning and saw us in bed sleeping. She was acting all funky at the wedding, but now I know her attitude had more to do with her being pregnant. I don't care what anybody says, including you. She's not having his baby."

"Is she supposed to have an abortion? You've always been against that, haven't you?"

"I have, but I don't know what she's going to do. All I can say is it ain't happening."

"There's a good chance that it will happen. I'm just trying to keep it real. I hate to see y'all going down this road again, so keep doing what you've been doing and keep your distance. Let Nokea make the right decision for her. If you try to force her to do anything, you're going to lose. As for Travis, what's up with that fool? Did she mention anything about how he feels?"

"I'm sure he'll be ecstatic, and the good doctor will have everything he wants. Meanwhile, I guess I'm supposed to just sit back and hand it all to him on a silver platter."

Shane kept trying to reason with me. "Again, if you push, you'll lose. And the good doctor may be good, but he ain't that good. We all have flaws, if you know what I mean."

"Well, I looked into his flaws and there ain't too many. This muthafucka must be Jesus' long-lost son, because I have never seen a man's record and profile so clean. Credit in good standing, and his ass got a fat bank account. Nothing like mine, but it would be more than suitable for most women."

Shane laughed and scratched his thinly trimmed beard that lined his jawline. "I must say, you have definitely done your homework. A-plus for sure."

I couldn't help but laugh. I also shook my head. "I had to do what was necessary to find out what was up. That fool got my woman wrapped around his finger. I got some serious problems with that shit, but you're right. I have to just chill and hope that the good doctor ain't as good as he seems."

"We all have skeletons. I guarantee you that he does too."

I tossed back my Rémy, drinking to that. At this point, I needed a miracle to happen. Nokea was slipping away fast. My gut told me it was for good this time.

Chapter 5

Scorpio

The wedding was a wrap, but the busyness continued. Mario and I had started to move our belongings into our new home. While the movers were a big help, I still found myself being hands-on. I wanted everything to be right. Therefore, when they put something in one place, I moved it to another. I was sweating all over. Talk about being tired, I was that and then some. The kids were running around, and with Mario in the back by the pool, talking to his father, I pretty much had to do a lot of furniture arranging on my own.

Regardless, I was happy. The wedding turned out so amazing. I'd never dreamed of having a wedding like that. Mario had made my day feel real special, but after what Jaylin had done to me, I could only make love to my husband for a mere ten minutes last night. I kept having flashbacks of my heated sex session with Jaylin, and I thought about the five orgasms I'd had throughout the night. Even during my wedding, the tenderness of my pussy wouldn't allow me to forget what had transpired between us. Trifling or not, I had no regrets.

"No, please, no," I shouted at two of the movers who wanted to put in the living room an old-fashioned chaise that Mario's mother had given us. "You can take that straight to the storage room in the basement. I'll find somewhere else to put it later."

"Yes, ma'am," one of the men said. "Downstairs we go."

I wiped across my sweaty forehead while standing near the stone fireplace in the great room. My loose-fitting T-shirt stuck to my skin, as did the sweatpants I had on that were comfortable as ever. With tennis shoes on, I started to tackle the staircase that sometimes made me tired. I could hear the kids having a pillow fight, but as soon as I'd made it upstairs, Mario yelled my name from downstairs. I looked over the rail and saw him standing next to his father.

"Papa is getting ready to go, sweetheart," Mario said. "Come say goodbye."

I marched back down the stairs, and as Mr. Pezzano stood in the foyer with a red and black gangster hat on, along with a black suit, I reached out to hug him. His potbelly was in the way, his embrace was lukewarm, and his beady eyes expressed how much he really didn't approve of me. With gold rings on nearly every finger, he held the sides of my face, squeezing it.

"Take care of my son," he said. "Good care of him, because he means the world to me."

I nodded, and he planted a soft kiss on my forehead before releasing my face. Mario opened the door for him, and after his father left, he reached for my hand. With a pair of white pants on and a blue silk shirt that stretched across his muscles, he wasn't much help to me today.

"Come with me," he said. "I need to show you something."

While keeping a grip on my hand, he took me to our bedroom. The hundreds of presents from our wedding were piled high near an arched window and another stone fireplace. Our bed had arrived, but we hadn't had a chance to dress it with the satin white and gold sheets I'd purchased.

"Sit," Mario said, gesturing for me to sit on the bed. I sat, and as he stood in front of me, he softly brushed his fingers along the right side of my face. "You're so beautiful. I am truly a lucky man, and I hope you know how much I love you."

I turned my head to the side, pecking his wrist where *La vita è bella* (life is beautiful) was tattooed. "I do know. And I love you too."

He removed his hand then squatted in front of me. "There is no question in my mind that you do, but I have to ask you something. I need for you to be completely honest with me, babe, because it is important that we do not lie to each other."

There was a queasy feeling in my stomach. Something trapped in his eyes gave me pause. I didn't like where this conversation was going. "I agree. It is important for us to be honest with each other. I would never lie to you."

"Good." Mario stood and moved away from me. He looked outside while massaging his hands together. "How was your bachelorette party?"

My heartrate increased the second I heard him say "bachelorette." I could almost predict what was on his mind, but I wasn't so sure if I was prepared to be honest about anything. Besides, no one had seen me with Jaylin. I was sure of that. All the people at the party who had probably said something to Mario, they were speculating about why I could have left.

"My party was spectacular. I had a great time, but I did have too much to drink."

Mario was still gazing outside as if something out there held his interest. "If you were having so much fun, why did you leave?"

"I left because I got a call from Jaylin. He said there was something urgent he wanted to discuss. When I got to his place, we discussed Mackenzie going to a different private school. We could've talked about that some other day, but when he called, he said it was important."

"I see." Mario finally turned to look at me. "So, whenever Jaylin calls and tells you something is important, you just walk away? If you were having such a good time, why not tell him to wait? More than that, why not just talk to him over the phone?"

"I wanted to do that, but whenever it involves the kids, you know how I am. Besides, I was starting to feel a little sick from all the alcohol I had been drinking. I wanted to get some rest before our big day, but I didn't know how to tell everyone I was getting tired."

Mario shrugged. "You should've just told them. Like you should've told Jaylin to wait."

I wasn't sure if Mario believed me, but if anyone thought I was going to mess this up and tell him the truth, they were sadly mistaken. If anything, I had to put him at ease and persuade him to put a halt to this conversation. Before he said another word, I got off the bed, making my way up to him. As I eased my arms around his rock-solid waistline, I looked into his eyes.

"Maybe I should have told him to wait, but at the time I didn't think it was a big deal. I guess some of your relatives told you that I left. I did. I'm glad you came to me about this. I don't ever want you to be jealous of my relationship with Jaylin. It's over. I couldn't be happier, and there is no man on earth who makes me feel the way I do when I'm with you."

I placed my lips on Mario's. We indulged in a passionate kiss. If he had known specific details about my visit at Jaylin's house, I was sure he would have rejected my actions. He was also willing to accept much more than that when I moseyed over to the door and locked it.

"Got time for a quickie?" I said with a smile.

Mario tugged at his shirt, which was tucked into his pants. "How quick do you want me to be?"

"Real quick, but give it to me nice and slow like you always do it." I pulled my T-shirt over my head, exposing my firm breasts. My sweats were removed next, and the second I got on the bed, Mario slithered his sexy body between my legs. His shirt was open, and his pants had been dropped to his ankles. His dick tapped at the center of my slit, and within seconds only a portion was in there.

"Go alllll the way in there, baby," I moaned. "We don't have a lot of time, but I need to feel all of you."

Mario parted my legs, holding them high while feeding me more of his hard meat. His strokes were slow and measured, making me shut my eyes and arch my back each time he pushed forward. He loved to suck my breasts, and as they wobbled around, he latched on to one, massaging it with his mouth. I had a tight grip on his ass, and for the next twenty minutes or so, I had the pleasure of making my husband forget about Jaylin. Too bad I couldn't. And just as Mario dropped low to taste me, my mind ventured to Jaylin's oral skills for a few minutes. Mario switched me back on his team when I felt myself on the brink of an orgasm. My thighs tightened around his head, and my fingernails raked through his hair. His tongue finally hit a homerun, causing my juices to burst in his mouth. I loved the slurping sound Mario made while tasting me.

"Mmmmm," I moaned as he brought his shiny lips to mine. Our tongues tangled. Everything felt as if it would be okay.

"I feel as if I'm on top of the world," he confessed while gazing into my eyes. "You are so precious to me, and I am unequivocally the luckiest man in the world."

I touched his bottom lip with my finger. He opened his mouth to suck it. "We're both lucky," I said. "But me way more than you."

Mario disputed my argument, especially when he rolled me on my stomach and worked me so well from behind. Our quickie never happened, but a few hours later we got back to business with our new home. The kids helped, and by eleven o'clock that night we all hit the bed. I was exhausted. There was so much more to do. Mario kept telling me that we were not going to have everything done overnight, but I couldn't rest until I made this house feel like home.

I also couldn't rest until I had a chance to speak to Jaylin about my conversation with Mario earlier. I was nervous as hell, but I did my best not to let it show. I thought he believed what I'd said, but just in case, I wanted to make sure Jaylin and I were on the same page. Something told me Mario was going to question Jaylin about my visit. I figured he wouldn't tell Mario the truth, but I wanted to let him know about the lie I'd told in reference to Mackenzie's school. Truthfully, we loved her school. She wasn't going anywhere, but Mario didn't have to know that right now.

While Mario was sound asleep, I tiptoed out of bed, making my way upstairs. I checked on the kids. They were all in one room knocked out. Their furniture had yet to be delivered, so they had sleeping bags and pillows all over the floor. I quietly closed the door, and then I went to Loretta's room to make sure she was there. She was asleep as well. I tiptoed back downstairs, making my way into the kitchen.

When I called Jaylin on my cell phone, he didn't answer. I sent him a text but got no reply. I suspected that he wasn't asleep this early, so instead of returning to bed, I grabbed my jacket from a closet and left. Jaylin's place was nearby. I was there in a flash.

Just as I was getting ready to ring the doorbell, Shane pulled the door open. He looked shocked to see me, as I was to see him. A towel was wrapped around his broad shoulders, and his dreads were contained by a blue bandana on his head. The wife-beater he wore revealed his muscular biceps, and as he smiled, his dimples came through in a major way. I had been there and done that several years ago. It was fun while it lasted, but it was no secret that I still had deep feelings for Jaylin when Shane and I dated. Yet again, I didn't have any regrets, especially after having the pleasure of being with a man as fine and intelligent as he was. Seeing him always brought back memories.

"What's up, Scorpio?" He looked me up and down in my pink pajama pants and sheer top. The jacket I wore covered my top, since I wasn't wearing a bra. "Is Jaylin expecting you?"

"No, he's not. I called him a few times, but he didn't answer his phone."

"We were playing ball on the court. I think he's still down there."

"Okay. Thanks. And good seeing you, Shane."

"Likewise."

As he walked off to get in his car, I had to take another look. If I weren't married, he could have gotten it again for sure. I fanned myself before going inside and locking the door behind me.

The moment I reached the stairs to the lower level, I could hear a basketball bouncing. Still tired from earlier, I hit the elevator button, allowing it to take me to the basement area. As soon as I got off, I walked to the court where Jaylin was. I stood in the doorway, watching him shoot the ball into the basket. His shirt was off, his body had a glowing tan, and his sweaty hair was wet. The Speedo compression shorts he wore hugged his big muscle, which sat real pretty on his right thigh. My dirty mind wandered just from looking at it, and when he missed the next shot, I laughed. He quickly pivoted to see who I was.

"Maybe you should call LeBron James to come over here and help you with that."

His eyes scanned me. "No need for LeBron to be here, but maybe I should call his wife over here so she can give you some lessons on what it means to be one hundred with the man you're married to."

I walked on the court, and catching Jaylin off guard, I snatched the ball from his hand. "I am one hundred, and one night with you doesn't change that."

"From the look of your hard nipples, it looks like you're shooting for another night. I'm not in the mood for fucking, so check back with me another time."

I rolled the ball on the floor, making sure I had his attention. "I didn't come here for that, so please don't flatter yourself. I came here because I may have a little problem. I need you to do something for me."

Jaylin crossed his arms in front of him. "Let me guess. You're pregnant too. It's my baby, and you don't know how to tell Mario."

I rolled my eyes at his foolishness. "No, I'm not pregnant, and if I were, it wouldn't be yours."

Jaylin shrugged. "Could be, because I put a whole lot of my goodness in that pussy. That shit probably still swimming, who knows?"

"I know it's not sooo . . ." I paused, thinking about something he'd said. "Pregnant? You said I'm pregnant too. Who is pregnant who you know?"

Jaylin jogged away to get the ball. He bounced it while coming my way. "Nokea," he said.

My eyes shot wide open. "Is the baby yours? I mean, I didn't think the two of you—"

"We're not. If she's pregnant, the baby is Travis's."

"This shouldn't be a surprise, but for real? How do you feel about that?"

"I don't care to discuss my feelings with you, but tell me why you're here again. My babies are okay, aren't they?" Jaylin shot the ball. This time it went in. He boasted and pointed to himself. "LeBron needs me on his team. Championships would come every time."

"I don't know about that, but the kids are fine. The reason I'm here is Mario asked me why I left my bachelorette party. I told him I came over here, but I mentioned that you and I discussed Mackenzie going to another school. If he happens to ask you, please tell him the same thing. You can understand why I don't want him to know the truth, don't you?"

Jaylin shook his head. "How long have you been officially married? Between twenty-four and forty-eight hours, and your ass lying already. I tried to stop you from throwing that hot coochie at me. But you refused to accept no for an answer. Now you want me to lie for you. That's fucked up, Scorpio. Real fucked up."

"You did not try to stop me, so quit lying. If anything, you were happy that I was here giving that boring room of yours some action. Your bed was happy to be squeaking again."

He laughed. "If only you knew. And when you don't know, you say silly shit that makes no sense. As you did with your lie to Mario, which sounds like bull. That man ain't stupid. He knows the truth. His ass probably had somebody watching us, but that's your problem, not mine. I can't promise you that I'm going to stick to your lie. It depends on if, when, or how he approaches me. After all, you do know how I am."

"I do know how you are, but please do it for me. That's all I ask, because I don't want any trouble."

I heard Jaylin's cell phone ring. He walked over to it, removing it from the floor. He took one glance but didn't answer.

"If I make this shot, her bed will be squeaking tonight, not mine. Mine don't squeak anyway, but I'm sure yours does." Jaylin shot the ball. It was all net. He smiled and winked at me. "Sorry, but she wins. Gotta go, all right?"

He walked off, taking the stairs to the upper level. I took the elevator. By the time I got to the main floor, he was already on the second floor, heading into his bedroom. I assumed he was about to take a shower and leave. I left as well, and the second I got back home, I went upstairs to check on the kids. They were still asleep. I then headed back to my bedroom. The moment I cracked the door to go inside, I felt someone reaching for my arm. Nearly jumping out of my skin, I quickly turned around, seeing Mario.

"Where did you go?" he asked in a groggy tone. "I got up looking all around for you."

"I couldn't sleep, so I went back to the penthouse to grab a few boxes I needed."

"You shouldn't be out this late. The movers will get all of that stuff. Be patient and everything will come together soon."

"I know. I just want this place to feel like home. I need to get comfortable. With all these people running around every day, it's starting to work me. I'll be glad when they're done. I'm eager to see the finished product."

"Soon enough, sweetheart. Now, go get in bed and let me massage you all over. I can help with some of the stress you're feeling, you know."

"You always do. That's why I love you so much."

For the moment, Mario massaged my stress away. I lay on my stomach with my eyes closed, in deep thought. I hoped he would never find out the truth, and I had faith that Jaylin would do as I'd asked. Then again, when it came to him, who knew what he would say or do?

Chapter 6

Nokea

I had been a nervous wreck. I felt kind of bad after what I'd done to Jaylin, but after saying what he did to me, he deserved it. I don't know why I thought I could tell him about the baby and he would provide me with some comforting words. Yet again, he made it all about him, but this baby had nothing to do with him. It was about me and Travis. While I definitely saw a future with him, I just wasn't ready to have another child and do all of that marriage stuff again. When the doctor told me it would be difficult for me to conceive another child, and I'd terminated one pregnancy, I surely thought that was it. I hadn't been taking any kinds of birth control, and when I missed my period last month, I could've died. Then I started feeling sick. My doctor confirmed my pregnancy a few weeks ago. I wanted to be happy, but I was so disappointed that I'd found myself in this situation again. That was one of the reasons I had been so moody.

The situation with Jaylin and Scorpio didn't help either. I started thinking about our failed marriage. I blamed him for putting me in the predicament I was in. Had he gotten it right, there would be no Travis, and there would be no baby. I wasn't about to have an abortion, so I had to come to grips and face my reality. The next thing I needed to do was tell Travis. I wasn't sure how he was going to react, but since he was coming over this evening, I made plans to tell him. I decided to cook a small meal and see what was on Netflix so we could watch a movie. While waiting for him to arrive, I called Scorpio to see what the kids were up to.

"They're fine," she said. "Keeping me real busy over here. We're about to sit down and have dinner."

"If you want them to come over here, that's fine. I know you're busy trying to get the house together and everything."

"Actually, they're helping me out a lot. They're having a good time, so no worries."

"Okay. And as soon as I have time, I'm going to stop by to see your place. I've been so busy lately, but maybe next weekend."

"Whenever you're ready. I know you have a lot on your plate, especially with the baby on the way."

I paused and was slightly taken aback by what she'd said. Had Jaylin told her about the baby already? He had to. How else would she have known? "I guess Jaylin told you. It's just like him to run his mouth. But yes, I am pregnant. I'm not ready to tell the kids yet, so please keep this between us."

"Will do, and congrats to you and Travis."

"Thanks."

"Hold on for a minute, because Jaylene said when you called she wanted to speak to you."

Jaylene came to the phone, telling me what a good time they were having. I spoke to LJ for a few minutes and even Justin who just wanted to say hi. After I spoke to Scorpio about an outfit she wanted at my shop, we ended the call.

I started to call Jaylin to see if he was okay, but then I changed my mind. I didn't want to hear any negativity right now. I couldn't talk to Nanny B because she always sided with him, so I called my mother to check on her and my father. Her diabetes had been giving her trouble, but she'd started to feel better. Now my father had something going on. That was why he couldn't make Jaylene's competition with my mother. Then again, I figured he just didn't want to be around Jaylin. My father still liked him, but I didn't think he was happy with Jaylin due to our divorce. He never said much else to Jaylin about it, but deep down I knew how my father felt.

"Hi, Mom," I said as she answered the phone. "What are you and Dad up to?"

"I'm watching TV, but your father is in the room, lying down. Where are my grandbabies at?"

"They're with Scorpio. She moved into a new house, and the kids are helping her."

"That's nice. How was the wedding? I wanted to stay, but I didn't want to be away from your father for too long. Was the wedding everything it was hyped up to be?"

"Actually, it was. Probably one of the most extravagant weddings I've ever been to. The kids enjoyed themselves, and I'm going to send you some pictures when I can."

"Please do. I showed your father those pictures of Jaylene during her competition. He started crying because we really don't get a chance to see our grandbabies that much. I wish we could travel more, but we don't like getting on those planes and flying all the time. It would be nice if you all would come here more often. I don't know why you don't, especially since y'all have that big ol' house in the Bluffs. I get lost in that house, but your father likes to go there all the time to show off with his friends from the church."

"That's Jaylin's house, not mine. It is nice, but I think it's a waste of money."

"What's Jaylin's is yours. He's the one who told me that. I don't think it's a waste. It's an asset, a huge asset."

I had my opinion, and she had hers. My mother was always Team Jaylin too, so deciding not to say much else, I hurried to end our conversation without telling her about the baby.

"Give Daddy a kiss for me, and I hope to see you two soon. Maybe the kids and I will come to St. Louis in a few more weeks or so."

"That would be nice. Tell Travis I said hello. Will he be coming with you?"

"I'm not sure. His schedule at the hospital is hectic. But I'll let you know for sure."

Right then there was a knock at the door, so I said goodbye to my mother. I was sure it was Travis. When I opened it, he stood with a bundle of roses in his hand. He was still in his green scrubs, looking tired as ever. His eyes were real glassy looking. I could tell he had been drinking. The good thing was there was a smile on his face. He was happy to see me.

"Seeing you is like a breath of fresh air." He kissed me on the lips. I forced my tongue in his mouth, just to give him a little something extra to help lift his spirits. "I needed that, more than you know."

I smiled and removed the roses from his hand. "Thank you. I needed these, too."

Travis followed me to the kitchen. As he washed his hands, I found a vase for my roses. The kitchen was lit up with the smell of baked chicken and rice. I had steamed some broccoli, and dessert was a surprise.

"Take a load off," I said, inviting Travis to have a seat. "From the look on your face, I can tell it wasn't a good day."

He cocked his tense neck from side to side. "It was a horrible day. I lost two patients today, and a thirteen-year-old boy lost his life to gun violence. Telling his mother was tough, real tough, and I'll never get used to that."

I stood behind him, raising his shirt over his head and massaging his broad, stiff shoulders. "I'm sure it doesn't get easy. But maybe it will when you've been at this for twenty or thirty more years. You're the new kid on the block. I know a lot of this is very new to you."

"It is, but no matter how long I stay in this profession, I can't ever see it getting easier."

I felt horrible for Travis. There was no question in my mind that the stress from his job was causing him to drink more. I wished he was in a better mood, but maybe my news about the baby would help perk him up. I started to prepare his plate, and after I piled it high with food, I prepared mine. We sat at the table, holding hands as we prayed. Afterward, we dove right in.

"How's business?" he asked.

"Business is good. We're still trying to fill orders from the fashion show. I'm glad I decided to keep the shop closed on Sundays because I need one day to rest. But as of tomorrow, it's back to work for me."

"Must be nice to get one day off. You know I'm always on call. I try to get in a nap every now and then at work, but things have been on a roll lately."

Travis was really feeling beat. We continued to make small talk that didn't revolve around the baby. I wasn't sure if this was the right time to spill the beans, but when I got up to get his ice cream, that was when I went for it. I placed a bowl of black walnut ice cream, his favorite, in front of him. He stirred it around, and I watched as he put a scoop in his mouth. Seconds later, he stirred the ice cream again. When he saw something in it, wrinkles appeared on his forehead.

He reached in the ice cream, pulling out a miniature pacifier with the word "Congratulations" on it. Travis raised his head, looking at me with wide eyes.

"Did you . . . Are you having a baby?"

I slowly nodded. "Yes. I'm pregnant, soooo what do you have to say about that?"

He reached out to grab me, holding me tightly in his arms. "Oh, my God, baby. This is . . . this is wonderful. I can't believe you're having a baby. I love you sooo much. No words can express how much I love you." After he released me, he pounded his fist against his hand. "Yes, yes, yes!"

His reaction made me feel a whole lot better. He kept kissing and praising me. "You're amazing, completely amazing, and I can't wait for you to be my wife. We have to get married. I want to get married, and we need to do it soon."

Just that fast, my mood had changed again. I didn't know how to say this without raining on his parade. "I love you too, Travis, but when it comes to getting married, I'm not so sure about that yet."

He inched away from me. Obviously, my words were not what he wanted to hear. "Why not, Nokea? What's so wrong with us getting married? I thought we had a great relationship. Tell me if I'm wrong."

I placed my hand on the side of his scrunched face, moving in closer to him. "It is great. It's wonderful, and I have never been this happy or at peace in any relationship I've been in. But that's the problem. I've been married, twice, and I came so close to being married three times. I can't keep rushing into marriages. This time I just want to take my time. I know you think two years should be enough, but Jaylin and I knew each other for many years, and it still wasn't enough to save our marriage."

"That's because he's a jerk. I'm nothing like him, and you know it. I appreciate you. I respect everything about you, and I would never do to you what he did. So what you've been married twice? Those marriages were never meant to be. You were too good for Jaylin, you didn't really love Collins, and that crap with Stephon was a big mistake. But that mess is in the past. It's done. I don't want you to use that as an excuse to not marry me."

I took a deep breath, backing away from him. I really thought he would understand why I didn't want to rush into this. "All that you're say-ing is true, but the fact remains that I've had two failed marriages. I have to be one hundred per-cent sure that if I go there again, it's a done deal."

Surprisingly, Travis started to throw a fit. His fist pounded the table, and his voice went up several notches. "It will be a done deal! I don't know why you think it wouldn't be. Tell me why, Nokea. Why aren't you willing to give us a chance?"

I placed my hand on top of his, trying to calm him down. "There is no need for you to get all worked up over this."

He snatched his hand away and shot up from the chair. With anger in his eyes, he paced the floor and then halted his steps to look at me. I sat in disbelief behind his actions. I'd never seen him throw a tantrum. That was what Jaylin often did when he didn't get his way.

"Don't make me give you an ultimatum," he threatened. "I don't stay in relationships with women for years just to play house. If that's what you want, you need to find yourself another man."

No words could express my frustrations. These demands were killing me. "Listen, okay? I will give what you said some serious thought, but you just don't know about these things, Travis. Please respect my take on this and understand why I feel as if marriage should be on hold right now. If the shoe were on the other foot, you would understand how I feel."

"I doubt it, because the love we have for each other supersedes everything, including your past. Get over it, Nokea, and stop feeding me crap about you *almost* being married three times."

"You view it as crap. I see it as my reality. I said I would think about it, so drop it."

With an attitude, I walked past Travis to head to my room. I thought we were done until he reached for my arm, spinning me around so I could face him.

"Why do I get a deep-down feeling that this has something to do with Jaylin? You've been talking to him, haven't you? You also told him about the baby, didn't you?"

His fingers were pressed hard on my arm. I peeled them off and stepped back. "Why do I have a feeling that this is more about the alcohol you've been drinking than it is about Jaylin? You can't yell at me and expect me to respond. If I do respond, I assure you that you won't like what I have to say."

He threw his hands up in the air. "Yep, you told him. And just so you know, trying to put me on the defensive doesn't work. Neither does talking about my drinking habits."

I shrugged. "Well, something is going on, because you're not your usual self. You keep bringing up Jaylin, and he is the least of my worries. This is about my future with you. I told him about the baby, but he didn't—"

Travis immediately cut me off. He stormed over to the chair, snatching his shirt from it. "That's what I figured. I knew he would try to talk you out of this. How could you tell him about the baby before telling me? Did you tell him because it's his baby instead of mine?"

At this point, I'd heard enough. I marched to the front door, opening it. "Come back when you're sober and thoughts of Jaylin aren't occupying your mind. I'm ready to celebrate our baby whenever you are. As for getting married, don't count on it anytime soon."

Travis slipped into his shirt, mean mugging me as he approached the door. He stopped right in front of me. "I'm going to allow you some time to change your mind. Hopefully, you'll come to your senses and decide to be with a man who really and truly loves you. If you don't, Nokea, it will be your loss, not mine."

He gave me a hard kiss on the cheek before leaving. I wiped it off and slammed the door behind him. I was pissed. No man, none whatsoever, was going to dictate my life and make any decisions for me. Not now, not ever, and not anymore.

Chapter 7

Jaylin

Shane and I had just left an old warehouse in Miami that we were going to purchase and convert into office spaces and loft apartments. The warehouse had much potential. When I saw it for myself, it was a go. Shane agreed, and as we got in my car, he made a phone call to see if we could quickly finalize the deal. The purchase cost was only $3.7 million. We could end up making a fortune in the long run.

While Shane was on the phone with the sellers, I looked out the window and saw a silver Mercedes speeding toward us at a distance. As the car got closer, I noticed Mario was inside. Within a few seconds, he positioned his car next to mine.

Shane looked at me, removing the phone from his ear. "What does he want? You good?"

"Always."

Mario stepped out of his car, and I got out of mine. There was no smile on his face. I wasn't smiling either.

"What's up, man?" he asked and lit a cigarette. He took a puff then leaned against his car.

"You tell me. I take it that you're interested in buying this property, since you're all the way out here by yourself."

"No, no, nothing like that. I'm not into the property business. It's too petty for me."

We were about to get off on the wrong foot. I could feel that Scorpio's request wouldn't get honored today.

"Petty, but legal. I'm all about doing shit that's legal, but I don't have a beef with those who don't."

Mario chuckled and raked his fingers through his hair. He took another long drag from the cigarette before whistling smoke into the air. "No beefs, Jaylin, no beefs at all. I just kind of thought we were cool, man, real cool, but I'm starting to have a change of heart. Something hasn't been right, and my lovely wife hasn't been completely truthful with me about certain things."

I shrugged my shoulders. "If you feel as if she hasn't been truthful with you, then why are you out here having this conversation with me? It may be wise for you to go home, have some wine, fix her a plate of pasta, and chat."

"We did all of that last night, but I still got some fucked-up feelings inside. Feelings about the day of her bachelorette party, where a little birdie told me she freaking spent the night with you. Scorpio says a simple conversation took place, but what do you say?"

I didn't like the question-and-answer bullshit, so it was time to wrap this up. "I say I'm not your wife. Scorpio is. Whatever she says happened, then that's what happened. Now, if you don't mind, I need to get back to some important legal business."

I tried to keep my cool, but when Mario held the door to my car so I wouldn't open it, shit was about to turn ugly. Shane got out on the passenger's side. We both delivered a look of death to Mario, who needed to think twice before he did anything stupid.

"No need for bodyguards," he chuckled then flicked the cigarette on the ground. "And you can leave your cousin Pooky and them on the sidelines for now. All I want is the truth. The t-r-u-t-h. Truth!" He slammed his hand against my car and had the audacity to move closer. So did I, and as we stood within inches of each other, Shane rushed over to my side. He stood beside me and Mario, trying to keep the peace.

"Pooky and them will kick ass if need be," he said to Mario. "But there is no need for us, as grown men, to settle our differences like this."

Shane was always trying to be the peacemaker. Me, on the other hand, I didn't give a fuck. Mario had no business confronting me with this bullshit. Therefore, he'd get an earful.

"Instead of knocking you on your ass for inter-rupting my business dealings, here's the truth as I know it. If or whenever I want to fuck your wife, I can. If I want her to leave you, she will. If I had an urge to satisfy my dick on your wedding day, I did. And if she begs for sex with me again, I may possibly deliver and give her the five explosive orgasms she so desperately needed. How I pro-ceed with this depends on how you treat me. So think hard about how we end this conversation. The ball is now in your court, but my balls may return to her mouth."

Mario raised his fist, attempting to throw a punch at me. Shane caught it midair and shoved him back. He staggered, trying to keep his bal-ance.

"Sorry, but it ain't going down like that," Shane said calmly. "You need to check out of here immediately."

I stood with a smirk on my face, waiting for Mario to make another move. All he did was spit something from his mouth and continue to talk shit with his hands in the air, as if one of us had a gun. A crooked smile was on his face.

"You win, Jay-lynnn. Today you win, but going forward, you grimy cocksucker, I do."

Words with no action didn't mean shit to me. I left Mario's pathetic ass standing there, looking like a fool. Shane and I got in the car, and as I backed up, Mario continued to stand with his hands in the air. He then lowered them and started shadowboxing.

"*La vita è bella,* my friend. No matter what, my life is beautiful. You'd better hope yours is too."

I drove away thinking about how Scorpio needed to intervene and get his punk ass in check soon. I wasn't about to trip with him over no pussy, and yet again, I was in the middle of her and Nokea's messes.

Shane said the same thing. "I don't get why they always coming to you. You need to tell them to stop running to you, man. I saw Scorpio at your crib the other night. I was on my way out, and she was going in. I guess Mario ain't having it. And to be truthful, Jay, I don't think it's a good idea for you to start fucking with her again. You really need to let that shit go."

Just that fast, Shane's words had gotten underneath my skin.

"Before you put your foot in your mouth, Scorpio and I shared one night together. That was it. When she came by the other night, it was with regard to this shit with Mario. I did not touch her, but you know what, Shane? If I choose to have sex with her again, I will. But I don't want to, and I'm happy as fuck that she is with his ass. So don't talk that nonsense to me right now about what I need to let go. Talk to me about what else we need to do to finalize this deal. That's what's important. All this other bullshit don't matter."

To no surprise, he wouldn't let it go. "It doesn't matter, but you need to pull back on your tone when speaking to me. I'm not Mario, and I really do not have a beef with you. All I did was make a suggestion based on what I thought. Nothing more, nothing less."

I fired back. "Your assumption was incorrect. And when you want to offer me advice, you need to be working with the facts."

"The facts can be muddled sometimes, and your tone is still up there. Bring it down or else."

This fool was tripping. I had to pull my car over so I could figure out where he was going with this. "Or else what?" I shouted, feeling irritated.

"Or else I'm gon' kick yo' ass, Jay, like Mario would have done back there, had I not intervened. In case you forgot, he was a professional boxer."

"Who gives a damn? Mario couldn't kick a fly's ass, and you need to reflect on years ago when I had to get you straight over Felicia."

"Get me straight? No, I got you straight and let you have that bitch. She became your problem, not mine. As is Scorpio, who I had to toss back to you too."

"You must be smoking something, right? You cried your heart out when Scorpio left you. That's why you're in your little feelings over there, talking about fighting me. But no worries. You're good, and so is she. I won't ever touch her again, so you and Mario can relax. Besides, the pussy was just okay that day anyway."

Shane laughed. "What? Just okay? Are you telling me Scorpio wasn't up to par? That she didn't whip that snapdragon on you and make you lose your mind like you used to?"

"No, she made you lose your mind, not me. Again, your facts are twisted."

"If you say they are, cool. But we both know the truth, and we have to face reality. The reality is that muthafuckin' pussy had us both doing some fucked-up shit. I don't know what she got between her legs, but whatever she got is like magic. It messed us up pretty bad."

I had to laugh. I also shook my head, briefly thinking about the past. "That was then, and this is now. Now, things aren't what they used to be, but if she had more practice, I'm sure she'll be able to revive herself in no time."

"Sorry to hear that. What a shame. Mario seems satisfied, though, and you have to be careful because a pussy like that can make a man want to kill somebody. That's the only reason I suggested that you back off. You don't need the hassle, and Scorpio needs to find a way to get control of this."

I agreed, and all this talk about Scorpio was put on the back burner when we got to my house and found out the sellers for the warehouse accepted our offer for $2.9 million instead. We lifted our glasses of alcohol, tossing out a toast.

"Here's to the next five years," Shane said. "May our pockets keep getting fatter."

"I damn sure will drink to that."

Later that day, I was in my office when I got a call from Nokea. My spirits were up until she started talking about what I didn't want to hear.

"I hate when we argue with each other," she said, "but you have to understand that this isn't about you, Jaylin. I just . . . just need someone to talk to about this. I told Travis about the baby. Now he wants to get married. I'm not there yet, and giving me your honest opinion, do you think it's too soon?"

I answered by hanging up on her. We were close, but how dare Nokea think she could keep coming to me with bullshit like that? She had to work that craziness out on her own, because any advice I gave would be beneficial to me, not her.

She called back, but I didn't answer. A few minutes later, I received a text message from her: What a shame that after all we've been through, U won't even talk to me. Every time U were going through something, I was there for U. My, have things changed. I'm leaving for a few days. Call U when I return. Maybe you'll be ready to talk.

I didn't see anything shameful about it, so I deleted her text and didn't bother to respond. I was too much in a good mood, so I went to the golf course with LJ. We returned home around seven, and by then Nanny B had already cooked. We all sat down to eat a late dinner.

"Jaylin, I need you to do me a favor," Nanny B said while chewing her food. "Jaylene needs her backpack for school tomorrow. I told Nokea I would stop by earlier to get it, but it's getting late, and I don't like driving at night. Will you go over to her place and get it? She's out of town on business for a few days, so I'll give you the key to get in."

"My backpack is in the closet in my room," Jaylene said. "I can go with you, Daddy."

"No, I'll go get it. After you eat, you need to take a shower and go get ready for bed."

Jaylene nodded and continued to eat. Justin, however, eased down from the chair and walked to the refrigerator. He opened it and started moving things around.

"He's looking for another soda," Jaylene said. "Do we have any?"

"No, not one," I confirmed.

Just then, Justin pulled out a soda and stretched his hand toward Nanny B, speaking softly. "Nanna, will you open this for me?"

She looked at me. My eyes were already fixed on her. "What is it that y'all don't understand?" I asked. "He does not need to be drinking no damn soda. There's too much sugar in that shit, so why do you and Loretta insist on giving it to him?"

Nanny B cut her eyes at me. "Jaylin, please. It's just a soda. It ain't like it's gon' kill him."

"It may not, but it damn sure can cause a lot of damage in the long run. I said no more sodas, and I mean it. Stop giving it to him. This is my last time saying it."

I got up and removed the soda can from Justin's hand. After I tossed it in the trashcan, he threw a fit. I tried to pick him up, but he wasn't having it. Tears poured from his eyes. He could barely catch his breath.

"Look what you done to that poor child," Nanny B said, reaching out for him.

He rushed into her arms, squeezing her neck while his head was resting on her shoulder. His gray eyes, identical to the color of mine, were narrowed, and as snot dripped from his nose, his sniffles continued.

"Daddy, you're mean," Mackenzie said. "Meanie, meanie, meanie. All he wants is just one soda."

"Yeah, Dad," LJ added. "Like Nanna said, it won't kill him."

Jaylene was the only one who hadn't said anything. And just when I thought she'd had my back, she didn't. "Why throw it away? That's wasting drinks, and you're always talking about wasting food and drinks."

"Well, we're going to waste plenty of food and drinks tonight," I said. "Get up from the table and let's all go to sleep. Anybody don't like it, call DFS on me."

"What's DFS?" LJ asked.

"Division of Family Services," Mackenzie said. "Somebody called them on my aunt Leslie before because she spanked her kids."

Jaylene scratched her head. "Should I call them too? Mommy spanked my hand, and it really hurt."

"Thanks for letting me know," I said. "I'll be sure to spank her when I see her. Now, off to bed."

They fussed and whined as they marched out of the kitchen, still referring to me as a mean dad. Nanny B tagged along with Justin still crying as if I had beaten him with a damn bat. All I could do was shake my head, but it wasn't long before I started feeling bad about my actions. Maybe one little soda wasn't going to hurt.

I opened the fridge to look for another one. I knew Nanny B had been hiding them somewhere, and sure enough, when I moved a few things out of the way, there was another can of orange soda. I opened the can, pouring half of it into a cup. I guessed compromise wasn't a bad thing after all.

Justin was in Nanny B's bedroom with her. As she sat in a comfortable suede chair, he was snuggled against her chest. I stood next to them with the cup in my hand. Justin looked at me but didn't move. I reached out my arms to him, but he turned his head, tightening his grip around Nanny B's neck.

"G'on with that soda," she said, shooing my hand away. "You done hurt our feelings, so forget it now."

I put the cup down then grabbed Justin from Nanny B's chest. As I lifted him in the air, he started to laugh. I dropped him on the bed, tickling him all over. He giggled loudly, and this time when I reached out to hold him, he came right into my arms. I grabbed some tissue to wipe his wet face.

"Listen, I don't know why you like so much soda, but water, milk, and some juices are much better. Soda has too much sugar. If you keep drinking it, the sugar is going to fill your whole body and turn you into a sugar monster. You don't want to be a sugar monster, do you?"

He moved his head from side to side. "No, Daddy. I don't want to be a sugar monster."

"Cool. Then drink one more soda and that's it. Okay?"

He nodded, and when I reached for the cup to give it to him, he rejected it. "Juice, Daddy. I want juice."

I winked at Nanny B, who sat with a smirk on her face. "See how simple that was?" I said.

"We're going to the kitchen to go get us some juice."

I carried Justin to the kitchen and got his juice, and then we returned to Nanny B's bedroom. She took Justin before giving me the key to Nokea's place. I wouldn't dare tell anybody I already had my own key. Nokea gave it to me a while back. I guessed she forgot to take it back after she made the decision to break it off with me.

"Thanks, Jaylin," Nanny B said. "I'll make sure the kids go to sleep, but when you get back, you can tackle that messy kitchen."

I surely didn't mind. And only because I hated to see things left in such a mess, I cleaned the kitchen before I left. It was spotless. I could have made a fortune being a maid.

I arrived at Nokea's place nearly thirty minutes later. Her condo was pitch-black. I was surprised that she didn't leave any lights on. I flicked the light switch in the living room and then hit up a few lights as I made my way down the hallway. I glanced in her bedroom. It was empty. All I saw were a few magazines sprawled on the bed, an empty glass on one nightstand, and what looked to be a journal on the other. I made my way into the room, and as I picked up the journal, I flipped through it, noticing her unique penmanship. I didn't really want to read what she had written, but just for the hell of it I sat on the bed and indulged myself.

Starting from several weeks ago, the majority of what she wrote about was her excitement about the fashion show, her amazing time with the kids, and sex between her and Travis. How good he made her feel, how passionate he was, how she was so in love with him, and how God had finally blessed her with the man of her dreams.

I love everything about him. So kind and gentle. Sex is the bomb, and my personal doctor has skills. Never had a man who utilizes his penis in such a unique way. I want more, and I can never get enough! Can't wait until later so I can serve him more of my sweetness.

My blood boiled while reading this bullshit. *How in the fuck is he utilizing his penis better than I do? And what kind of skills is she referring to?* She also mentioned his drinking habit and had written about an argument they'd had. Right after that, she expressed her anger with me. I was the bad guy for sure. I was the one who had broken her heart, but she was over that now. That was until she saw me and Scorpio together.

She hated me. She hated Scorpio. I wasn't shit, but why, she asked, did she even care? She hated that she still cared for me, and she questioned, time and time again, her level of love for me.

I keep telling myself no. No, I do not love him anymore. How could I love a man who has caused me so much pain? I can't and I won't. Screw him. I need to thank him. Thank him for freeing me so I can be with the one I love.

She went on and on about the baby. It was all my fault for putting her in this predicament. Her words left me very confused. I didn't know that Nokea still harbored this much anger toward me. It was so crazy, because I thought that after all this time things were good between us. Well, as good as it could get, considering all that had happened. Maybe it was wise for me to listen to her instead of hanging up the phone. She seriously needed to get certain things about our past off her chest.

Refusing to read more, I closed the journal. I headed to Jaylene's room to get her backpack. Barbie dolls and books were on her bed, so I put her dolls in a toy box then put her books back on the shelf. I went into her closet and saw her backpack on the top shelf. As soon as I grabbed it, I heard a door slam. It startled me because Nokea was supposed to be on a business trip.

The first thing I thought was somebody was breaking in. My gun was in the car, so I tiptoed down the hallway, trying to see who had entered her apartment. The closer I inched my way to the living room, I heard laughter. I heard whispering and a whole lot of giggling. I could officially say the laughter was Nokea's. And by the time I peeked into the living room, I saw that it was her.

Travis was with her. A bottle of Hennessy was in his hand. He appeared drunk. Nokea was giddy too, but there was nothing in her hand. Her clothes, however, were disheveled, and her wrinkled shirt had been ripped away from her chest. Her left breast was exposed, and as she plopped back in the chair, her skirt gathered at her waist, displaying her goodies. With her legs open, Travis had a clear view. So did I. He appeared mesmerized and turned the Hennessy bottle up to his mouth. He took a deep swallow before dropping to his knees in front of Nokea and placing the bottle on the floor. He wiped his hand across his mouth, and within seconds he and Nokea started to vigorously go at it. She ripped his shirt off while he took passionate bites at her neck that made her moan. They laughed as she rushed to unhook his belt buckle.

"Naaaah, you don't want none of this," he slurred. "You can't hang, and the last time I tore into your pussy, you was begging me to stop and go."

Really? She was begging for it, huh?

"No, I was begging you to fuck me, like I am now," she said aggressively as she yanked down his pants, shoving him back on the floor.

Her ass ain't ever begged me to fuck her. She knows better.

She crawled on top of him, and with her pretty bare ass now in my view, I watched her reach for his dick, readying herself to take it all in. My stomach rumbled and was queasy as fuck. There was no way in hell I was about to watch it go down like this. With Travis packing very close to the same size as I, I knew Nokea would put on an interesting performance. I had never, ever witnessed her have sex with another man. Even though I knew she had, I refused to stand there and be a witness to this.

I charged into the room, snatching Nokea off of him. I shoved her on the sofa, lying over her while holding myself up. She was so shocked that her eyes were wide, and her body appeared frozen. The sweet aroma of her pussy slapped me in the face, and with her breasts so close, I was so tempted to go there. Travis, however, had a grip on my arm, trying to pull me away from Nokea.

"What in the fuck are you doing?" he shouted. "Have you lost your gotdamn mind? Get off of her, now!"

I ignored him while searching deep into Nokea's eyes. My heart was beating fast, a sheen of sweat covered my forehead, and my words were stern. "I'm putting it all on the line today, and I'm asking you to help make me whole again. I can help you get there too, but you first have to put an end to this. If you want to have sex, I prefer that you think about making love to me. I've already said, time and time again, that I was sorry for hurting you. With everything there is in me, I truly am. I love you, baby. I will never stop loving you. I can't. I tried, but I can't."

"Well, you fucking need to," Travis barked. "And you need to get the hell up before I . . ."

He snatched the Hennessy bottle from the floor. That was when Nokea placed her hands on my heaving chest to push me back. By then, he threw the bottle, causing it to shatter against the wall. Brown liquor splattered and rained down the wall. He stood like a madman with his chest rising and falling.

"Leave, Jaylin," Nokea said as I stood up. She knew I was about to deal with this fool, so she hurried off the couch, trying to push me away. I looked over her shoulder, staring at Travis without a blink. His twitching eyes were locked on me too.

"Did you not hear what she said?" Spit sprayed from his mouth as he yelled. "She said get out!"

I fought hard to remain calm and ignore his pitiful ass. My eyes shifted to Nokea, who stood in front of me so I wouldn't move. "As I was saying," I continued, "no man will ever love you like I do. We share too much history to let go. Please think about what I'm saying to you, and if you still have an ounce of love left for me, allow me to make you fully love and trust me again. I can do it, Nokea. Just give me the opportunity to do it, baby, all right?"

She stood gazing at me with her big and beautiful doe eyes. Her tongue appeared tied. She didn't snap out of her inner thoughts until Travis started to make noise again.

"Will you please speak up and put this shit to rest! Damn! Tell him who you love, Nokea! For God's sake tell him it is over! Geesh!"

Nokea swallowed while keeping her eyes locked on me. She slowly moved her head from side to side. "I . . . I'm not going there again with you, Jaylin. I've given you too many chances to do right by me, and you failed me every time. How can you stand there and think that I'm supposed to drop everything and come running back to you? I'm in love with—"

"No," I quickly cut her off. My stomach was in knots. It hurt, but I needed to say what was on my mind. "I don't want to hear that. What I need is for you to help take away my lonely nights. I'm having too many of them, and your relationship with him is too much for me to handle."

She fired back, expressing anger. "Listen, I know all about those lonely nights, Jaylin. I had them too, and I cried plenty of nights over you. Soft music is therapeutic, so go try it. Hopefully, it'll be able to get you through some of those painful nights like I had time and time again."

I shook my head, realizing that I wasn't getting through to her. "Yes, I failed you but, baby, you made some mistakes too. Regardless—"

"Mistakes?" Travis roared from behind her. "Having an affair and a child during a marriage is not a mistake! It's called having your freaking cake and eating it, too! The only mistake she made was trusting you! And if she has any damn sense, she'll tell you right now to go fuck yourself!"

Unfortunately, I couldn't let this drunk-ass, slick-mouth fool slide. I rushed around Nokea and lit his ass up with a hard punch to his gut.

More spit and alcohol sprayed from his mouth. He doubled over, grabbing his stomach. As he coughed and staggered back to the wall, Nokea rushed to his side. Fury was trapped in her eyes, and daggers were flying fast.

"I'm so sick of you doing this," she said tearfully. "Why can't you just—"

"Because I can't," I shouted. "Have you not heard one fucking thing I've said to you? I guess not, but you know what, Nokea? If this is what you want, and he is who you truly want to be with, then stop calling me, stop asking me to be there for you, stop making me a part of your world, and leave me the hell alone. That's all I ask, so you'd better be sure this is the route you want to take."

With gritted teeth, she rushed toward me to respond. I stopped her dead in her tracks when I grabbed her face, bringing it close to mine. I put my mouth over hers, and as I sucked her lips, they trembled. I could feel her body slowly melting, but she didn't reciprocate the kiss.

"This is crazy!" Travis yanked at Nokea's arm, pulling her in his direction. She nearly lost her balance he pulled her so hard. He secured his arms around her waist, giving me the evil eye. "This, motherfucker, is how you kiss the woman you truly love!" He hugged Nokea's lips with his while rubbing his hands all over her body. She rejected his moves and slightly pushed him back. I spoke up before she did and unhooked my belt buckle.

"That was a weak-ass kiss, but if you want me to show you how to make love to her, I can do that very well. Been doing it for years, and I intend to do it for many more years to come."

Nokea had seen and heard enough. She pointed to the door and spoke sternly. "Go home, Jaylin. Don't come here again unless I invite you. And just so you know, I am with the man I want to be with."

"No, you're not," I countered. "When you're ready to wake the fuck up, you know where I'll be."

I walked out with Jaylene's backpack in my hand, thinking. Call it karma, payback, whatever. I called it bullshit.

Chapter 8

Scorpio

The house was finally coming together, but Mario had been walking around acting real strange. He didn't seem like his perky self, and his ongoing questions about my bachelorette party were starting to annoy me. No, I didn't tell him the truth. I wholeheartedly believed that only Jaylin and I knew what the truth was. Therefore, I was sticking to my lie. I would never tell Mario what actually happened, only because I didn't want him to know that I'd betrayed him.

Did I think he would divorce me if he knew the truth? Absolutely not. He would be upset for sure, but I didn't want to upset him. We were still in the honeymoon stage right now. This was our time to enjoy our new life together, in addition to our new home. Instead, I found myself watching my back and being a little fake with my husband just to help him take his mind off things. Usually, sex would do the trick, but for the past two nights, he'd gone to bed without even holding me.

It was up to me to turn this situation around, so when we woke up the next morning, I asked Loretta to cook him breakfast so I could feed him in bed. I also ran some soothing bathwater so we could take a warm bath together. He was still sleeping, and when Loretta lightly knocked on the door, I opened it. I removed the tray of food from her hand, thanking her for hooking us up.

"You're welcome," she whispered. "If you need anything else, let me know. I'll be in my room."

I closed the door, and with my turquoise silk robe on, I laid the tray on the nightstand then got in bed. Mario stretched his arms and yawned. He slowly sat up, rubbing his eyes. I removed the tray from the nightstand and placed it on my lap.

"Good morning." I leaned closer to peck his lips. "You slept kind of late today."

He raked his hair away from his face, but a long, curly part of it fell in front of his eye. "I've been tired. Haven't been getting much sleep because there's too much on my mind."

I pecked his lips again. "I don't know why you've been stressing so much, especially with this thing about my bachelorette party and me being at Jaylin's house. Why is it so hard to believe that I went there to discuss an ongoing issue with Mackenzie? I always go to Jaylin's house. You act as if I've done something differently, and I haven't."

Mario tossed the covers aside and got out of bed naked. Not an ounce of fat was on his body. I took a quick glance at his tight ass before he opened the doors to the bathroom and went inside. I heard him take a leak and wash his hands. He also took a while longer. I assumed he was brushing his teeth. When he came back, he didn't return to the bed with me. He sat on the chaise with his elbows resting on his knees.

"Just so you know"—he paused to rub the minimal, silky hair on his chest—"I spoke to Jaylin a few days ago. It didn't go well. He said some shit that got underneath my skin. I thought he was cool, but I don't wanna fuck with him anymore. I don't want you fucking with him either, and if you screw me, Scorpio, you will pay a costly price."

My brows shot up. I was surprised by his threat. He had never spoken to me like that, nor had he ever threatened me.

"I don't know what Jaylin said to you, but whatever it was, you have no right to speak to me like that. I've done nothing wrong, Mario.

It really hurts that you don't believe me. I have everything that I need and want right here, and I'm not trying to complicate things in any way."

Mario reached for a cigar that was on the table next to him. He lit it and lay back on the chaise, taking a puff of the cigar. His eyes were focused on me.

"I don't know why I don't believe you. Something doesn't add up. I called you early that morning, and you never answered your phone. I called you three fucking times." He held up three fingers. "Yet there was no answer. You've always answered your phone when I called. Why didn't you answer it then?"

I released a deep sigh. This was becoming ridiculous. We couldn't even enjoy ourselves, and day by day, there was one question after another. I started to wonder what in the hell Jaylin had said to him.

"I don't know what I will have to do to make you believe me, but—"

"But my naked ass, Scorpio." He removed the cigar from his mouth, and while holding it between his fingers, he pointed at me. "What you can do is tell the fucking truth. That's what you need to do, especially since Jaylin said he could have you. Said he could screw you when he wanted to. Said he did, and he would continue to do it, because you, my sweet, little, beautiful fucking wife, would allow him to do it. Is that true? Tell me if what he spoke was the truth."

I couldn't believe Jaylin had told him that. Maybe Mario was exaggerating. "No, it's not true, and I know for a fact that he didn't say that to you."

Mario got up from the chaise and walked to where I was. He laid the cigar in an ashtray before grabbing my face and squeezing my jaw with his strong hand. "Are you calling me a liar? I hope not, sweetheart, because you're not going to like me when I'm angry. I ask you again: did you fuck him? Did you come for him five times and put his filthy balls in your mouth?"

Mario's tight grip on my face hurt, so I smacked his hand away. Now knowing that Jaylin had said something foul to Mario, especially since he knew about the number of orgasms, I didn't have much else to say. I placed the tray on the nightstand, and instead of responding to him, I moved to the other side of the bed and got out of it.

"Answer me." Mario raised his voice as I walked into the bathroom. The Jacuzzi tub with four thick columns surrounding it was still filled with bubbles and water. I dropped my robe to the floor and stepped inside of it. As I lay back on the contoured pillow, I closed my eyes, ignoring Mario as he stood in the doorway, awaiting an answer.

"Your little silent treatment won't work. And if you won't speak, many others will."

I opened my eyes and shrugged. "You can talk to anyone you'd like to, but my words still stand, even though you're ignoring them. I said no. No, I did not have sex with Jaylin. It never happened. So if all you want to do is argue, put your hands on me, and make threats, I'm going to ignore you. I'm trying to avoid going down this road with you, and maybe after breakfast you'll feel much better. For now, I'm done talking."

I closed my eyes, relaxing and attempting to enjoy my bath. Mario stepped away from the door, but when he returned, he dumped the tray of food in the tub with me, causing me to jump up and hop out of the water. I damn near slipped on the wet floor, especially when he grabbed my arm and swung me around to face him.

"Fuck breakfast. You eat that shit. You didn't prepare it anyway, but you have very little time to prepare an explanation for what happened that night. I'll wait, but I won't wait long."

Mario let go of my arm, but catching me completely off guard, he shoved me so hard that I fell back into the tub, causing water to splash all over the floor. I hit my elbow on the tub, my ankle bumped the column, and my head jerked back. I wiped my hand down my wet face, looking at Mario as he went into his walk-in closet.

"Is this how you treat me because I don't want to argue with you?" I shouted and tried to hurry out of the tub without slipping on the floor. Once I was out, I grabbed a towel from the heated rack, covering myself with it. This time, Mario ignored me as I stood in the doorway to his closet, watching him get dressed.

"Don't you ever do that crap again! If you're that angry, just leave. This is so ridiculous. I don't know what else you expect me to say."

He zipped his jeans and tossed a shirt over his shoulder. He walked by me as if I weren't even standing there. I followed him into the bedroom, and after he picked up his wallet from the nightstand, he headed toward the door.

"Mario," I shouted. "I said no! No to all of your questions. No, no, no, so why won't you listen?"

He halted his steps at the door and turned around. "Because you're a gotdamn liar."

He walked out, leaving me speechless.

Nearly an hour later, I stood in Jaylin's kitchen, watching him eat from a fruit cup and appearing unfazed by my comments.

"You didn't have to say anything to him," I said in a snippy tone. "All you had to say was what I asked you to say. It couldn't have been that difficult for you to do, Jaylin. Instead, you just had to tell him some crap about how you could fuck me whenever you wanted to. And why mention how many orgasms you made me have? So what? Why say that to him when you knew it would piss him off and stir up an argument between us?"

Appearing real calm, he just stared at me and continued to eat his fruit. "Scorpio, don't make me disrespect you. If you don't mind, I'm enjoying an afternoon snack. I would also like to get some more work done today, so forgive me if I don't react to your drama."

He pissed me off so bad that I reached out and smacked the fruit cup from his hand. Juice splashed on his face. The fruit and cup hit the floor. He jumped from the chair, and I sprinted toward the front door, hoping he wouldn't catch me. Unfortunately, he did. In a matter of seconds, he pinned me against the wall with his hand gripped around my neck. I couldn't even breathe. I scratched at his hands, trying to get him to release me.

"You're never fucking satisfied unless there is drama in your life. I don't have time for it, so don't bring that shit over here, Scorpio! Keep that shit in your own household. If you didn't want any of this to happen, you should have thought carefully about the consequences when you brought yo' hot ass over here begging me to fuck you!"

He released his grip, and as a tear ran from my eye, I reached out, slapping the shit out of him. His head stayed still, and his face tightened even more. When I saw his eyes narrow and his fist clench, I turned toward the door. He reached for the back of my neck, squeezing it and pulling it toward him. His lips were right at my ear as he spoke sternly in it.

"You are dead to me," he said, "to me and to our kids. Until you and your man get y'all shit together, they will not be staying over there. Don't like it? Talk to my attorney about it. Talk to your husband about it, too, because when I get done bringing up all the illegal shit going on behind the scenes, it will be a cold day in hell before you ever see your kids again."

My neck was in a lot of pain, and the more I tried to pull away from him, the tighter his grip got. "You won't win this battle, Jaylin. How dare you bring our kids—"

"I've already won, so go home, tell your husband the truth about how good I was to you that night, and use all that good pussy you got to win him over again. He's weak, so that shouldn't be difficult for you to do." Jaylin opened the door, inching me to it. "One, two, three, go!"

He shoved me forward, and as I quickly pivoted, I was face-to-face with the door. Maybe, just maybe, a battle with Mario would have been much easier.

Chapter 9

Nokea

For the past few days, Travis hadn't been speaking to me. He felt as if I hadn't done enough to stop Jaylin from interfering. Said I lay there on the couch without saying a word, and when I refused to call the cops and press charges against Jaylin, Travis left again. Ever since I'd told him I was pregnant, things had been going downhill. We hadn't argued this much since we'd been together. It was as if Travis was changing right before my eyes. It very well could have been the issue with me not wanting to marry him, too. I wasn't sure, but we needed to get back on track fast.

As for pressing charges against Jaylin, I honestly didn't think that was necessary. But I understood Travis's concerns about Jaylin's actions. I was totally shocked, and all this time, I thought he was okay with the way things were. Not overjoyed, but I figured he understood my decision pertaining to us being together again. I'd heard every word he'd said that day, but the truth was it was too late for us. Too much damage on both of our parts led me to believe that we had no business trying to rekindle our relationship and go there again. More than anything, Jaylin knew I was in love with Travis. This was no game. And unlike my past relationships, I wasn't trying to use Travis to get over my hurt. I'd made my decision, and I regretted that Travis felt caught in the middle.

Thinking about him, I called his cell phone again, but he kept saying he was busy. He threw himself into work. So did I. I worked long hours at the shop, and I had only been by Jaylin's house three times this week to hang out with the kids. Both times he wasn't there. Nanny B said he was in Detroit. Thank God for that. The kids and I were going to a water park this weekend, but I wasn't so sure if Travis was still going with us. Even if he wasn't, our plans remained intact.

One of my customers needed help with a dress, and when I looked up, I saw Scorpio come in. There was no smile on her face. I could tell something was on her mind. I called my assistant/ designer, Jazz, to help the customer. Scorpio came up to me, looking stressed.

"Do you have a minute?" she said. "I really need to discuss a few things with you about Jaylin."

"Sure," I said. "Let's go to my office."

She followed me to my office. Once we were seated, she removed her sunglasses and started to tell me about an unfortunate situation between her and Jaylin.

"He's trying to stop the kids from coming to my house," she said. "We got into an argument, and he doesn't want the kids with me on the weekends anymore. He also said I'm not welcome at his house, so I don't know how he thinks that's going to work. I just wanted to let you know that he's not getting his way this time. He doesn't control when I get to see my children, so there very well could be a legal battle coming soon. I wanted to make you aware of it."

I sighed. There was always something. I could only imagine what started this argument. "What was the argument about?"

Scorpio started to give me details about what had been transpiring. She had the audacity to lie to me about why she was at Jaylin's house the morning of her wedding. I already knew the truth, but I let her continue with her lie until she was finished.

"This sounds horrible," I said, "but in my opinion, if you don't mind me saying, Mario has every right to be upset. I know why you were at Jaylin's house, and it had nothing to do with Mackenzie. You spent the night with him, and the two of you had sex. Jaylin already admitted it. When I came over that morning, I saw you and him in bed together. The two of you were naked, so I'm pretty sure that Mackenzie hadn't been discussed."

Scorpio swallowed hard before trying to clean up her lies. "I did have sex with him, but the whole world doesn't have to know about it. I just wanted to hook up with him before I walked down the aisle and married Mario. Since then, I haven't even thought about going there again with Jaylin. I'm trying to work through this little problem in my marriage, and I don't want the kids involved."

I refused to bite my tongue on this matter. Scorpio needed to hear what I had to say, whether she liked it or not.

"You can get over the hump by telling Mario the truth. If you say you haven't thought about Jaylin, fine. I don't believe you, but you don't have to convince me. Convince your husband, and after all he's done for you and for our kids, he deserves better. I really don't know him that well, but from what I can see, the two of you have a pretty decent life together. I don't know why you would allow Jaylin to mess that up. Was sex with him worth it?"

Scorpio was silent. She nibbled at her nails, looking away as if she was in deep thought. "No, it wasn't, but it was something I needed to do. I guess it wouldn't be fair to blame it all on Jaylin, because I participated too. But he said some things to Mario that he shouldn't have said. That's why we got into an argument. That's what led to all of this."

"Well, I'll try to talk to him about the situation with the kids. He really has no say-so about the weekends, because we've already worked that out. If he wants to stop you from coming to his house during the week, ask Nanny B to meet you somewhere. That's what I would do, because there is no way he would stop me from being with the kids either. The only reason things are the way they are now is because the kids love it at his house. Their happiness is more important to me than mine."

Scorpio agreed. She hung around to do some shopping, and after she spent almost two grand in my shop, she left. I thanked her for the purchase and invited her to go to the water park with us. She told me to count her in.

After Scorpio left, I returned to my office so I could reach out to Jaylin. The first two times I called, he didn't answer. When I called him a third time, he did.

"I'm in a meeting," he said. "What's up?"

"I wanted to speak to you about this little problem with you, Scorpio, and the kids."

"You and I don't need to discuss that. Are you still pregnant?"

I didn't appreciate his question. "Of course I'm still pregnant. Why wouldn't I be?"

"Because it's not my baby."

"Soooo, what does that mean?"

"Nothing, I guess. Have you thought about what I said?"

"Yes and no. I already told you how I felt, Jaylin. I think it's best that we remain friends and leave it at that."

There was silence before he spoke up. "All right. Is there anything else?"

"Yes. Please don't put the kids in the middle of your so-called battle with Scorpio. We always tend to work things out, and I think it's so unfair to the kids, especially when you make threats about them not being able to spend time with their own mother."

"Are you done?"

"Not really, but I have a feeling that you're not listening to me."

"That's because I'm not. When you want to talk about us, let me know."

The phone call ended there. Since I didn't have time to deal with Scorpio's and Jaylin's problems, I left the shop to go to the hospital and see Travis.

The hospital floor Travis worked on was extremely busy. Doctors and nurses were moving at a speedy pace through the hallways, phones were blaring, visitors were everywhere, and an old man in a wheelchair was sitting in the middle of the floor, asking for help. A nurse quickly attended to him. I wasn't sure if Travis would have time for me, but the minute I saw him coming down the hallway with two other doctors and a nurse by his side, all I could do was smile. He smiled too. He excused himself from the others and walked up to me.

"Why haven't you been responding to my calls?" I asked.

"I've been busy, but I'm responding now." He wrapped his arms around me, squeezing me tight. A delicate kiss was planted on my forehead, and then he clenched my hand together with his. We made our way to the elevator.

"Let's go to the cafeteria," he said. "I need to grab a quick bite to eat."

We went to the cafeteria, and nearly everyone in the area said hello or stopped to chat with Travis. His personality was the best. Every time I saw him in action, I loved him even more.

"I'm settling for chips and a sandwich," he said. "Would you like anything?"

"No, I'm fine. I'll get something later."

"What about the baby? The baby needs to eat too, you know."

"The baby does eat, every day at four in the morning when I'm craving something sweet. I can't believe I'm having food cravings already."

"That happens. By the way, when is your next appointment? I want to go with you."

"Not for another two weeks. I'll let you know ahead of time so you can schedule a few hours off work."

Travis nodded. I followed him to a two-seated booth in the far corner. It felt so good to share a pleasant conversation with him.

"So is everything okay between us?" I asked. "I hope so. I don't like how upset you were the other day."

"Yeah, I was pretty darn upset. More so with Jaylin. It's like he thinks he can come and go as he pleases. I mean, what kind of man lies on top of my woman, kisses her, and talks crap to her in front of me? He's pretty bold, and he truly fits the definitions of a control freak, an egomaniac, and a narcissist. His pompous behavior is unsettling, and it took everything I had not to crack that bottle upside his head. That's why I threw it at the wall instead. I apologize for that."

Travis barely used curse words, so I knew he had to be upset that night. "You don't have to apologize. What Jaylin did was wrong on so many different levels. I regret that it happened. It will never happen again."

"You can't promise me that, because your ex is out of control. He may catch a bullet one day from doing crap like that. I'm just saying."

I didn't like that kind of talk, so I reached over to touch Travis's hand. "I know it will never come to that. To make sure it doesn't, I will continue to let Jaylin know where things stand between us."

"Have you spoken to him since then?"

"It was brief, but long enough for me to tell him that I'm with you and only you. I'm not going back to that relationship, Travis. So whether you like it or not, you're stuck with me."

He smacked on his chips and smiled. "I'll be stuck with you any day, anytime, and anywhere. And since I'm stuck with you, I assume you're referring to the rest of our lives together. Any update on us getting married?"

"No updates, but I'm getting there. I'm almost there."

"Get there, especially before the baby comes. We need to be a family. All of us, including Jaylene and LJ."

I didn't know why the fact that he didn't include Justin and Mackenzie bothered me a little. They were my kids too. It was like a package deal that included them all. And even though I wasn't getting closer to the marriage thing, I had to say that in order to stop the bleeding in our relationship. Hopefully, this madness was now behind us.

Chapter 10

Jaylin

For the first time in a long time, I could honestly say I was fed up with Nokea's and Scorpio's shit. All the phone calls, all the text messages, all the pop-up visits, and the ongoing finger-pointing had started to work me. I was dead smack in the middle of their relationships. It was time for me to remove myself in a major way. Since Scorpio and I weren't necessarily on good terms, I picked up the phone in my office to call her first. I leaned back in the chair, waiting for her to answer the phone.

"What?" She spoke in a nasty tone.

My voice was mellow. "I need to see you tonight. Can you come over?"

There was dead silence before she answered. "Come over for what, Jaylin? I hope this doesn't have anything to do with sex, because I'm not interested."

"Yes, you are. You're always interested in sex with me, but don't get excited, because that's not the purpose for my call."

"Go to hell," she said then hung up.

With a smirk on my face, I called right back. She answered but didn't say anything. I cleared my throat, trying not to sink to the level her heart often desired.

"On a serious note, I thought we didn't hold grudges anymore. What I want to discuss is important."

"Yeah, well, probably not important to me. Besides, the last time I was there, you said I was dead to you. Remember?"

"I do, and you still may be dead. Wake up for a few hours and come see me. Seven o'clock if you can make it."

"Whatever. I'll try to make it, but the truth is, after how you treated me, we shouldn't even be having this conversation."

"No, the truth is whenever I call to say that I need you, you need to be here no questions asked. Don't be late. See you at seven."

I hung up on her then called Nokea. She answered, but I heard people talking in the background. I assumed she was at work.

"Hey, Jaylin. Can I call you back in a few minutes? The shop is really busy right now."

"I'll make it quick then. I need you to come over around seven tonight. It's real important. Can you make it?"

"If you say it's important, then I'll be there. Besides, we do need to clear the air about a few things."

I agreed and told her I would see her later. Her response reminded me again why I continued to love her so much.

After I'd spoken to Nokea, I ran a few errands and asked Nanny B to hook up a few things for me, and then she left for a weekend vacation to St. Louis with the kids. The water park had to wait. Nanny B had been talking to Nokea's mother and father. They were all supposed to meet at my house in the Bluffs.

Once everybody was gone, I took a shower that lasted nearly forty-five minutes. I then changed into a pair of jeans, a white T-shirt, and a dark blue, slim-fit blazer. My goatee needed a trim, so I hit it up with a razor then brushed my hair, which was already lined perfectly. With the smell of Clive Christian wafting around me, I jogged down the stairs and went to the kitchen to check on the food Nanny B had prepared. It was warming in the oven and had the whole kitchen smelling delicious. I went into the dining room, dimmed the lights, straightened the pink roses in vases, lit some cinnamon candles, and waited for my guests to arrive. Ten minutes later, Nokea was right on time. I opened the door, greeting her with a welcoming smile. She checked me out from head to toe, smiling right back at me.

"You look handsome. Are we going somewhere?"

"Yes. Right here in the dining room. Come in and have a seat."

She halted her steps at the door. "Jaylin, I don't want—"

I placed two fingers over her lips. "Shhhh, just chill, all right? I know what you said, and I respect that. Just follow me to the dining room, okay?"

Nokea followed me, and when she got to the dining room, her eyes widened. She looked at the neatly wrapped gifts on the table and at the beautiful roses that screamed romantic.

"Okay, Jaylin. You have some explaining to do, right now."

I pulled the chair back, inviting her to have a seat. "I'll explain in a minute. Just relax and give me a minute to get everything in order."

As I started to walk away, Nokea reached for my hand, pulling me toward her. I squatted next to her in the seat. She stared at me as if something was on her mind. But as our eyes stayed connected, I felt anger inside. I could see her pregnancy starting to take effect. Her face was a little fatter, her hips had spread, and her belly was starting to protrude. She blinked to look away, and then she reached for the diamond cross necklace that rested on my chest.

"Didn't I give this to you?" she asked.

"As a matter of fact, you did. On my thirty-fifth birthday, at Café Lapadero."

"That's what I thought. I have never seen you wear it before."

"I've worn it. You just probably never noticed." Nokea shrugged and released the necklace. "Maybe not. But, uh, what are your plans for your birthday this year? I wanted to do something special for you and LJ since the two of you share the same birthday."

"I already have plans, but if you wish to do something for LJ, let me know, and I'll work around my plans."

"Do you mind telling me what your plans are?"

I stood and wrung my hands together. "I do mind, but as I said, let me know what you want to do with LJ."

Nokea appeared slightly taken aback by my response. Her only reply was, "Sure."

I headed toward the kitchen, thinking about what I needed to say to her tonight. Maybe it was what she needed to hear, and if so, releasing all that was inside of me would do us both some good. I felt the same about Scorpio, who was already fifteen minutes late. Purposely so, I assumed, just to annoy me. Her plan didn't work, and just as I removed the food from the oven, the doorbell rang. I hurried to it right after Nokea yelled and asked if I wanted her to see who was at the door.

"I got it," I yelled. "I already know who it is!"

I opened the door, displaying another smile. Scorpio's expression was flat.

"Sorry I'm late, but you should be glad I'm here after what you did to me."

I ignored her snobby comment and reached for her hand. "Thanks for coming. Follow me and cease the attitude."

Scorpio walked with me into the dining room. She was surprised to see Nokea, who was now standing and looking at the fish tank that was built into the wall. When Nokea turned her head and saw Scorpio, they both appeared perplexed.

"I've waited long enough, Jaylin," Nokea said. "What's going on?"

"That's what I want to know." Scorpio crossed her arms. "Why did you ask me to come over here?"

"I have a lot on my mind that centers around the two of you. I thought it would be a good idea if we talked it all out together."

My words seemed to momentarily calm both of them, especially since most women loved to talk. Nokea sat back down, and Scorpio took a seat in the chair across from her. The dim chandeliers above and the scented candles set the mood. I returned to the kitchen to prepare both of their plates exactly as I wanted them. Shortly thereafter, I entered the dining room, serving Nokea first. I glanced across the table at Scorpio, who shot me a mean mug.

"You don't mind if I serve her first, do you?" I asked. "After all, she's been working all day. I'm not sure what you've been doing. Maybe you've already eaten something."

Scorpio cut her eyes and snapped, "You can serve who you want, but don't insult me. I've been working my butt off helping to paint rooms for your kids and decorating."

"Then maybe I should've served you first." I winked then placed Nokea's plate with steak, salad, and a baked potato in front of her. She liked her steak medium well, with onions on top and a slice of provolone cheese. Her potato always had to have sour cream and just a little butter. Salad was with ranch dressing and blue cheese chunks on top. I opened a pint of milk that was next to her, pouring it into a wineglass.

After I gave it to her, I went back to the kitchen and returned with Scorpio's food. She liked her steak well done with cranberry sauce on top. Her baked potato needed shredded cheese, sour cream, and butter. Salad with blue cheese dressing, croutons, and real bacon bits. I popped a bottle of rosé wine that was next to her, pouring it into a glass. Busying myself like a waiter working for tips, I returned to the kitchen to get my food. I kept it simple: a chili cheese dog and some fries. I also grabbed a bottle of Rémy for me, and as I finally sat at the table, slightly out of breath, Nokea and Scorpio glared at me as if I had lost my mind.

"Enjoy, ladies. I prepared all of this for the two of you just so we could celebrate what I would like to call the End Celebration. I am tired of being blamed for shit, sick of being thrown up in the mix, and I'm really fed up with the two of y'all running over here with men problems."

I looked at Scorpio first. "I regret having sex with you. Big mistake. All it did was cause more problems, problems I do not need. Do whatever you must to get your marriage in order, and please understand that until your husband gets right with me, I will not, and I do not, trust him around my kids. My final piece of advice to you is to tell the truth, deal with the repercussions, and recognize that you are the one with the upper hand. It may take some time for you to realize how, but once you correct your attitude problem, take responsibility for your actions and wise up. You'll figure it out soon."

My eyes shifted to Nokea. "No more talks, Nokea. You've made it crystal clear that we are done, so proceed in your relationship and be happy."

I reached in my pocket, pulling out the wedding band I hadn't removed from my finger until a few months ago. She asked me to, claiming that it was disrespectful to Travis. I laid it on the table in front of her and continued. "Do whatever you want to with that. If I keep it, it will wind up in the trash. Have your baby, Nokea, and good luck. I sit here today, telling you that you have my blessings. With Stephon and Collins, I interfered. The only reason I did was because I knew you didn't love them. With Travis, I know how you feel, and I know when the woman I love is truly in love with someone else. My final advice: go do you, and keep begging for dick belonging to the man of your dreams. This friendly shit we got going on is over. I'm done apologizing to you for the past, and the truth is, unexpected love for one woman, just one, who is sitting across from you right now, caused me to do things that I couldn't control. You of all people know how love can make you do some crazy shit at times, so surely you can stop hating me so much and finally begin to understand why my heart made me take risks. Wrong or not, I did."

I lifted my glass to both of them. "To the end, and to the beginning of a life that I need to go live. That life starts today. As a matter of fact, it starts right now. So enjoy dinner, drink some wine and milk, chat a little with each other, open your gifts, and have a great fucking time tonight. I have somewhere else I need to be. When the two of you leave, somebody please blow out the candles and turn off the lights. Take the roses to Travis and Mario. I'm sure they'll appreciate them."

I bit into my hot dog, tossed back a shot of Rémy, and then stepped away from the table. Nokea and Scorpio sat without saying one word.

I jetted in a flash, and within the hour I was on my yacht where I'd told Kenyatta to meet me earlier when we spoke. She was waiting for me on the top deck, rocking a bright orange bikini that displayed her mocha-chocolate skin and curvaceous figure. Her hair was cut short, and her light brown eyes told me to stop tripping and get with the program. I wasted no time walking up to her and easing my arms around her waist.

"I was starting to think you weren't coming," she said.

"My word, my bond. I told you I was coming, and even though I'm a little late, I hope you don't hold that against me."

The only thing she held against me was her naked ass when I escorted her to the master suite and had sex with her. This was long overdue. I had been depriving myself too much when it came to sex. My decision had a lot to do with Nokea. The good thing was she wasn't even on my mind tonight as I lay on my side behind Kenyatta, holding her slender leg straight in the air. My dick had seduced her and was curved into her warm pussy, hitting multiple sensitive spots that made her whine. Her wetness covered every inch of my shaft, polishing it as I glided in and out of her.

From one position to the next, we had ourselves a ball. I watched her ass clap while on top of me, and as appealing as it was, I had to reach out and guide it. My meat got lost in her sweet, tight hole, and every time my steel disappeared, it reappeared wetter and harder than before. Her flexibility was a big plus. But as I stroked her in a butter-churning position that enabled me to penetrate deep inside of her, she expressed her enthusiasm and roared my name. The sound was piercing but sweet.

This was the kind of shit I missed, but I had to be perfectly honest with myself. Even though my dick was eager to break free and run wild tonight, my heart was in another place. Still, I focused on where I was going to venture to next with Kenyatta, especially since we'd made plans to sail the high seas for a few days. Once we returned, there was no reason for me to pursue a relationship with her. This was simply a fuck thing, and as long as she knew it, we were good.

Chapter 11

Scorpio

Honestly, the food was too delicious for Nokea and me to walk away from, so we sat at the table and finished eating. We talked and laughed about Jaylin's crazy self. The "end" was what he wanted to celebrate, and I was perfectly fine with that. So was Nokea. We kind of understood where he was coming from, because neither of us had closed that door and shut it tight.

I, myself, had continued to run back to him for everything. That included sex that had me in deep trouble with Mario. Maybe it was time for me to tell him the truth. I needed to get it over with, and as Jaylin had said, I was the one with the upper hand. I knew exactly what Jay Baby meant. If Mario tripped and did something stupid, he would lose. I would divorce him, and he'd have to pay up. I wasn't trying to go there, but then again, I had played the fool once before. Never again.

"Is your steak as juicy as mine is?" Nokea asked while chewing. "Nanny B must've cooked this."

"I agree. And yes, mine is delicious. This whole little scenery is nice, but it's too bad Jaylin didn't want to stay and enjoy this with us."

"Obviously he had plans. There's no telling what he's up to, and it appears that he won't even be around for his birthday."

I clapped my hands. "That's a good thing. Besides, he's already celebrated enough of his birthdays with us. Remember when his slick self had sex with us on the same day? I was livid. Could have killed him when I saw him pull into his driveway with you in the car."

Nokea shrugged and shifted a bit in her seat. She appeared slightly bothered by my comment. Then again, I wasn't so sure. "Yeah, that was crazy. I have a feeling that his birthday wasn't the only time he had sex with us on the same day. It was probably more times than that."

"Maybe so, but let's be thankful for 'the end' of that."

I raised my wineglass, clinking it against Nokea's with milk inside. We laughed, and she proceeded to tell me about what had happened when Jaylin interrupted her and Travis about to have sex. My eyes were wide. I was tuned in. I was also a little jealous, too. I had always been slightly jealous of Jaylin and Nokea's relationship. If he'd felt the same way about me, we would be together for sure. I wasn't ashamed to admit how much I loved him, and I appreciated him for expressing how much love he had for me. In the beginning, it was all about sex, but over the years, for both of us, it grew into so much more than that. Married or not, Jay Baby would always have a huge piece of my heart.

"I know Travis was pissed," I screeched. "I'm surprised he and Jaylin didn't start fighting."

"Travis was too drunk to do anything. I have some serious work to do when it comes to my relationship with him. I think he's getting kind of tired of my close relationship with Jaylin, so cutting ties with him and strictly making it all about the kids may be best for all of us."

Nokea picked up the ring Jaylin had placed on the table, staring at it. I wondered if she still loved Jaylin or if all of this love she claimed to have for Travis was fake. I wouldn't dare tell her how I still felt about him, only because it really didn't matter anymore.

"I agree that cutting ties with him is a good thing," I said. "The men in our lives deserve better. After I leave here, I'm going home to have a serious conversation with Mario. Things have been rocky since our wedding day. We used to have so much fun. I miss that, and I know the problems in my marriage are on me."

"It seems that way, and if you don't mind me saying, I kind of agree with Jaylin about the kids taking a break from being over there. If you and Mario are arguing a lot, that's not good."

"I understand what you're saying, but the kids weren't around when we were arguing. I'm not mad at you or Jaylin for being concerned, but I'll work this out soon. You both can be sure that I will never have the kids in a place that's uncomfortable or unsafe for them."

"I trust that you wouldn't, so here's to you and Mario working things out, and to Travis and me staying on the right track."

She lifted her glass, and we toasted again. I couldn't help but think what a sweet person Nokea was. As I had gotten to know her on a different level, one where we weren't clashing all the time over Jaylin, I finally understood why he was so in love with her. I never regretted meeting Jaylin, but I did have regrets about the hurt I'd caused her. It felt good to let her know why I had a difficult time letting him go. Now, I truly believed that she understood me as well.

After we finished dinner, we ripped open the gifts he'd given us. My gift was a soul food cookbook. Nokea's gift was a newborn baby outfit for a girl. We chuckled at Jaylin's foolishness and left the dining room messy for him to clean up. I blew out the candles, turned off the lights, and left with a bouquet of roses in my hand. I was home in less than twenty minutes.

The second I walked through the front door, I saw Mario talking to his father while chilling in the great room. A bottle of Hennessy was on the table, and the smoke from their Cuban cigars permeated the air. When they saw me enter the house, silence fell over the room. Both of their expressions were flat. It was apparent that they'd been discussing me. With the roses in my hand, I strutted into the room, feeling upbeat.

"These are for you." I placed the roses on the table in front of Mario. "I stopped to purchase them after I left Nokea's shop. We also had dinner. That's why I'm late."

Lies continued to roll off my tongue, but I figured if I told him dinner was at Jaylin's house, Mario wouldn't like that. Instead of him responding to me, his father did.

"I love how this house seems to be coming together," he said then smashed his cigar in an ashtray. He stood and reached for his cane, which was next to him. "Now that you're home, why don't you show me what you and the decorators have done? Mario said I should wait for you to come home so you could give me a grand tour."

"Sure," I said, kicking off my heels. I was positive that Mr. Pezzano had already seen the entire house, but what the hell? Maybe he wanted to say something to me in private, so instead of asking Mario to join us, all I did was bend over and pucker for him to kiss me. He gave me a quick peck before raising the glass of alcohol to his lips. He sniffed it twice then tossed the liquid down his throat, clearing it afterward.

"Papa is waiting." Mario nudged his head toward his father, who was standing behind me. "Go show him what you've done."

I was proud of how well the decorators had done the modern kitchen, so I decided to start there. As I moved in that direction, Mr. Pezzano followed me. He limped when he walked. Mario said he'd been injured several years ago, but without getting into specifics, all I knew was his father had been shot. He was on the hefty side, too, but that didn't stop him from wearing tailored suits like the black one he had on today. His healthy, salt-and-pepper hair was slicked back, and his chiseled face was always clean-shaven.

We stood in the spacious kitchen, which had an eighteen-feet ceiling and two granite-topped islands. I had chosen a unique metal backsplash that matched the stainless-steel appliances. As I started to tell Mr. Pezzano what had been done to the kitchen, he appeared disinterested. I paused to ask if everything was okay. He rubbed his chest and squinted while studying me.

"No, not really, Scorpio. Everything is not okay. Mario seems troubled by something that was brought to his attention. I hope the two of you are able to settle things quickly, because the last thing I want is for people to get hurt. I'm sure you wouldn't want that either."

My face appeared contorted. Talk like that annoyed me. Threats went in one ear, out the other. I was married to Mario. Therefore, I didn't have to explain a damn thing to Mr. Pezzano. I didn't care how wealthy he was or what kind of crap he was involved in. He wasn't about to intimidate me. He needed to know what kind of woman his son had married.

"Mr. Pezzano, I know you and Mario discuss an array of things, but if he is upset with me about anything, we'll work it out. For you to say someone could get hurt, I'm not sure who you could be referring to. That kind of talk is unnecessary. Mario and I will be fine, so please do not worry about a grown man who is more than capable of taking care of himself."

Mr. Pezzano released a cackling laugh. He abruptly silenced himself and swiftly lifted his cane, positioning it near the tip of my nose. I guessed he assumed I would back away in fear. I didn't.

His tone was stern, and his eyes were devilish. "Family, Scorpio. All we care about is family. If you hurt one of us, you hurt all of us. I told my son not to marry you. You are not a loyal woman, and you will never be loyal to him. He's so freaking pussy whipped that he can barely think straight. But when he wakes up, my dear, don't you dare say that I didn't warn you."

The tour was over. I marched back into the living room where Mario was. He was chilling back on the couch with one leg crossed over the other. The cigar dangled from his mouth, and when he removed it, he whistled three circles of smoke into the air. I stood in front of him, darting my finger while shouting my demands.

"You need to get your father in check. He's disrespecting me in my house, and I do not appreciate it. Do you mind asking him to leave?"

Mario sighed. He placed the cigar in an ashtray, and as the direction of his eyes traveled from me to his father, there was a smirk on his face.

"Papa, what did you say to my lovely wife? You have her tight panties in a bunch, and she's highly upset. I don't like it when she's this way. Nor do I condone the way her loud voice squeaks when she speaks to me. I do apologize to you. Because she should know better than to ask my own father to leave this house." His eyes were now fixed on me. "That's not going to work, sweetheart, but nice try."

Steam was pouring from my ears. I was seething with anger, but instead of arguing with Mario for not taking up for me, I decided to leave.

"I'll tell you what. He can stay, and I'll go. Call me when he's gone, and if you decide not to call me at all, I'm good with that too."

I wasn't playing with Mario. While lying to him wasn't the right thing to do, I still didn't owe his father a single explanation. I always sensed that he was going to be a problem for us. I told Mario a long time ago that his father had issues with me.

I slipped my heels back on and made my way to the door. Mario called after me. I didn't bother to turn around. I got in my car and sped off. He knew how to reach me, and I wasn't going to step one foot in my own house until Mr. Pezzano was gone. Maybe by then Mario and I could get to the root of our issues.

I drove around for a while before parking to call the kids, who were still in St. Louis. Nanny B said Nokea's parents were enjoying their company, and after Mackenzie told me Nokea was on her way there, I told them to have a good time.

Afterward, I took a long walk on the beach. My thoughts were on Mario. He didn't bother to call me, and when I returned home nearly two hours later, his sports car wasn't in the driveway. There were very few lights on in the house, only because Loretta was still there. She informed me that Mario had left, and she said he would be back later.

"Did he say where he was going?" I asked.

"No, he didn't say. Mr. Pezzano left, and a few minutes later so did Mario. Is everything okay between the two of you?"

"Not really, but don't worry. Things will be back to normal soon enough."

Loretta reached out to give me a hug. She was so sweet. Jaylin hired her years ago to help me with the kids. She was like family to me, and she was never the type of woman to stick her nose in my business. I watched as she made her way upstairs, wearing a blue nightgown that was too big for her petite frame. Her hair flowed midway down her back, and her round face displayed worry. I was starting to worry too. There was no way in hell we were going to turn this beautiful house into a hellhole.

I tossed and turned all night. Periodically, the roaring thunder caused me to jump from my sleep and look out the window. I also glanced at the spot beside me, seeing that Mario hadn't come home yet. I'd thought about calling him, but my eyelids were so heavy that I fell back on my pillow and went to sleep.

What seemed like only a few hours later, I woke up again. This time, the smell of cigar smoke filled my nostrils. My eyes cracked open, and I could see Mario sitting in a chair right in front of the bed. He was stark naked, and his legs were wide open. The cigar dangled from his mouth, and something was in his hand that I couldn't quite see. The lighting in the room was faint, and with every window wide open, I felt a cold chill. Goosebumps covered my arms, and something with my hair felt real strange. It wasn't until I turned on the lamp next to me that I saw hair, my beautiful, wavy hair, spread out on the sheets. My heart raced as I touched my head, feeling how short my hair was. Without looking in a mirror, I could only imagine.

"What in the hell did you do?" I shouted as I feverishly patted my head. "Mario, noooo! Why would you do this?"

I yanked the covers back, but as I charged out of bed, he cocked a gun to the side, aiming it in my direction.

"Don't move," he demanded. "Get back in bed and stay there until I say go."

Not knowing what to expect, I eased back on the bed with my heart racing faster. All I could think was who in the hell had I married? This was not the same man who had been nothing but kind to me for the past few years. I didn't even know this side of him existed.

"Let me make one thing clear," he spoke calmly and laid the gun on his lap. "You don't get to speak to me in a nasty tone, my dear. You're not allowed to make demands, especially when you're the one in the hot seat, not me. Not me, Mrs. Pezzano, so I need to ask you about the night of your bachelorette party again. This time, you need to get it right and speak the truth. You need to tell me if I should believe Jaylin when he tells me he has you wrapped around his little fucking finger. Does he or doesn't he?"

I swallowed a lump that was stuck in my throat. With anger trapped in my teary eyes, I wanted so badly to tell Mario to go to hell. I also wanted to cry, but crying would do me no good. The last thing I wanted to do was show weakness. If Mario ever viewed me as weak, he would take full advantage of it.

"Be . . . before I answer anything, why, Mario? Why cut my hair off like this? I would never—"

He slammed the gun on his knee. "Fuck your hair! You needed to cut that shit anyway, and didn't you say that's what you were going to do? I did you a favor, so stop your griping and don't change the subject. Get back to what I asked you. Does he have you twirling around his finger like a little stripper girl on a pole?"

"I'm not going to answer any of your ridiculous questions."

Mario's face crumpled. His eyes narrowed to slits, and he charged at me so quickly that I didn't have enough time to scurry off the bed. He grabbed my leg, pulling me toward him. This time, he lay over me with the gun planted at the center of my forehead.

"If you want to keep screwing me around, I'll show you what happens to people who screw me. I'll show you right now! Is this what you want?"

"No," I said softly while looking into his eyes, which displayed pure rage. I could feel beads of sweat building on my forehead. For the first time ever, I feared for my life. My chest heaved in and out, and so did his.

"Tell me!" he shouted. "Tell me the fucking truth!"

I shouted back. "Not like this, Mario! We don't have to go out like this!"

He removed the gun from my forehead and rubbed it against my trembling lips. "You're right, we don't. So open your mouth, talk real slow, say the right things, or else this gun will find a better place to create a bigger hole."

My eyelids fluttered when he lowered the gun, raised my wet nightgown, which was clinging to my sweaty skin, and pressed the gun at the center of my pussy lips. My mouth opened wide. I was ready to talk.

"Yes," I rushed to say. "I had sex with Jaylin the day before I became your wife. I needed to do it for my own personal reasons, and . . . and I will never go there again. As for what he said to you, none of it was true. He said those things to upset you. The only man I want is you."

I wasn't so sure about that after this, but I had to say anything to get Mario back on my team. He continued to lie over me without saying a word. The gun was still at the folds of my pussy. He didn't move it.

"Personal reasons, huh? I have a personal reason to shoot you and that slimy motherfucker, and if he—"

"Sex," I bellowed then hurried to correct my tone. "It was just sex, Mario. This has gone too far, and think about what you're doing to us over one night of sex. I know I was wrong, wrong for lying to you and everything. I was ashamed to tell you what I did, but I can promise you, right here and now, that it will never, ever happen again."

He added more pressure from the gun against my folds, causing me to squeeze my eyes tighter.

"It better not happen again. Not ever, and if it does, he dies and so do you."

Mario slowly got up and carefully laid the gun on my stomach, which was tied in knots.

"If it takes a toy gun for you to speak the truth," he said, "maybe you shouldn't be Mrs. Pezzano after all."

As Mario turned toward the door, I lifted the gun from my stomach. It was a heavy plastic toy gun that looked real as real could get. I had been tricked. Damn! Mario left the room, and I threw the gun at the wall. It broke into pieces, just as my marriage had done. I couldn't help but wonder if I had made a big mistake marrying Mario, or if he had made a mistake marrying me.

Chapter 12

Nokea

I was in St. Louis, sitting patiently and waiting for Jaylin to arrive at Café Lapedero. It was his birthday, and yet again we found ourselves at odds with each other. We hadn't been to this restaurant in years, even though this was the place we often dined at to celebrate his birthday, settle some of our differences, and find solace again. That was why I invited him to meet me here, regardless of him proclaiming it was "the end."

I didn't want to say much around Scorpio during dinner the other night, but when it came to Jaylin and me, there was no end. We would always be there for each other, and for him to try to cut off what we had was ridiculous. I was somewhat disappointed that he had returned his ring to me, but since I was moving in another direction, why not return it? So many questions about my future flooded my mind. I was starting to feel confused again. Travis was in St. Louis with me, but he had met up with his uncle to attend a St. Louis Cardinals baseball game. As I had done in my past relationship with Collins, I kept this intimate dinner arrangement with Jaylin private. He said he would be here, but as expected, he was late.

"Will Mr. Rogers still be joining you?" said the poised waiter, Romero. He was so nice and had served Jaylin and me almost every time we came here.

I looked at my watch, seeing that Jaylin was only ten minutes late. "Yes, he will. He should arrive soon."

"Okay. Meanwhile, I'll go get you some more water. Would you like anything else?"

"No. The water will be fine. Thank you, Romero."

I released a deep breath as he walked away. And to be honest, I was a bit nervous. I wasn't sure how Jaylin was going to behave today, especially since he seemed adamant about us going our separate ways. I bit my nail while scanning the restaurant, which in a weird way was too quiet. There were only two other couples inside, and their conversations were just above a whisper. Romero was the only waiter working the floor tonight, and every now and then the chef came out of the kitchen to converse with him. The whole atmosphere felt strange, but it was very romantic in a sense. The lighting was faint, and scented round candles in the middle of every table in the room provided a cozy atmosphere. Crisp, white tablecloths covered the square tables, fine china was on top, and every table was surrounded by two or four velvet wingback chairs. Wall-to-wall beveled mirrors made Café Lapedero appear larger than what it was, and with marble flooring traveling from one area to the next, the whole place represented elegance.

I felt underdressed in my sleeveless, flared dress that dipped low in the front. It was a glittery gold, cut right above my knees, and it meshed well with my caramel skin. My fresh haircut was slayed, and with feathered bangs close to my left eye, I kept moving my hair to the side so I could see Jaylin make his appearance at the door.

It wasn't long before he arrived, but to no surprise, there was no smile on his face. His serious demeanor traveled with him, and his fine hair, particularly the hair that formed his goatee, was trimmed meticulously. He smoothly walked my way with overconfidence on display.

The navy pinstriped slacks he wore were tailored to fit. His Persian blue shirt grasped the muscles in his arms and chest. A beautiful sight he was. I stood to greet him. A smile emerged on my face, but it wasn't enough to make his demeanor change. When he arrived at the table, all I could do was spill the words, "Happy birthday."

"Thanks, but you didn't have to waste your time coming here," he said before taking a seat in the chair. No hug, no kiss on the cheek, no thank-you . . . nothing. I sat back in the chair, clearing my clogged throat.

"I don't believe that I've wasted my time, and I'm glad you're here. It's been a long time since we shared an intimate dinner like this together, and it is my hope that we can leave here on a more positive note. Will that be so difficult for us to do?"

"That depends on you, Nokea. I'm just here because you asked me to come. I thought you may have some good news for me, too, but I guess this may be just another opportunity for you to tell me how much in love you are with another man."

"No, I didn't come here to talk about Travis tonight. Actually, I wanted to talk about us. I want you to know how important it is for us

to still confide in each other, be there for each other, and never let anyone or anything come between us. Our friendship means the world to me. I could never see myself being without it. I know my relationship with Travis is difficult for you to accept, but I need your support, Jaylin. Please tell me what I can do to help us both heal and get us back to the place where we used to be."

Without a blink, Jaylin's eyes penetrated my thoughts from across the table. He leaned forward and circled his lips to blow out the flickering flame of the candle in front of me.

"Time's up and lights out. There is only one way for us to get back to the place we used to be. I don't have to tell you what you must do to make that happen. Unfortunately, you won't do it, so stop wasting my time with this. I meant what I said about us moving on, and the time is now. Right now, Nokea, so stop trying to make all these pieces to your little fucked-up puzzle fit when they won't. I'll never accept your relationship with Travis. I can't support you, but what I can do is keep my distance so I don't offend anyone. That's all you're going to get from me, so have a nice evening and please don't call me with this nonsense again."

He was so darn stubborn. I couldn't believe when he stood to leave. I nearly lost it and stood too.

"You know what?" I said with a heavy heart. "You expect too much from me. All I'm attempting to do is make our lives run a little more smoothly than what they are now. Every time we find ourselves here, all you do is drop your measly dollars on the table and walk away. You can't have your way, so you walk away and go to your little corner and hide. If that's what you want to do, fine!" My voice cracked, and my tone went up a few notches. "Go be by yourself and deal with your hurt the best way you can. It's what you've always tried to do, but guess what, Jaylin." I pointed to my chest. "In the end, you needed me. You've always needed me, and now I need you too!"

He spilled his anger through gritted teeth. "Need me for what? What in the hell do you need me for when you insist that you are in love with the man of your dreams? That shit hurts, and how in the world can you stand there and say I'm the one expecting too much from you? Damn, baby, what is wrong with you?"

"You are expecting too much. I remained with you through thick and thin. Stayed through all the good and bad. Never turned my back on you, but now you think it's okay for you to run away from me because you can't cope with my relationship? Really? Is that how this works? Please help me understand why I need to always be there for you, but you can't find it in your heart to be there for me."

My words seemed to anger him more. His face appeared distorted, brows bushy and furrowed. "Wake the fuck up, Nokea. Are you really that clueless? Just in case you are, let me spell things out for you, all right?" He stepped up to me, now nearly face-to-face. I could see the damage in his eyes. Mine showed the same. "I will love you until the day I die and thereafter. There is no other woman for me, and it hurts like hell to sit back and wait until you make your next move. I'm devastated about you being pregnant, and do you have any idea how I'm going to feel if you become Travis's wife? I give you major props for sticking by me throughout our relationship but, baby, I simply cannot do it."

He tried to walk away again, but I grabbed his collar, forcing him to stay there and face me. Avoiding eye contact, he turned his head, looking toward the door. "Okay, so what is it that you want then? Look at me, damn it, and tell me what you need from me."

*Jaylin's breathing increased. His lips quiv-
ered. He was fighting his words. Just as he got
ready to release them, a lingering tear rolled
down his face. He blinked his long lashes, looking at me with his heart-piercing eyes. "I need
you," he said softly. "All I need is you again,
and I give you my word that I will never hurt
you again. I promise, just . . . just don't give up
on us. You've given up on us and I can't. Stop
this pain from burning through my soul, baby.
Please put a halt to my pain."*

*My eyes were filled with tears and a mag-
nitude of sorrow. Seeing him like this took me
back, way back, to when we were children.
Through every painful experience he'd had, I
was there. Even on the day of our divorce, I felt
everything he felt. Today was no different, and
on Jaylin's birthday, I couldn't allow him to
walk away from me for good. As his head was
lowered, my forehead touched his. My hands
still grasped his collar. I tugged it to get his
attention.*

*"You want me, you got me," I confirmed. "But
now what, Jaylin? Where do we go from here?"*

*He moved his head from side to side. "I don't
have you like I need you. Travis does, and you
can't dispute that."*

"No, Travis doesn't have me. You do, and shame on you for believing that I could ever love another man more than I love you. Now, let me ask you again. What do you want? It's your birthday, so be as wishful as you want to be."

Jaylin reached up and wiped another tear that had fallen from his eye. He then brushed away mine, and with my face cupped in his hands, our quivering lips made a connection. The kiss went from deeply passionate to severely intense. So intense that I could feel an electrifying tingling sensation rising from the tips of my toes to my hotspot, which felt as if it were being tickled.

I was eager to feel Jaylin inside of me again, and not even giving a care who was in the restaurant, I aggressively yanked at his shirt, ripping it down the middle. I grabbed all over his carved chest. His hands were underneath my dress, gripping my soft mountains. My panties were in the way, but right after he hiked me on the table, they vanished. I unhooked his belt buckle, snatching his belt from the hoops. His pants were loose, and in a matter of seconds, I unzipped them and dipped my hands inside to massage his ass. From there, I journeyed to his loaded weapon that stood at attention in his briefs. I felt it grow from nothing to something,

something that I could no longer resist. My strokes on his steel energized him.

In one swoop, his arm cleared the table. The wineglasses, china, and candles crashed on the floor, causing the couples around us to gasp. I expected someone to interject, but pure silence followed. I leaned back. Jaylin was right there between my legs, inching closer. He breathed in. I breathed out. My arms were latched around his neck, and with no space in between us, he released his package, finally bringing it home. I wheezed out loudly, and with my arms secured around his neck, I reached up to tighten my fingers in his curled hair. I pulled tighter as our bodies rocked together without missing a beat. Our breathing increased with every long stroke he delivered. My mind was swirling in circles. I couldn't believe this was happening. Why now, why was I doing this, and why did it have to feel so good? Jaylin held my legs wide in his arms, and with his wrinkled shirt hanging on one shoulder and pants down to his ankles, he set my whole body on fire. Sparks sprayed from my wet coochie. I could hear fireworks in the background sounding off. I gyrated my hips to adjust to his pace, but as his thrusts strength-ened, the way I was positioned on the table didn't work.

"I . . . I feel you, Jaylin, all of you. But I need to feel more. Take your clothes off. Do me from behind and show me what I've been missing."

Just for a few minutes, he shut me down. He backed out of me, exposing his dripping wet muscle heavily glazed with my syrup. Hurrying to resume, he raised my dress over my head, tossing it aside. His shirt, pants, and briefs were stacked in a pile near his feet. I needed to feel his nakedness close to mine, so I pulled him closer and clasped my legs around his waist. I uncontrollably massaged his chest, clutched his ass, and stole numerous kisses from his lips and tongue that tasted like sweet honey.

"Jaaaylin," I cried out between each sensual kiss that left me craving for more. I just couldn't get enough, and in a fit of passion, I reached for his package, resting it between my moist folds.

"Wait a minute." He stepped back and pivoted to address the couples behind us who sat in utter shock and awe. All eyes were focused on us, including Romero's and the chef's, who had obviously exited the kitchen to get a glimpse of the action. They stood like mannequins and hadn't said one word.

"Dinner, wine, dessert, diamonds, or whatever is on me," Jaylin said to the couples. "Just leave your business cards on the table, and I'll pay generously for the inconvenience. I need some privacy right now. Will you all please exit?"

The two white women sat in a trance with their mouths wide open. Their eyes were bugged and zoomed in below Jaylin's waist. The men took peeks at me, but they were the first ones to make a move. Each of them left cards on the table, and everyone stood to exit. It was a slow exit, one that brought about a little confusion when one woman asked the other a question that her date didn't approve of.

"Was that thing real?" she asked. "I've never seen anything like it."

Her man was offended. They argued on their way out, and after they left, Romero and the chef disappeared. Jaylin turned around, facing me again. The look in his eyes told me how he wanted to serve me, so I positioned my body over the table, resting comfortably on my stomach. My legs were spread wide. I looked straight ahead at the beveled mirrors in front of us, viewing nothing but pure sexiness as he boldly stepped up behind me. I didn't dare want him to witness my facial expressions, but when he brushed his head against my folds, I clamped my eyes shut. Several deep breaths followed. His sudden entrance made me pause and contract *my stomach. My eyes shot open, and to muffle my murmurs, I bit into my lip, licking them to catch my saliva.*

"Keep your eyes open and look at us," he said, looking at the mirror too.

He bent over me, pecking his lips on my upper back. He dragged his wet tongue down my spine, and as he stretched my insides to full capacity with his super-hard muscle, my facial expressions spoke volumes. I kept opening my mouth to suck in air while forcing my fluttering eyelids to stay open. I immediately adapted to his rhythm, and for fifteen long minutes, we indulged ourselves. Wetness covered our bodies, and our enthusiastic voices sang out loudly. My face was shielded by my arm, but Jaylin wasn't having it.

"Look at me," he demanded.

"I . . . I can't," I mumbled. "Not now."

"Baby, look at me. I need to tell you something, please."

I slowly lifted my head to glance at the mirror so I could see him.

"I love you," he whispered. "Tell me you still love me too and that you never fell out of love with me."

"I dooooo," I admitted. "I said I do, and I meant every word that I said."

"*Good. Now hang in there, all right?*" *he said, encouraging me. His hands roamed and caressed my shapely curves. "Smile, too. You're so beautiful when you smile, and with all of this in you, why not smile?*"

I flashed my pearly whites but kept lowering my head and tugging at my flat hair. The feeling, the feel of his dick journeying deeper while brushing against my walls, left me feeling high. I could no longer "hang in there," and as his fingers wiggled over my clit, I stomped my foot on the floor and screeched loud enough to break every piece of glass surrounding us. Shards flew everywhere, causing my eyes to shoot open.

In a very confused state of mind, I saw and felt Travis vigorously shaking me like a ragdoll.

"Nokea!" he shouted as we lay in bed together. "Wake up!"

I was so startled that I quickly backed away from him and tumbled to the floor. My butt hurt, but I covered my mouth, thinking about what had taken place in the dream I'd had.

"Are you all right?" Travis rushed to say with frustration on his face. "You kept moaning and groaning. I couldn't even wake you up."

I removed my hand from my mouth, feeling so ashamed of myself for having such a dream. It seemed so real, and as sticky as my insides were, it felt real, too.

I rubbed my forehead as if it ached. "I . . . I'm okay. I just had a nightmare. Somebody was chasing me."

Travis sat on the edge of the bed, reaching for my hand so he could help me get off the floor. "Did you see who it was? I mean, I thought you were having a seizure or something."

That was putting it mildly. "No, I don't know who it was, but I'm glad it's over. I need to go splash some water on my face so I can get back to sleep. Sorry for waking you. I know how much you need your rest."

"I do, but I'll be fine. I can't sleep that well in this hotel room, but you know that staying the night at Jaylin's house was out of the question."

"I know, but let's not discuss that again. Okay?"

Travis agreed, and as I headed to the bathroom to get myself together, I thought about our conversation from earlier. The second we arrived in St. Louis, Travis said he didn't want to stay the night at Jaylin's house. We got a room at a hotel that was less than two miles away. I kind of understood why Travis had issues with spending the night there, but with the kids being there, it was more about me spending as much time with them as I could. Besides, Jaylin wasn't there. Nanny B said he was on vacation. I had no idea where he'd gone to.

I guessed our so-called "End Celebration" was weighing heavily on my mind. Did it bother me so much that I had to go there like that in a dream? I was so shocked by the dream that I couldn't even think straight. All I wanted to do was calm myself and do something, anything, to work off this dire need I had for sex right now. I was sure Travis could help with that, so after I gathered myself in the bathroom, I stood in the doorway with no clothes on, calling his name. He turned around, looking at me with a sly grin on his face.

"If you can't sleep," I said, "maybe I should get back in bed and take advantage of you."

Travis yanked the covers back and patted the spot next to him. "Maybe you should. And if I'm the one chasing you, good things will come once you're caught."

I made my way to the bed, and as Travis brought me back to reality, I felt better. Thoughts of Jaylin had been pushed to the back of my mind.

The following morning, Travis and I put on our clothes and were ready to tackle a busy day. He seemed a little on edge, and when I inquired about his demeanor, it appeared as if he was grasping at straws to create an argument.

"For some reason," he said, sitting on the edge of the bed while putting his shoes on, "I just have a feeling that you're not as excited about this baby as I am. You haven't even told your parents yet, and I would think your mother would be the first person you would want to know."

I sat on the bed next to him, trying to explain why I wasn't ready to tell my parents. "I will tell them in due time. My parents never wanted me to have children out of wedlock, and it was a disappointment for my father when I told him about my pregnancy the first time. He loves LJ more than anything in the world, but I've never forgotten my father's reaction that day. If I tell him about our baby, I'm not sure how he'll respond. I just want to give it a little more time. Hopefully you can understand that."

"Your father won't feel the same way if we're married. I don't know what the holdup is, but just like everything else, Nokea, you continue to make excuses that trouble me more than you know."

He got up from the bed and walked away. I felt horrible about this. I thought my reasons were legit, but no matter how Travis felt, I didn't feel comfortable telling anyone else about the baby yet.

On the drive to Jaylin's house, Travis sat quiet as a mouse on the passenger's side. He didn't seem like himself lately, and even though I figured he was still bothered by his last encounter with Jaylin, I wasn't sure if he harbored ill feelings toward me about that day as well.

"I hate to keep asking you this, but are you upset with me about something? If so, Travis, please tell me. I'm sensing something with you, and I'm trying to deal with all of this as best I can."

"You're not the only one trying to deal with it." He turned his head to look out the window. "I'm trying to deal with a lot. The first thing is being in your ex's house all day. I hope we get a chance to go somewhere else while we're here."

His bitterness was starting to annoy me. "You can go wherever you wish. I told you the reason I was coming to St. Louis was to spend time with the kids and my parents. You didn't have to come, especially since you're acting as if you don't want to be here. Yesterday you seemed fine. Today, however, is a different story."

"I have no problem with the kids, and you already know that. I just can't deal with your ex. I don't like how he conducted himself at your place that day, and I haven't been able to get over it. Being in his house seems awkward to me.

The less time we stay there, the better. I'm only hanging around for a few hours today. Then I plan to go find something else to do."

Without even knowing it, Jaylin had me in a bad spot. I wished he hadn't gone there that day, but for now, I had nothing else to say to Travis about it. The bottom line was if he didn't want to be in Jaylin's house, he never should've come to St. Louis with me. I did, however, take what he'd said into consideration.

We stayed at Jaylin's house until noon. After that, we piled into the SUV with the kids and went to the zoo. The kids were having fun. Travis seemed a bit more at ease. He laughed with the kids, bought ice cream for them, and pointed out several animals as we rode the train. The only thing that pissed me off was what he said to LJ as he was standing up on the train.

"Sit the fu . . . Sit down!" Travis shouted. "If you fall and bump your head, boy, that's on you."

My head snapped to the side. I was getting ready to put Travis in check, but LJ spoke up before I did.

"Travis, you're not permitted to speak to me like that," he said politely. "You're not my dad. Therefore, I don't have to listen to you."

I quickly spoke up while pulling on LJ's arm so he could sit down. My eyes, however, were zoned in on Travis. "Don't you ever speak to my child like that. Your tone was unnecessary, and there's a better way to speak to people, especially children, when you want them to do something. Furthermore, you'd better make sure that never happens again."

LJ sat with his brows furrowed. He wasn't too happy. Neither was Travis. He looked at me with fury in his eyes.

"I was only trying to prevent him from hurting himself. Since I'm not his father, I guess I'm supposed to sit here and let him stand up when the signs around us clearly say everyone must be seated."

I snapped back. "It's not what you said. It's how you said it. You were out of line, period."

"For the record, your kids fall in line, I don't. And when all is said and done, he shouldn't have been standing up."

"You're right. But when all is said and done, maybe you should've stayed home."

Travis nodded but didn't respond. I couldn't believe what was happening to us. We had never experienced anything like this. I mean, we had minor disputes from time to time, but something about this was different. Travis had never raised his voice at my kids, and I didn't like it one bit. It surely dampened the mood, and when we returned to Jaylin's house, Travis changed clothes so he could go with my father to play golf. The golf course was located within the subdivision. They couldn't have asked for a better day. At eighty-one degrees outside, the weather was perfect.

Since the kids were a bit disappointed about our abrupt departure from the zoo, we decided to hit up the kitchen and make a variety of cookies. My father and Travis ate some before they left, and Nanny B and my mother were outside on the screened-in porch that viewed the Missouri River. I could hear them laughing and talking about some of my mother's church members she didn't get along with. She and Nanny B could stay on the porch for hours and hours, drinking wine and listening to music. I also loved the peacefulness this house provided. It was one of the best pieces of property Jaylin had built from the ground up, and it was unfortunate that no one lived here on a daily basis.

The kids and I had the spacious kitchen in a mess. Several bowls were on the island, flour was on the hardwood floors, cracked eggs were on the table, and more cookies already were baking in the double ovens.

"Time to clean up." I wiped my dirty hands on the apron. "Jaylene, you go get the broom.

Mackenzie, why don't you start cleaning off the table." I looked around for LJ, who had suddenly disappeared. "Where did LJ go?"

Just then, he came into the kitchen, extending his cell phone to me. "Here, Mom," he said. "Dad wants to speak to you."

I sighed, already knowing what this was about. Before I spoke to Jaylin, I told LJ to help clean up. Justin and I went into the parlor room that was structured like a half circle. I sat on the sofa, put Justin on my lap, and then put the phone up to my ear.

"Yes, Jaylin. What's up?"

"One question and you'd better have the right answer. Why in the hell is that muthafucka yelling at my son?"

"Look, I don't care if my answer is satisfactory to you, but I already spoke to Travis about his tone. It was inappropriate, and it will never happen again."

"It better not happen again, and if it does, I'm going to drill my foot in his ass and yours. You know I don't play when it comes to my kids, Nokea, and the way I see it, that bastard shouldn't even be in my fucking house."

"Well, he is, and you know what, Jaylin? I really don't have time for this. He made a mistake, and I corrected him. Now we move on. I don't even know why LJ called—"

"Because I'm his fucking father," he roared. "He's supposed to call me, and if you want to pretend that this ain't no big deal, that's you! It's a big deal to me, especially when I know that when Travis looks at my son, all he sees is me! It's no secret how he feels about me, and—"

I quickly cut him off. "Stop this, okay? Travis would never do anything to hurt our kids, and you know that. Besides, everything was fine until you did what you did at my place that day."

"No disrespect. Then again, why not, especially since you're sounding like a damn fool. You're the one who trusts that idiot, not me. All I'm going to say to you is this: you'd better keep your eyes and ears open, just as you do your legs. If something like this happens again, and any of my children calls me, upset about some bullshit Travis said to them, I'm coming for you first. You first, Nokea, and I guarantee you that it won't be pretty. Now give my son back his phone so I can speak to somebody around there who's got some fucking sense."

"Call him back in five minutes. I don't take orders from you, and your insulting words won't get any action from me."

I hit the END button then gave the phone to Justin, who had been reaching for it. "Go take that to your brother," I said as we exited the parlor together. "And let's go see if our cookies are ready."

Justin ran in front of me. He handed LJ his phone, and when LJ looked at me, I reached out to rub his wavy hair, which was sharply lined.

"I'm sorry about what happened earlier," I said again. "I hope you know that I will never allow anyone to mistreat you. You could have told me how you felt. I know Travis hurt your feelings when he yelled at you."

"I know you wouldn't, but I just wanted to talk to my dad."

"That's fine, too. Now give me a hug, and let's find out who made the best cookies."

LJ and I gave each other a squeezing hug that put a smile on his face. I hoped this situation was put to rest, but deep down it seriously left a bad taste in my mouth.

It was getting late. The kids were exhausted, so they turned in early for bed. With it being dark outside, I was surprised that Travis and my father hadn't made it back from the golf course yet. Nanny B and my mother were now in the kitchen. I asked if either of them had heard from my father or Travis.

"No," my mother said, "but knowing them, they probably went for a drink somewhere or decided to go watch a game at one of the restaurants around here."

Since Travis had mentioned staying away from here, that could have been the case. But when the doorbell rang nearly twenty minutes later and we saw two police cars outside, my heart raced. We all went to the door, and after I opened it, I stood face-to-face with a police officer who wasn't there to share good news.

"I'm looking for Mrs. Gloria Brooks."

My mother nervously stepped forward with her hand pressed against her chest. "I'm Mrs. Brooks. Is everything okay?"

"I'm afraid not, ma'am. Your husband collapsed on the golf course earlier. He was rushed to the hospital. You need to go there immediately."

My mother's face was like stone. Tears welled in our eyes. "Collapsed?" she stuttered. "Is he going to be okay?"

"We don't know yet. But you need to get to the hospital soon."

I hurried off to go get my purse and car keys. Nanny B said she would stay with the kids, and the police assisted me in escorting my visibly trembling mother to the car. She was very fragile and seemed so out of it, so I did my best to be strong for her.

That all changed when we arrived at the hospital. From a distance, I saw Travis coming our way, walking in slow motion. The blank expression on his face told me this wasn't going to be good. He opened his arms, and as I totally zoned out of it, all I heard was him whisper the words, "I'm sorry. I did my best to save him, but he died on the way here."

I heard my mother's cries, and my legs weakened. I immediately crashed to the floor.

Chapter 13

Jaylin

Shane and I had just left my house and were about to head to his when I saw a white man walking up my driveway. He had on an unflattering brown suit that was too big, a white, dingy shirt, and silver-framed glasses. Several papers were crumpled in his hand. He completely looked like a nerd. He straightened his glasses as he approached me and cleared his throat. Not only was I looking at him like he was crazy, but Shane was too.

"Jaaaaaylin Rogers," he said with a dragging voice.

"Who wants to know?"

"My name is Mr. Suuuuummersville. I'm with the Division of Family Services."

Thick wrinkles appeared on my forehead. I hoped like hell that he wasn't here to tell me no bullshit about Scorpio and her damn husband or Nokea and Travis.

"Yes, I'm Jaylin Rogers. What's the problem?"

He started fumbling with the papers in his hands, trying to straighten them. "The problem is, sir, we received a phone call from one of your children, a Jaaaaylene Rogers, who said there were some serious problems here. Her complaints were about being starved and not being able to have sodas. She also mentioned that she'd been spanked."

I winced at the man while standing in disbelief. "Man, get the hell out of my driveway with that mess. My daughter didn't call you with no bullshit like that, and I know damn well you didn't come here to fuck with me over a soda."

He nodded and extended a piece of paper in my direction. I refused to take it. "I'm afraid she did call, sir, and per State's orders, I'm going to have to go inside of your home and look around. Do you mind opening the door so I can go inside to speak to your kids?"

My pressure was already up from the phone call from LJ. This man had definitely shown up at the wrong place, wrong time. "Hell yeah, I mind! This is bullshit, and you got one muthafucking minute to march your ass back down my driveway and get the hell out of here."

He didn't move. "I . . . I can't do that, sir. I'll have to contact the police if I'm not allowed to go inside."

"What?" Shane yelled. "This is crazy."

"You're damn right it is, and you're down to thirty seconds now before shit turns ugly."

Shane snatched the paper from the man's hand, and as the man attempted to move toward my door, I grabbed him from the back of his jacket. He crouched down and lifted his hand to cover his face. I started pulling him down the driveway until Shane rushed after me, grabbing my arm.

"Jay, I think you may want to look at this."

He reached out to give me the paper. I snatched it from his hand, and with a frown on my face, I looked at it. In big, bold letters was: YOU'VE BEEN PUNKED!

I looked at Shane and the man, who were now laughing their asses off. I started laughing too, and then I snatched the blank papers from the man's hands, hitting Shane with them.

"You muthafuckas play too much," I said.

"I couldn't resist," Shane said, patting my back. "Yo' ass was hot!"

The man removed his glasses and swiped his hand across his forehead. "Real hot. I just knew I was about to get my ass kicked before you had time to tell him the truth."

I agreed. "Yes, you were, especially when you mentioned going into my house. And then to lie on my baby Jaylene like that. Shane, you know better. I'ma get you back for this shit."

I hit him with the papers again, and we continued to laugh. He introduced me to the man, who was actually there to see if we were interested in purchasing some property from him. We stood around talking, and when my cell phone rang, I stepped away to take the call because it was Nanny B. She told me Nokea's father had been rushed to the hospital. According to her, it was serious. I cut my conversation short with Shane and Mr. Summersville, telling them that I needed to go to St. Louis right away.

No sooner had I made it to the airport than Nanny B called back, telling me Mr. Brooks had died. I was stunned. All I could think about were Nokea and her mother. I was sure my kids had taken the news pretty hard too, but Nokea and her father were tight. I couldn't imagine the pain she was feeling right now. I also felt bad about my recent conversation with her. I kind of wished I hadn't said some of the things I'd said. If only I could've taken them back.

Nonetheless, I couldn't allow her to deal with this alone, so I took a private plane to the Spirit of St. Louis Airport, which was close to my house in the Bluffs. Nanny B met me there, and from what she'd said, Nokea and her mother had taken the news real hard.

"Gloria hasn't gone home yet because she says it's too hard for her to go there," Nanny B said. "She's been talking to numerous church members and family. Nokea has been cooped up in the guestroom. I've been checking on her all day, and Travis is with her. The kids are okay, but LJ is taking it the hardest because he was the one closest to his grandfather. All we can do is pray and do whatever we can to be there for them."

I agreed, and I was going to do my best to keep my distance from Travis so nothing unfortunate popped off.

"Was Mr. Brooks sick? Nokea kept mentioning that something was going on with him, but she never specified what it was."

"He was complaining about being tired all the time. He'd been having some migraine headaches, and Gloria said his blood pressure had been way too high. When he left with Travis to go play golf, he seemed fine. All week he's been fine. I'm so glad that the kids and Nokea came to St. Louis when they did."

My face displayed a frown. I hated death. This whole thing made me think about when my mother was killed, and when Nokea and I found my father dead. I remembered how devastated I was. I was grateful to Nokea for being there for me both times.

Nanny B keyed in a code that opened the gates to my property. As she drove up the steep, curvy driveway, my stomach felt queasy inside. I didn't have the right words to say to Nokea or her mother at a time like this. I wasn't even sure if they wanted me here, especially since Mr. Brooks wasn't always fond of me. We'd had our ups and downs over the years. Still, he knew how much I loved his daughter, and that was good enough for me.

Nanny B parked in the garage, and as we entered the house through the front doors, I could see Nokea sitting on the couch in the great room. Her head rested on her arm while she gazed out of the curved picture windows. Much sunlight lit up the room, and as Nokea sat on one side, Travis sat by the fireplace in a chair on the other side. Nanny B shut the door behind us, causing Nokea to slowly turn her head. There was so much pain in her teary eyes. They were so contracted I figured she could barely see. Her tearstained face looked swollen, and her breathing became heavy. I took several steps forward, but by the time I reached the carpeted area that led to the great room, Nokea darted toward me, rushing into my arms. I was caught off guard by her reaction, and I staggered a bit from her tight hold on me. My embrace was just as tight. I secured her in my arms and didn't let go.

"He's gone," she cried out. I had to hold back my own emotions after seeing her like this. "What am I going to do, Jaylin? What am I going to do without my father?"

She backed her head away from my chest, searching into my eyes for answers I didn't have. Tears poured from her eyes. I couldn't recall a time when I had ever seen her so broken. I cupped her face with my hands, hoping that she wouldn't collapse when I released her waist.

"I'm so sorry, baby, deeply sorry. I'm going to help you get through this for as long as it takes. Okay?"

She nodded and continued to release staggering cries. I wrapped my arms around her again, this time closing my eyes while holding her close to my chest. I swallowed a sizeable lump in my throat, and as Nokea's body weakened in my arms, I held her up while transitioning her over to the couch.

"Go get her some water," I said to Nanny B. "Please."

Nokea's mother entered the room with sadness written all over her face. She sat next to Nokea, who leaned on me for comfort.

"I'm sorry," I said to Gloria. "And if there is anything—"

"I already know, Jaylin," she said. "Once we get through these next few days, we'll be fine. Just pray for God to give me and my child all the strength we need right now. This is horrible. I just don't understand."

She rubbed Nokea's back to help calm her. Slowly but surely, her mother's rub and my embrace helped to put her at ease. I was so out of it that I barely had time to look at Travis. When I did, he sat with his eyes closed, hands behind his head, and one leg crossed over the other. His foot tapped the floor. He appeared zoned out as well.

Nokea slowly sat up and reached for the glass of water Nanny B had given to her. My shirt was wet from her tears, but I surely didn't mind. I watched as she drank the water, appearing to be in a daze.

"Where are the kids?" I asked Nanny B.

"They're downstairs. Before I left to pick you up, I told them to go bowl for a while or go to the game room and play."

I wanted to make sure they were okay, so I stood and looked at Nokea. "I need to go check on the kids, but can I get you anything? Have you eaten or would you like to—"

"No, I don't want anything. I just want my father to be alive. All I want is him."

I was getting ready to sit back down, but Nanny B told me to go see about the kids. She sat next to Nokea, telling her that everything would be okay. I was sure it would be too, but there was no doubt in my mind that these next few days would be difficult for all of us.

Around ten o'clock that night, the kids were all settled in bed. They seemed to be okay and were handling this situation much better than I thought they would. Nanny B had fallen asleep on the sun porch. I tried to wake her so she could go to her room, but she insisted she was perfectly fine where she was. Gloria was in one of the guestrooms, as was Nokea, who had gone to the room around seven. Travis went back to the hotel, and in an effort to keep the peace, I didn't say one word to him. I wasn't sure what kind of support he had offered Nokea. If you asked me, he seemed real bitter about something. It was the wrong time to catch an attitude about anything, but Nokea was the one who had to deal with his shit, not me.

Feeling tired, I hit up a quick shower and changed into a pair of beige silk pajama pants. I chilled on a chaise in my bedroom, watching TV for a while. I didn't have much time to continue my conversation with Shane earlier, so I reached for my cell phone to call him. He mentioned that he and Tiffanie were in bed, so I didn't want to keep him long.

"We're just trying to keep the fire burning, and you know we're working on another little one," he said. "But before I go, how's Nokea doing?"

"Not well. Her father passed away before I arrived."

"Damn, I'm sorry to hear that. Please offer her my condolences. You too. I know how you felt about Mr. Brooks."

"I'm fine. Nokea not so much, but she'll get through this. I just hate to see her like this. There's nothing that I can really say or do to help take away the pain she's feeling right now. To some extent, I feel helpless."

"All she needs is support, your support. When you speak to her, get her to cheer up. Talk to her about the good times between her and her father. Make her reflect on those memories. If anybody knows about some of those good times, I'm sure it's you."

I nodded and thought about some of my past experiences with Nokea and her father. Most of it was laughable, but some of it not so much.

Nonetheless, I understood exactly what Shane was saying. We ended the call after he said he would be in St. Louis tomorrow.

I sat quietly for a while, thinking more about Nokea's father. He was a good man, and it was such a shame that his life ended so abruptly. Things like this always made me think what if it were me? What would happen to my kids, and how would they make it without me? Financially, I had definitely prepared for that, but I quickly shook the thoughts from my head. I dimmed the recessed lighting, tossed back a shot of Rémy, and then I went to the guestroom where Nokea was. When I opened the door, she was lying sideways in bed with her clothes still on. She lifted her head from the pillow to look at me.

"I just came to check on you," I said. "Why don't you get out of your clothes, take a bubble bath, and get comfortable?"

"I will," she said softly. "Just not now. Right now, I prefer to lie here in thought."

With the exception of one lamp on, the room was somewhat dark. I turned on another lamp before getting in bed, facing her. Her eyes were barely open, and small bags were underneath them. A handful of tissue was gathered in her hand, and the pillow she'd laid her head on was soaked from her tears. I touched her pretty face, softly rubbing her cheekbone with my thumb.

"As I was lying in the other room," I said, "I was in deep thought myself, thinking about the kind of man your father was. He was . . . nice."

"Yeah, you're saying that now, but I remember you always talking about how mean he was."

I had to chuckle. She was right. "He had a mean side for sure. So do I, so in no way can I be critical of him. I was thinking about when we were kids. Do you remember how everybody in the neighborhood used to run up on y'all porch to get money when the ice cream trucks came? He kept a lot of change in his pockets, but for some reason by the time I reached him, he would always say he didn't have any more. My feelings were crushed, and then he would smile and tell me I'd better not cry over no ice cream. He then dug deep into his pockets, and somehow the change would appear. I got my ice cream, and I always shared it with you."

Nokea smiled. "Yeah, you got your ice cream, but I got in trouble for always being around you. That's why he didn't want you to have any ice cream, because he knew you would use it to get on my good side. I never knew why he wouldn't give me the money so I could buy my own ice cream. That would have made more sense, and I never would have followed you around as much as I did."

"Maybe he wanted us to share, who knows? And you didn't follow me for my ice cream. You followed me because I was fine and you knew I would grow up to be somebody real special one day."

Nokea blushed, making me feel real good inside. "No, honestly, I followed you because my father forbade me to do it. He knew you were trouble, but I refused to listen to him."

"You did listen. You listened when he said we were destined to be together. He was right about that, but he was wrong for spanking you for making a mud pie with me. That was the only time I can recall him being upset with you. Mud was all over our clothes, on the floor, in our hair. All you got was a tap on your leg though."

"Yeah, kind of like what Jaylene gets when she's in trouble, huh?"

"Yeah, something like that."

We lay silent for a minute, in deep thought. Nokea spoke up again. "I'm so upset with myself for not spending more time with him. I didn't even tell him about the baby. Now I wish I had. I am, however, glad that I came to St. Louis. Something inside told me to come here. I don't know what I would've done if I was in Florida when this happened."

Hearing her mention the baby was like a punch in my gut, but I knew she meant no harm. "It's interesting how things operate sometimes. I'm glad you and the kids were here. Your mother needs you, so we're all going to stay here, support each other, and try to get through this together."

Nokea wiped the tip of her runny nose with a tissue. "Thank you so much for coming. I wasn't going to call you, especially after our 'End Celebration' the other day. I'm glad Nanny B called you. When you came through that door, I was so happy and relieved to see you."

"Same here, but please know that the 'End Celebration' is still in full effect. I'm just here now because I know your father would want me to be here."

"I don't know about that," she teased. "Daddy was hot, and if he could've taken off his belt and spanked you like he did when you and Stephon went to the store and stole that candy, he would have."

I cocked my head back. "What? Your father never spanked me. He hit Stephon one time, and that's because he cursed in front of your father. We were like . . . like eight years old or something. Stephon called a woman who was walking down the street a fine, freaky bitch. Your father was standing in the doorway, and when he heard that shit, he rushed out that door, pulling his belt from his waist. I ran my ass off, even though I wasn't the one who'd said it. Stephon was too slow, and before I knew it, that belt tore him up. Then he got it, again, when your father told Aunt Betty. Unfortunately, I got in trouble too for lying and saying he didn't say it."

Nokea nodded. "You may be right about that. Maybe he didn't spank you, but he should have because you and Stephon were baaaaad."

"Trust me, we got our share of spankings and then some. And you, Miss Lady, were bad as well. You just got away with a lot of shit, that's all."

Nokea showed her pearly whites. "I kind of did, didn't I?"

We both laughed, but seconds later, silence fell over the room again. More tears fell from her eyes. I moved closer to hold her, and to my surprise, she snuggled her head against my chest.

"I told myself that I would never tell you this, but when I asked your father if I could marry you, he said no. As a matter of fact, he said, 'Hell no.' I didn't know how to respond until he started laughing. I thought he was serious, especially when he asked why I even called to get his approval. He told me that with or without it, I would probably marry you regardless. He put me on the spot when he asked if that was true. I told him that his approval meant volumes to me, but I loved you so much that I didn't care who approved. He hung up on me that day, hurt my damn feelings. About fifteen minutes later, he called back. He said your mother's father never approved of him marrying her, but he loved her so much that he couldn't allow no one to stand in their way. I asked if that meant he approved, and he told me to let him think about it. I didn't hear back from him, but an hour before we got married on the beach that day, he called to give me his approval. I really appreciated him for doing that, because I was worried about going against his wishes."

Nokea didn't respond. All I heard was snoring. When I lifted my head, thinking she had fallen asleep, she giggled.

"Oh, okay," I said. "My boring little story put you to sleep, huh?"

"No, I heard you. My father called me several times that same day, asking me how much I loved you. I kept saying, 'A whoooooole lot, Daddy. Don't you already know how much?' Then he said, 'Do you love him more than you love yourself?' I replied, 'No, but still a whooooole lot.' He reminded me to always love myself first, and then he told me that you were going to ask me to marry you. He didn't know you had already asked me the first day I came to Florida to be with you, but I appreciated his heads-up."

"I'm sure you did, but I asked him after the original proposal. I just wanted his approval, that's all. I really didn't care about anybody else's, just his."

Nokea lay silent in deep thought again. Minutes later, she asked if I would go run her some bathwater. I knew exactly how she liked it, so I removed myself from the bed to go take care of that for her. As I was in the bathroom getting the tub ready for her, I could see her sitting on the bed. She removed her shoes, and after pulling her shirt over her head, she sat in a hot pink lace bra that showed her hard nipples. My mind traveled straight to the gutter, especially when she stood to remove her jeans. Her lace panties revealed her sweet goodies, and I could see her protruding belly, which caused me to shake my head. When she went to go flick on the lights, my thoughts turned positive. I stood mesmerized by her blemish-free, toned body and shapely ass, which left me with so many memories. The lights came on. She looked in my direction and saw me leaning against the doorway. We stared at each other without a single blink. I hadn't a clue what she was thinking, but the seduction in her eyes told me something was still there.

"I had a dream about us the other day." She spoke in a whisper. "We were making love at Café Lapedero and—"

She paused when she heard a light knock at the door. The direction of our eyes traveled to it, and seconds later, in walked Travis. His eyes scanned Nokea before he shifted them to me.

"I didn't know you were coming back tonight," Nokea said.

The tight expression on his face said it all, as did the thick wrinkles on his forehead. He was pissed. "Obviously not. I came back so you wouldn't have to be alone tonight. But it looks like you're already covered."

Just so Nokea wouldn't have to explain anything to this fool, I spoke up. "I was just running her some bathwater. But now that you're back, I'm sure she wouldn't mind you handling things instead of me."

I moved toward the door in slow motion. I took one last glance at Nokea, and as I approached the good doctor, I got a whiff of the strong alcohol he'd been drinking. A glassy film covered his eyes, which displayed nothing but fury. I hesitated to leave him alone with Nokea, but instead of interfering, all I offered was my support to her. "Try to get some rest tonight. If you need anything else, you know where I'll be."

I left the guestroom, returning to my bedroom. I could hear Travis and Nokea talking, maybe even arguing, but I stayed put. Their voices calmed less than ten minutes later, and that was when I made my way to the kitchen to get something nonalcoholic to drink. I opened the fridge, removed the orange juice, and placed the carton on the island. As I reached in the cabinet for a glass, I heard a door slam. I jetted toward the guestroom where Nokea was, but by that time Travis was already standing near the foyer with his jacket thrown over his shoulder. His eyes shot daggers at me. I fired right back.

"You really shouldn't drink and drive," I said. "But if you care to stay, my *twelve-car* garage has heated flooring."

"Fuck you, nigga, and no thanks. I'll gladly sleep elsewhere, but you can be sure that me and my *twelve* inches will be back later to give my woman all the support she needs. Until then, have a nice night, sucker."

He marched toward the door, leaving me with a smirk on my face. "I promise you I will. And by *twelve* o'clock tonight, I may be making all of her dreams about me come true. She did give you explicit details about her dream, didn't she?"

"What dream?"

"The one where I put *twelve* bullets in your head for disrespecting my kids. If you value your life, don't you ever say shit else to my son again."

Travis didn't respond. The door slammed on his way out, and after I locked it, I returned to the kitchen to get my orange juice. I watched TV for a while, and an hour later I returned to the room where Nokea was, seeing that she was asleep. I closed the door, pleased that she was resting peacefully.

Mr. Brooks's funeral was too much for me. That was why I'd made a decision to not let the kids go. With him being a deacon, the church was packed to full capacity. The choir was live, and people were screaming and shouting, including the pastor. He was racing up and down the aisles as if hot coal were underneath his feet, while everyone clapped. A few people looked as if they were about to pass out. It could've been because it felt like it was a hundred degrees in there. Hand fans waved all around, even on the piano player, who kept hammering away at the keys.

I sat stone-faced, hoping that this would be over with soon. All I could see was Nokea dying inside. I sat right behind her, and as she was bent over, holding her stomach as if she was in enormous pain, I just wanted it all to stop. Travis sat next to her like a bump on a log while two ushers fanned her. Gloria's head was dropped back, and with her eyes closed and tears pouring down her face, she was being fanned too.

"Jesus!" she shouted with her arms stretched wide. "Help me, Jesus, please help me right now. Lord, I need you!"

"He got you, Sister Brooks! Yes, ma'am, He got you!" a woman bellowed in response.

"Amen," another said. "Got you and He got me too! Thank you! Thank you, Jesus, thank you!"

In a flash, the woman jumped to her feet and started stomping and shouting. The piano player performed like he was at a concert or something, and in a matter of minutes, things went from bad to worse, particularly for my baby.

She dropped to her knees. So much agony was in her eyes. I could no longer sit there and try to respect her relationship with Travis. I removed my suit jacket, giving it to Shane, who sat next to me in disbelief. My shirt stuck to my sweaty skin, and the frown on my face deepened when I went near the front pew where Nokea remained on her knees, rocking back and forth. I dropped to my knees, securing my arms around her quivering body. I had never seen her like this, and when I witnessed her eyes roll back, I helped her to her feet so she could get out of there and go get some fresh air. As I held her waist, Travis had the nerve to reach out and grab her arm.

"Thanks, but I got her," he said.

"No, you don't," was all I said before escorting Nokea down the aisle so she could suck in some fresh air outside and breathe.

Two nurses followed us. Many people looked on. One of the nurses suggested that I take Nokea to a room where she could lie down. The other suggested calling an ambulance, but the second I took her outside, she rejected an ambulance. She sat next to me on a bench.

"I need to go lie down for a few minutes," she said, holding her stomach again. "I feel weak. Sick as a dog, and I'm hurting all over."

She stayed outside for a few more minutes. After that, I helped her inside so she could chill in one of the rooms. It was much cooler in there than it was in the sanctuary, and as one of the nurses tended to Nokea, she asked me to go check on her mother.

"If you don't mind, Jaylin, please. I ju . . . just want to go, but I don't want to leave her or my daddy like this."

Feeling emotional, I left the room, hurrying to blink away tears that had filled my eyes. There was much tension in my body as I proceeded up the steps to enter the sanctuary again. Travis stood at the top stair, waiting for me. I attempted to walk past him without saying anything, but when he yanked my arm, I snatched his collar, pulling him face-to-face with me.

"Muthafu . . ." I paused, almost forgetting where I was. "Do not put your hands on me ever again!"

I released his collar, shoving him away from me. He staggered backward but managed to keep his balance. "My hands should be the least of your worries," he threatened. "I'm warning you, fool. I'm about to unleash some serious hell upon you."

"Not in the house of the Lord!" a woman shouted. "Y'all better take that mess out there on them streets! I mean it. There won't be no fighting up in here today."

As Travis and I stood within inches of each other, one man pulled me back, and another pulled on him. "Come on, brothers, we can do better than this. Can I get an amen?" the man closest to me said.

I cut my eyes at him and Travis before walking away. When I returned to the sanctuary, Mrs. Brooks wasn't in her seat. People were now viewing Mr. Brooks's body, and after taking one glance at him, I looked at Shane, nudging my

head toward the door. He knew that meant I
was ready to go. I met him by the church doors,
but before we left, I returned to the room where
Nokea was. Travis was with her. In an effort not
to upset Nokea even more, I figured it was time
for me to go.

Chapter 14

Scorpio

After what Mario had done, I was left speechless. I knew he was upset with me, but his actions had gone too far. We had barely spoken to each other, and most of the time he was gone. I regretted that it had come to this, but I was so furious about everything that I couldn't even contemplate how I was going to fix this. A part of me didn't want to fix it, but as I looked at the bigger picture, I had to admit that my wrongdoings got us here.

Nanny B called to tell me about Nokea's father, so I left the next day so I could support her and attend the funeral. It was so sad. There was no question that Mr. Brooks was loved by many. Several people got up during the funeral to say really nice things about him. Flowers were all over the church, and the songs truly touched my soul.

On the flipside, it was too hot in there, there were too many theatrics, and the funeral went on for hours. Nokea and her mother were so out of it, and when I saw Jaylin leave the sanctuary with her, I felt so bad for her. Tears were in my eyes. Jaylin glanced at me. I could see how upset he was. Probably because Travis had said something to him. I saw him standing up front watching Jaylin and Nokea with bewilderment in his eyes. Shortly thereafter, he stormed out of the sanctuary, breezing by everyone in his path. I didn't see Jaylin return, nor did I see him at the repast. I saw Nokea and offered her my condolences. She reached out to hug me. Sadness was written all over her.

"Thanks for coming, Scorpio," she said, standing near the doorway. "When did you get here?"

"Early this morning. I stopped by Jaylin's house first to see the kids. Then I came here."

She slowly nodded and kept looking at my short hair. "I like your hair. What made you cut it all off? It was growing and was so pretty."

Thinking about what Mario had done, I released a deep sigh. I wouldn't dare tell Nokea the truth. I was too embarrassed. "I just got tired of it. Needed a change."

"I know how that is. Definitely know what you mean."

She looked around, and as several people came up to offer their condolences, I told her I would catch up with her later at Jaylin's house. I spoke to a few other people, but as I walked back to my car, I heard someone call my name. I swung around only to see Travis a few steps behind me. He was really a handsome man, but stress was visible in his eyes, which told me he hadn't had much sleep. The wide smile he always presented wasn't there, and with a scruffy beard growing, he obviously needed to shave. Normally, his face was clean-shaven.

"I'm sorry to bother you," he said as he approached me, "but do you have a minute, maybe two?"

"Sure. What's up?"

"I . . . I'm a little confused about something, and since I saw you, I was wondering if you could shed some light on a few things and help me try to understand these feelings I have inside."

I shrugged, not really knowing where he was going with this. "Feelings about what?"

"About Nokea and Jaylin. I could be wrong about this, but I get a feeling that there's more to them than being friends for the sake of the children. I know their past is deep. Nokea told me all about it. But I'm starting to feel a little threatened by that past. I guess you of all people would know if there—"

I quickly spoke up, just to make Travis aware of something I had known throughout my entire relationship with Jaylin. "I don't want to hurt your feelings, Travis, but the truth is Nokea will always have deep feelings for Jaylin. He will always love her too, but from what I can see, the two of them have moved on. This is the first time I've ever seen Nokea so happy with another man. So instead of feeling threatened, why don't you step up instead of stepping back? She loves you, and you're making a big mistake by doubting that. I don't know what else to say to you, but please know this: if you leave a tiny crack open for Jaylin to make his way back into her life, he can and he will."

Having nothing else to say, and not wanting to interject myself into what was going on, I got in my car and drove off. From the rearview mirror, I could see Travis walking back into the church with his hands dipped into his pockets. Unfortunately for him, I didn't exactly speak the truth. That was, from what I saw at the church earlier, Jaylin had already slipped through that crack.

I arrived at Jaylin's house, parking my car in the garage area that wasn't connected to the house. I entered through a side door that was unlocked, and as I made my way through the kitchen, I heard Nanny B talking. I peeked into the great room where Jaylin sat suited up, looking star-studded and fine as ever. Worry was in his teary eyes as he looked at Nanny B with his elbows resting on his knees. He wrung his hands together and lowered his head to look down when Nanny B told him there wasn't much more he could do. Shane stood behind him, leaning against the fireplace. He was also suited up. They both were perfectly polished from head to toe. Justin was on Nanny B's lap, and as she continued to speak to Jaylin, Justin kept kissing her cheeks. She kissed his back.

"Nanna loves you too, baby, and I know why you're giving me all of these sweet kisses. You want a soda, don't you?"

Jaylin's head snapped up. "Please don't tell me he's drinking soda again."

"No, he's not. I just said that to mess with you. I want you to cheer up. Don't let this thing with Travis get you all worked up. You're getting too involved again. I keep telling you to just be still and let everything work itself out."

Jaylin wiped down his face then sat back on the couch, resting his arms on top of it. A few buttons on his shirt were undone, and the bottom of his shirt had been pulled from his slacks, which had cuffs at the bottom. Diamonds glistened on his cufflinks as well as from his watch. Looking slouchy, he was still picture perfect. Sexiness defined him even when he wasn't trying. With one leg bent and the other leg stretched far out, the hump between his legs was quite noticeable. I wasn't trying to go there, but this was one of those moments when I would have loved to prance into the room, straddle his lap, and ride the shit out of him. Thankfully I was married now.

"I feel what you're saying," he said to Nanny B, "but I just love her so much. I hate to see her going through this, and to see that muthafucka sitting there while she was going through it like that, I couldn't believe it. He sat like a fucking zombie or something."

Shane added his two cents. "I know, and since he was right in front of me, I wanted to tap his shoulder and tell him to get the fuck up and help. The whole scene was unfortunate. I don't care what anybody says. If that was considered a home-going celebration, count me out."

Jaylin turned to give Shane dap. "Count me out too. That was ridiculous."

"Well," Nanny B said, "that's how we do it, and it's what Mr. Brooks wanted. As for Travis, most people don't like to deal with funerals. Being there could have caused him to shut down. This is a tough time, not only for Nokea, but for all of us. He cares for her too, so I'm sure he's feeling some kind of way about all of this as well."

I nodded, silently agreeing with Nanny B. Seconds later I stepped into the room, causing all heads to turn toward me. My black dress was nothing special, but with my hour-glass figure, I always managed to bring attention to myself. I wasn't sure about my short hair, though. It would take some time for me to get used to for sure.

"Damn," Jaylin teased. "What's up, Halle? Where's Scorpio at?"

"Right," Shane said. "Or more like that, uh, Anika chick from *Empire*. She is fine."

"No doubt," Jaylin added and tossed me a compliment too. "So is Mrs. Pezzano."

I playfully cut my eyes but thanked him for the compliment. I guessed it took a few seconds for Justin to notice who I was, but when he did, he rushed off Nanny B's lap.

"Mommy," he said, rushing up to me. I picked him up and gave him several kisses on his cheek. When I stopped by earlier, he was asleep, so he didn't get a chance to see me.

"Muah, muah, muah! Don't you look adorable, and where is my picture at? I came all the way here to get that picture you've been telling me about."

Nanny B stood and tightened the string on her apron. She was such a jewel. Not only was she the matriarch of our family but she was a blessing to all of us. The only reason all of this worked out was because of her. Our situation seemed awkward at times, but without her none of this would've been possible.

She reached out to tickle Justin's feet. He giggled and went right back to her. "Let's go see what your brother and sisters are up to. Then, we'll give your mama those pictures you painted."

"Where my picture at?" Jaylin asked, sounding jealous. "I don't get a picture?"

"No," I said. "You get nothing but a blank piece of paper with your little name scribbled on the top."

Nanny B laughed, and as I turned to follow her, I could only imagine the expressions on Shane's and Jaylin's faces. I quickly turned my head just to catch them in action. Their eyes were focused on one thing: my ass. They tried to divert their attention elsewhere, but it was too late. I shook my head before leaving the room.

"What you shaking your head for?" Jaylin asked.

I didn't bother to reply. He already knew how the minds of many men operated.

A few hours later, Nokea and her mother returned. I wasn't sure where Travis was, but Nokea mentioned that he was at the hotel and planned on leaving this evening. I was leaving as well. I hadn't even spoken to Mario, and I was sure he was wondering by now where I'd gone. So after I spent time with the kids, ate a little something, and chatted with Nokea and her mom, who were on their way to Nokea's mom's house, I was ready to leave. Jaylin and Shane were standing near the pool area talking, so I walked up to say goodbye. I also needed to ask Jaylin for a favor, but I wasn't sure if this was the appropriate time. Since his mood had been all over the place today, I decided not to go into detail.

"I'm getting ready to leave," I said, standing in front of him. "But please give me a call when you get home. I need you to do something very important for me, and after this, I promise to never bug you again."

He sucked his teeth while staring at me. "No more favors, Scorpio. I told you that I'm done."

"I know, but like I said, this is important. I'll tell you more about it later. Just don't forget to call me, and be careful on your way back to Florida."

He tossed his head back. I waved at Shane, and after getting in my car, I left.

Later that day I returned home. The house was so quiet you could hear a pin drop. Loretta wasn't even there. She'd told me earlier that she had a few errands to run, and she mentioned something about staying the weekend with a male companion since the kids weren't here. After all that had happened, I was glad that they weren't here. Mario and I needed to deal with our messy marriage.

The second I reached for my phone to call him, I heard the front doors close. I rushed to the stairs, and when I looked down in the foyer, Mario stood with a Louis Vuitton suitcase next to him. He glanced at me before cutting his eyes, ignoring me.

"What's that suitcase for?" I asked.

"It's for me, my dear. I'm leaving you. Today. Just so I don't have to kill you."

He whistled as he marched forward, making his way to our bedroom. I hurried down the stairs, preparing myself to talk some sense into him. By the time I reached our bedroom, he was already in his walk-in closet, which was thick with name-brand clothes, shoes, jackets. Mario had it all. My closet, however, was double the size of his. He removed several pieces of his clothing from hangers. I stood in the doorway with my arms crossed, pouting.

"I can't believe our marriage has come to this," I said. "There has to be more to this. I refuse to believe that my having sex with my ex prior to us getting married has caused all of this."

Mario shook his head while standing with one of his expensive silk shirts in his hand. "Your lies caused this. Then you run off and go to St. Louis to fuck him again. Do you think I don't know where you've been? You must think I'm freaking stupid. I need to get the fuck away from you before I do something I'll regret."

"You're jumping to conclusions before having all the facts. I went to St. Louis to attend Nokea's father's funeral. Everyone was at Jaylin's house, so that's where I was for a few hours. My trip had nothing to do with me going to St. Louis to screw him. I rushed back here because I would love for us to just chill for a while and talk about this. If you still want to leave, fine, Mario, do whatever. But the bottom line is I do love you. I don't want to lose you. I made a horrible mistake by having sex with Jaylin. I apologize, and when I talked to him about it, he wants to apologize to you too. He said that when he comes back, he would like to have dinner with us and do whatever he can to help us get back on track. Like me, he didn't intend for things to turn out like this. He wants you to know that what's in the past is in the past. It was one night of sex that, honestly, shouldn't have happened."

Mario darted his finger at me. "But it did, and you lied to me about it. Aside from that, Jaylin's bombastic behavior is overboard. I did some fucked-up things the night before our wedding too. But if you asked me about it, I wouldn't have lied to you. I would've told you the truth regardless."

This was breaking news that caused me to cock my head back. "Fucked-up things like what? What did you do the night before our wedding?"

He waved me off. "It doesn't matter now. No matter what I did, it doesn't come close to what you did. You fucked him all night, exhausted yourself, and left nothing for me."

Mario slapped his chest as he walked up to me. He reached underneath my dress, cupping his hand over my pussy. "You gave me ten fucking minutes of this on our wedding day. I could feel that it wasn't the same. It didn't even taste the same, and you willingly put into my mouth what he put into you." He turned his head, releasing a gob of spit from his mouth. "Nasty, filthy shit that I refuse to taste, especially since you keep fucking him."

I reached for his hand, moving it away from my coochie. "That's not true. You're so upset that you keep reaching for something that isn't there. I can't blame you for this. After all, I did lie. But never in a million years did I think you would treat me like this. I know deep down that you're not the kind of man who would kill me. You're doing all of this because you're hurting, but allow me to help us put this to rest. I don't even care if you were with someone the night before our wedding. Let's call it even and be done with this. Can we at least try to do that?"

Mario responded by walking out of the closet. Since there were no clothes in his hands, I figured he'd changed his mind about leaving. He sat on the bed, searching me from head to toe.

"You let me know when Jaylin wants to talk. I want a fucking apology from him, and that shit better be sincere."

I wasn't sure how sincere it would be, and I damn sure didn't think Jaylin would apologize. I needed him to come through for me. Unfortunately, this seemed to be the only way for me to save my marriage, something I really wanted to do. Maybe Mario would listen to Jaylin, because thus far he definitely wasn't listening to me.

Several days later, Jaylin came back to Florida with the kids. His birthday had come and gone, and this time there was no celebration because of Mr. Brooks's death. It was a good thing that it didn't occur on Jaylin's birthday, but I wasn't so sure that five days later made a difference. Nokea hadn't returned. Mackenzie mentioned some unfinished business Nokea had to take care of regarding her father.

Mario and I had been speaking to each other more often, but it was clear that we still had work to do. He kept asking when Jaylin wanted to meet, so I had to hurry up and make our gathering happen fast. I went to Jaylin's house on Thursday afternoon while the kids were at school, with the exception of Justin, who was the only one being homeschooled right now.

He was in the playroom with Mrs. Mahoney and Nanny B. I figured Jaylin was probably in his office, and sure enough, when I made my way to it, the door was open. I saw him inside, leaning back in his chair. His hands were behind his head while he was speaking to someone through the speakerphone. I entered the room. The first thing he did was move his head from side to side, implying no.

"Man, see what you can do," he said to Shane. "I really want this deal to happen because a casino would be huge. I'm not prepared to dish out more than thirty or so million, and I think we should be able to find some other investors who can get us to that magic number. What do you think?"

"I think we don't mention what we're willing to put up until we find out how much the investors are willing to pony up first. Thirty is my limit. I'm almost to the point where I think that may be too much for a casino. Just think about how we can utilize that kind of money elsewhere."

"Maybe so. Let's sit on this for a minute. Hit me back later today to convey your final thoughts about this and whatever else you have in mind."

"Will do. Holla later."

After Jaylin hit the END button, he closed his eyes and lowered his head on the desk. "What do you want?" he mumbled as if seeing me was discouraging. "Didn't I tell you you were dead to me?"

"I'm never dead to you until you bury me six feet under. That hasn't happened yet, so I need you to listen to me without barking like a pit bull."

Jaylin's head remained on the desk. I scooted a chair in front of it. I tapped the back of his head, and when he wouldn't lift it, I rubbed my fingers through his curls.

"Oh, my God," I shouted. "Look at this! Is this a strand of gray hair?"

He quickly lifted his head and fell back against his seat. "Stop lying," he said. "You did not see any gray in my hair, but now that you have my attention, what do you want?"

"You do have a strand of gray in your hair. If you would like for me to get a mirror so you can see it, I will."

"What I would like for you to do is leave. Obviously, that's not going to happen."

"No, it's not, but before I ask you for a huge favor, how's Nokea?"

"I assume she's doing okay. Before I left, she told me Travis was upset, and the two of them needed some alone time."

"Well, I hope she'll be okay. Travis seemed pretty pissed. I'm sure he wasn't pleased with your actions at the funeral."

"Too damn bad. Now get to your favor that, most likely, will be rejected."

I sighed and cut my eyes at him. "Okay. I know what you said about the 'End' thingy, but I kind of need you to help me get through to Mario."

"Scorpio, you may as well leave right now. I'm not doing anything that revolves around your marriage. The only things up for discussion between us are issues with the kids. I have too much going on and—"

"Can you please silence yourself for a few minutes? Just hear me out, Jaylin, and if your answer is still no, so be it, okay?"

He didn't respond, so I started to tell him about what had been transpiring between me and Mario. I told him about Mario's aggressiveness toward me, about everything from my hair being cut off to the toy gun he used to force the truth out of me. I even told him about Mario pushing me in the tub, and about him possibly having sex with someone else the day before our wedding. Jaylin sat in silence, studying me, sucking his teeth and releasing deep breaths. I could see the anger and frustration building in his eyes, but I didn't know if it was directed toward me or Mario.

"So, with that being said," I continued, "I am begging you to have dinner with us. Tell him we are done. That it was sex that meant nothing to us. That you're now in love with someone else.

That you want him and me to stay together and that you are deeply sorry for encouraging me to have sex with you."

That prompted a quick response from Jaylin. "Get the hell out of here. Sorry my ass. Are you fucking serious?"

"I'm dead serious. I truly believe that hearing something like that from you will help Mario get it together. Whatever you told him that day angered him so much. You have to reverse those words and tell him that you didn't mean what you said. Please. Will you please do it for me?"

Jaylin sat perplexed with his index finger pressed against his temple. "I'm in total disbelief that you came here today, asking me to help you stay married to someone who is already showing you how reckless he can be. I did some fucked-up shit too, but Mario ain't wasting no time. I don't know what you're going to do with all of those extra rooms over there, because our kids won't be coming there anytime soon. I mean, what's next, Scorpio? And what are you going to do when the real guns show up?"

"I understand your concerns, but there is a lot of good in Mario. He's hurting, and this is how he's choosing to deal with it. In addition to that, sometimes you have to give a little to gain a lot. If things don't work out, there is no way I can lose, if you know what I mean."

Jaylin sat up straight, now giving me his full attention. "I do know what you mean, and you're finally talking what I want to hear. So, I'll tell you what. I'll meet you and Mario for dinner and tell him whatever you need me to say. But when you divorce him, I want half of what you're entitled to."

This time, I sat up straight and let his ass have it. "First of all, if I can stop the bleeding, there will be no divorce. Second, how dare you make this all about money when I'm sitting here pouring my heart out to you, asking you to do a simple favor for me? That's cold, Jaylin, and shame on you for even coming to me like that. You sound like a serious hustler."

I could see that he was becoming annoyed with my presence. "Cut the damn act, Scorpio, and just so you know, I am a hustler. But your ass is the one who is cold. You may like Mario a lot, but you are not in love with him. I recall you saying the same shit about Bruce, but we both know how that turned out. You're down with Mario's money more than you are anything else. You ain't even down with the sex, because the way that pussy yelled at me, I knew it had been deprived. If there will be no divorce, then you have no worries. But if there is, like I suspect there will be, I want half."

I thought he was kidding, but Jaylin was serious as ever. No way would I agree to anything like that. I was so mad at him that I jumped from my seat and snatched my purse off his desk.

"Bruce doesn't have anything on Mario, and yes, marrying him was a big mistake. But for half of what I'm entitled to, you'd better be down on your knees, kissing Mario's feet, crying and begging for him to accept your apology. I don't think you're willing to do all of that, so let's forget this stupid conversation ever happened."

"I'm willing to do whatever you want me to do, provided that if you divorce Mario or he divorces you within the next two years, I get half. I even cut the agreement to two years instead of a lifetime."

I planned on staying married to Mario for a lifetime, so this could very well blow up in Jaylin's face. He waited for a response. I gave him one when I put my purse back on his desk.

"Okay, Mr. Greed. Half is yours if I get a divorce within the next two years. In the meantime, I want you at the restaurant of Mario's choice, kissing his entire ass, paying for dinner, and telling him how deeply sorry you are for fucking me. Tell him it was your idea, not mine. That you refused to let me go. That you finally realize how much I love him, and you have no other choice but to move on. I may think of some other things before then, but that's a start."

Jaylin displayed a wide smile. "Hey, it's whatever you want, baby. Just tell me where I need to be and what time I should be there. In the meantime, I don't show up anywhere until you sign a contractual agreement my attorney, Frick, will happily put together for you. After you sign, the deal is done."

"No, the deal is already done. I don't know why you think I'm not in love with my husband, because I am. His money is surely an asset, but at the end of the day, with or without it, I'm good because I still have you as my baby's daddy."

"You got lucky, big deal. As for what you said about Mario, I'm not convinced. Hopefully he will be after I pay for dinner. Do I have to pay for your dinner too?"

"Hell yes you do, so be sure to bring a credit card that won't decline."

"That has never happened in my world. In yours, I'm sure it has, and I'm sure it will."

Jaylin snatched up his phone and hit a button to dial out. He put the phone on speakerphone so I could hear him talking to Frick. He gave Frick specific details about what the contract should include.

"She what!" Frick shouted. "This is a joke, isn't it? Please tell me this is a joke. That's like taking candy from a baby."

I hurried to speak up. "I'm so glad you know me well, Mr. Frick. I assure you that you don't. You're going to be wasting your time on that contract, and Jaylin will waste money paying you because my husband and I will be together forever."

Frick chuckled. "Anything could happen, sweetheart. You should rethink this. You may consider it a laughing matter now, but this could become serious if you're ever in a position where you have to honor the contract."

"Damn," Jaylin said. "Are you her lawyer or mine? Don't be giving her no advice. If this is what she feels comfortable doing, and she believes there will be no divorce, then what does she have to lose?"

"Nothing, I guess," Frick said. "But if the two of you want me to proceed with this, I most certainly will."

Jaylin looked at me. I looked at him. In unison, we both told Frick, "Proceed."

Chapter 15

Scorpio

The big day had finally arrived. The contract was signed, and Jaylin agreed to meet Mario and me for dinner. I'd come up with a longer, detailed list of things for Jaylin to say, and before dinner wrapped up, I expected him to make Mario feel like a king.

As for Mario, he'd been conducting himself much better. With all the drama going on, we hadn't finished getting our house together like we wanted to. Last night he finally helped me rearrange some of the furniture in the parlor. I wanted to use that room for reading. It was decked out with wall-to-wall bookshelves, a sofa, and numerous velvet chairs just in case the kids wanted to chill and read with me. Even when we'd gone to bed last night, Mario held me in his arms and whispered that he loved me. I returned the love, but for whatever reason, he didn't pursue sex with me. That was why I needed Jaylin to put the nail in the coffin today. If he failed to deliver in a major way, this time he would be dead to me.

Around seven o'clock that evening, Mario and I sat at one of the Italian restaurants his family owned. His aunt was the one who managed this particular restaurant, and she was delighted to see Mario and me come in. The first thing she did was compliment my short hair as well as the soft yellow baby-doll dress I wore that cut right at my thighs. It had thin straps, and with a round neckline, my breasts sat firm, as did my toned, soft legs that looked dipped in baby oil. A diamond necklace Mario had given me added bling to my neck. With my wedding ring weighing down my finger, couldn't nobody tell me anything. All they could do was take a glance at Mario and me. We certainly made an attractive couple.

The restaurant was packed, but Roseabella made sure our glasses were filled with wine, breadsticks were on the table, and our food, she said, would be ready in minutes after we ordered. We were seated in a cozy booth on the second floor, where classical music thumped through the speakers. The area was somewhat private, and behind a half-glass wall was a view of nearly everyone in the restaurant.

"Enjoy the wine," Roseabella said. "I'll be back to check on you two. When Jaylin arrives, I'll send him right over." She reached out to Mario's cheek, squeezing it. "Have you spoken to your papa today?"

He nodded. "*Sí*. I spoke to him around noon."

"Is he still upset with you?"

"He's always upset with me, Bella. But I can't do anything about that."

Roseabella shook her head before walking away. I looked across the table at Mario, who wore gray slacks and a light green silk shirt that matched his eyes. The shirt was partially unbuttoned, and a dog tag was draped around his neck. His hair was parted and slicked back into a ponytail. Fine hair on his chin suited it well. Based on what Roseabella had said, I jumped into a conversation with him that I didn't want to have.

"Why is your father upset with you?" I asked. "Does it have anything to do with me?"

Mario cocked his neck from side to side before lifting his wineglass to me. "I don't wish to talk about Papa right now. But as I said to Roseabella, he's always upset about something. You're just a small piece of his unfortunate problems."

I certainly didn't want to know what those problems were, and when Jaylin swooped around the corner, garnering attention with his stride, my attention diverted to him. He appeared real clean-cut in an embroidered, button-down shirt and jeans. He came up to the table, apologizing for being ten minutes late.

"My tardiness rarely happens, but I needed to take care of something real important," he said, looking at Mario, not me.

Mario extended his hand across the table where Jaylin stood before taking a seat. "No problem. Have a seat and let's talk."

Jaylin slid into the spacious circular booth next to me. I was slightly nervous. I wasn't sure how all of this was going to play out. For starters, though, Jaylin picked up the menu, looking it over.

"What's good, Mario? I've never been here, so tell me what I should order."

Mario quickly went on the attack. "Everything on the menu is good. My wife is too, so maybe that's why you can't keep your hands off her."

Jaylin released a soft chuckle and laid the menu down. "Yes, your wife is good, very good, and I wholeheartedly agree with you on that. She was so good to me that I couldn't imagine myself being without her. But what I knew was I could never make her as happy as you could. She has certain requirements in a man that I could never meet. I felt that it would be wise for me to finally release her, and when she met you, I was skeptical but pleased that a man of your stature had stepped in and persuaded her to fall in love with you. She loves you, Mario, and there's not a damn thing I can do about it. When I asked Scorpio to come over that night and make love to me, I did so because my ego was a little bruised. She continued to tell me no, but as I proceeded to pressure her, she finally gave in."

Jaylin was putting it on a little thick, so I had to send him a signal by lightly kicking him underneath the table. He turned his head to look at me. A grin was on his face.

"By the way," he said then winked at me, "you look lovely tonight. Mario is truly a blessed man."

I smiled but lightly kicked him again. He was being sarcastic. I didn't want Mario to notice how fake Jaylin was.

Mario tapped the table with his fingers. "If I can recall, we had numerous conversations where you pretended to be okay with me. We were cool, man, and not once did you tell me you still had deep feelings for my woman. I never knew how serious your relationship was with Scorpio. She told me it had always been a fuck thing, nothing more. No love, no nothing. Now I'm hearing differently. I'm hearing how you can't let her go, she can't let you go. I mean, who's telling the truth, man? You or her?"

"Truthfully, we both are being honest," Jaylin said then leaned in closer to the table. His hands went underneath it, and when I felt him pinch my leg, I moved it. "Our relationship started out as a fuck thing, but then, for me anyway, it grew into something more special. Maybe I did love her more than she loved me, or maybe she didn't love me at all. If she said it was just a fuck thing, then that's what it was for her. At this point, however, what you need to know is I will never interfere in your marriage. And as good as your wife may be . . ." Jaylin paused to softly rub my leg. I attempted to move it, but this time he gripped it tight, pulling it closer to his leg. I lifted my heel, adding pressure to his shoe so he would remove his hand. All that did was make his hand travel farther up my leg. I hurried to clamp my legs shut. "She is your wife, not mine. I get that now, and even though I have lost plenty of sleep over this, it is what it is."

Jaylin continued to rub my thighs, and in an effort not to make Mario aware of the festivities underneath the table, I sat real still with my legs as tight as they could be. I knew what Jaylin was aiming for. Before his hand got closer to my pussy, I reached for a cloth napkin, laying it over my lap. I then moved closer to the table and took a sip of water to wet my dry mouth.

"That's right, man, it is what it is. My biggest problem with the whole thing was the lies. I didn't appreciate the lies, nor did I like how you spoke to me when I tried to get at you about what I'd found out. You weren't really kind to me that day. That shit made me maaaad."

Jaylin shrugged. "Hey look, I was upset too. I was already having a bad day. Scorpio knows how I am when I'm having a bad day, don't you?"

He shifted his head to look at me again. His fingers crept up my leg like a spider, and he forced his hand between my thighs, massaging them. I coughed and cleared my throat.

"I do know when you're having a bad day, and that explains why you said what you did. Maybe you should apologize to Mario for not telling the complete truth. I'm sure an apology would go a long way."

Jaylin nodded and glided his middle finger up and down between my thighs. Was he finger fucking my thighs? Or was he signaling something else?

"You're right," Jaylin said. "I do owe Mario an apology. I owe you one too, and instead of telling the two of you to go fuck yourselves"—his middle finger between my thighs moved faster—"I should have been kinder. I shouldn't have made this all about me, but I'm known for being a selfish man. In addition to that, there was a time when I was pussy whipped. Scorpio had me making some very bad decisions, all because of that magic she has brewing between her legs."

Right then, Jaylin touched the upper crotch section of my silk panties. His words caused Mario to shoot him a hard stare. Jaylin quickly corrected himself. I, on the other hand, took a deep breath and lifted my butt from the seat, inching over.

"No offense," Jaylin said. "I was just thinking about some of the unfortunate mistakes I made during and after our relationship."

"That was then, and this is now," I snapped back. "We both made them, so let's just be thankful that you've moved on and so have I."

After poking at my pussy through my panties, he finally removed his hand. He placed his fingers on his lips, rubbing across them. I was sure my scent was on his fingers.

"We have moved on, and even though I won't be able to stay for dinner, I don't mind paying for dinner for you two. It'll be my treat. My way of expressing how deeply sorry I am, again, for what I encouraged to happen. I know how important trust and loyalty is to you, Mario. It is just as important to me."

Mario nodded and tossed back the red wine in his flute glass. "It is very important. Without trust and loyalty, a marriage is nothing."

His words were convincing. He truly believed what he'd said. Jaylin, however, snickered and narrowed his eyes as he glared across the table at Mario.

"Yeah, I know all about that trust and loyalty shit. I used to feel the same way until I finally realized one day that things ain't always that simple. That shit happens sometimes, and the people who truly love you can unintentionally hurt you as well. When it comes to loyalty, realistically, very few people are. The ones you think are loyal, they're really not. I'm surprised that you keep talking about how important it is to be truthful, Mario, especially if you haven't been totally honest with your wife about certain things."

Jaylin's words caused me to swallow and turn my attention to Mario. He repositioned himself in his seat, appearing slightly uncomfortable. I wasn't exactly sure why.

"I don't know what you mean by that," he said to Jaylin in a more timid tone. "But if you think trust and loyalty isn't important, that's your prerogative."

"I said it was important, but I also said it applies to very few individuals. For example, look at you. You go around pretending to live by your words, but you also had sex the night before your wedding. With three women, may I add, and to my surprise, one of those women is now saying she's pregnant by you. The least you could have done was use a condom, but I do understand if the pussy is so good, like your wife's is, you just want to hit it raw sometimes."

My heart sank, my mouth dropped open, and my eyes locked on Mario. He shot up from his seat like a rocket and threw his napkin on the table.

"You son of a bitch! Who do you think you are, digging into my business? How dare you spew your lies in front of my wife like this!"

"No lies," Jaylin said, sitting calmly. "Just facts, Mario. If you wish to dispute the facts, we can. I can make some phone calls and show your wife, right now on my phone, pictures of this fine, sexy-ass Brazilian woman you will soon call your baby's mama. Her name is Camila, right? I know she's been harassing you for money, threatening to tell Scorpio. You know, all of that exciting stuff that happens when you're not loyal to the person you're married to. What I'm going to recommend that you do is sit down, explain this little fucked-up situation to your wife over dinner, beg for her forgiveness, hope that she gives it, and then take her home so you can delve into more of that good pussy. As for me, keep me out of it. I already told Scorpio that she's dead to me. As far as I'm concerned, so are you."

Jaylin reached in his pocket and tossed a hundred-dollar bill on the table. "Eat light, and discontinue the wine. Hopefully, that should cover it."

After that, he strutted out of the restaurant as if he were the one who owned it. To say I was blown away by all of this would be an understatement. I never saw any of this coming, and the wideness of my eyes, as well as the visible anger trapped in them, represented how shocked and furious I was.

I hurried out of the booth to go after Jaylin. Mario snatched my arm. Having nothing to say to him, I raised my hand, slapping him so hard that his head jerked in another direction.

"I will deal with your lying ass when I get back. If you want to take this marriage there, muthafucka, by all means, let's do!"

I stormed away, trying to catch up with Jaylin. As soon as I got to the parking lot, I saw him leaning against his car with a bold stance and his arms across his chest.

I yelled at him from a distance, "You knew this all along, didn't you? That's why you asked me to sign that fucking agreement!"

He opened his arms and shrugged, speaking nonchalantly. "Hey, don't be upset with me if you didn't do your homework. Whenever anyone threatens me, I go to the extreme to do mine. Whether you like it or not, the agreement stands. Either you deal with that muthafucka in there for the next two years or prepare yourself to divorce him and give me my money."

My face had to be beet red. I was so damn mad. I couldn't believe Jaylin had done this. It was totally unbelievable to me. I spoke through clenched teeth with my finger pointing at him.

"I am the mother of your children, and as much as I've always had your back, you damn well should have had mine. If you knew something, anything about Mario, you should have told me! You knew this was going to hurt me. I don't understand why you continue to do shit that always hurts me! Then to create a gotdamn agreement to benefit yourself off my pain is gut-wrenching! Who in the fuck are you, Jaylin? Why do you keep doing shit like this?"

"Look, if you want to yell at somebody, I suggest you take your ass back into that restaurant and have a real talk with your husband. You're wasting your breath and your tears on me, because I do not give a fuck anymore. I told you that I'm sick of this shit and I meant it. But you just kept pushing. You stooped to an all-time low, asking me to apologize for making love to you, basically telling me to concoct lies to appease your stupid-ass husband. You should have known better coming to me like that, and just in case you've forgotten, my name is Jaylin Jerome Rogers. I do not apologize to anyone unless I feel it's necessary, I only make love to and/or fuck women who mean something to me, and I love making money but not as much as I love my kids."

"You don't have to remind me who you are. I know, but never did I—"

"You don't know shit. If you did, you wouldn't be out here talking about all the pain I've caused you. You'd be inside with Mario, telling him about your pain. But before you go tackle your overwhelming problems, here's something I want you to know pertaining to the last time, and I do mean the last time, we had sex. I told you I regretted it, but I didn't. I wanted you to believe that it meant nothing to me, but it did. It did because I've always loved the connection between us, and when you came to me that night, I was ecstatic. You kept asking what I was thinking during sex. My thoughts reflected on how much I loved you. On how I will always love you, Scorpio, yet I didn't say it because I didn't want my words to hold you back anymore. The whole night was special, and years down the road, I figured I'd look back on that day to reflect on the memories of our last intimate time together. So when you asked me to apologize for it, when you made it seem like it was nothing but sex, when you wanted me to sum it up as wrong, I couldn't. Wrong or not, I just didn't want to view it that way, all right?"

His words caused me to pause and slowly lower my finger. I was left speechless. My chest rose and fell as I stared at Jaylin. A tear rolled down my face. I'd felt the same way about that night, and if I had to do it all over again, I would. As I opened my mouth to speak, Jaylin placed two fingers over my lips.

"Never doubt the happiness I want for you, and you already know why I will never be able to give you what you deserve. Maybe Mario can make some adjustments and do it, and what I do know is, like most men with money and power, he has a happy dick that is difficult to control when you have women coming at you from every angle. He got some anger issues, too, and in no way am I'm standing here defending him. Forgiving him will be for you to decide, and for the last time, if you divorce him, our agreement will be enforced."

Jaylin opened the door to his car, got inside, and drove off. I stood there thinking about all that he'd said. I wondered what in the hell I was going to do about my husband and possibly about his baby on the way. Call it karma. Hell yes, it was.

Chapter 16

Nokea

I wouldn't wish the ill feeling I had inside on my worst enemy. Death this close was hard. I couldn't stop thinking about my father, and as my mother and I started going through his things at their house, it was so painful. I tried my best to stay strong for her, but I was unable to do it. One minute she was up and the next she was down. I was up, then down. We both were down together, and in the moment all we had was each other. I didn't want her to stay in St. Louis by herself, so I begged her to relocate to Florida with me. She said she would give it some thought, and after staying with her for nearly two weeks, I had to return home.

The first thing I did was go spend time with the kids. Jaylin was out of town. I was glad about that because we were getting too close again. I didn't want memories from our past to interfere with my future, so I asked him to leave St. Louis and give me some space. He wasn't happy about it, but it was the only way for me to put Travis at ease. Previously he'd been so supportive, but every time he turned around, Jaylin and me were somewhere talking, reminiscing, or hugging. Of course it bothered Travis, and to be fair to him, I had to do what was necessary to save my relationship.

I felt Travis slipping away from me. His actions were clear as day, especially on the day he'd left St. Louis. He kept apologizing to LJ for raising his voice, and he also apologized to me. But while at the airport, he seemed distant. My mind was all over the place. I was in a daze, thinking about my father. Travis implied that I must've been thinking about Jaylin, but in that moment, I hadn't been. Surely I'd thought about that dream, but a dream was just a dream. I couldn't do anything about it, and every now and then, Travis jabbed me with a comment about Jaylin. Ever since Travis saw Jaylin and me in the guestroom that day, he hadn't been right. I kept smelling alcohol on his breath. The way he acted alarmed me. He told me that years ago he'd had a drinking problem. I certainly didn't want him to travel down that road again, so I tried to explain that Jaylin was only trying to help. It seemed like more than that to Travis. He was livid that night, and he stormed out of the room with something eerie in his eyes. I didn't bother to go after him, but I called his cell phone to apologize. That apology led to another one right after the funeral. He'd told me about his confrontation with Jaylin. I simply couldn't take much more. It was one big mess that was happening at the wrong time.

I left Jaylin's house around midnight. The kids and I had a great time, Nanny B included. She always said the right things to me. Her comforting words about the loss of my father made me feel better. More than anything, I was glad to be home. I wanted to clean up before the kids came over later, and in addition to cleaning up, I had so much to do businesswise. I also had to reschedule my doctor's appointment. I still hadn't said much to anyone about the baby, not even my mother. The timing didn't seem right. She was already dealing with so much. I didn't want her to worry about me. She worried about every little thing, but I hoped that with a little faith and prayer, we both would bounce back soon.

During my time in St. Louis, Jazz called every day to keep me informed about my business. I was glad to have her as well, and I looked forward to returning to the shop in a few more days.

Thirty minutes had passed. My condo was cleaner than it was when I arrived. Before going to bed, I poured a glass of milk, drinking it while leaning against the counter. My thoughts turned to the last time I'd seen my father. That was when I was in the kitchen, baking cookies with the kids. He snatched up one of the cookies, tasted it, and rubbed his belly. He'd looked me right in the eyes and said, "Don't tell your mama, but you are the best when it comes to making cookies." I laughed, thanked him, and told him I loved him. He kissed my cheek, telling me he loved me too. That was his final goodbye. I guessed closure couldn't get much better than that.

My thoughts were interrupted by a knock at the door. It was almost one o'clock in the morning, so I wasn't sure who it could be. I set the glass on the counter, but it fell and crashed to the floor. I didn't have time to pick up the glass. I was interested in knowing who was at the door. I looked through the peephole and saw that it was Travis. I hadn't called to tell him I was back yet, but I'd planned on calling him before noon. I opened the door, feeling hyped about seeing him.

"Hi, honey," I said, opening the door wider so he could come in. "Are you off work?"

"Yes, finally," he replied. He sluggishly strolled in with his scrubs on and his face clean-shaven. Alcohol was on his breath, but he'd attempted to tone it down with mints.

"You look tired. Maybe you should've gone home to get some rest instead of driving over here tonight."

Travis grabbed me in his arms and moved back to sit on the arm of the couch. "I came here because I wanted to see you. That's okay, isn't it?"

I pecked his lips and placed my arms on his shoulders. "That's perfectly fine, but it worries me when you drink and drive. You have been drinking, haven't you?"

With a glassy film over his eyes, and with very strong breath, he couldn't deny it. "One. I only had one drink. That's it."

"Well, why don't you take a shower and get some rest with me? I was getting ready to get in bed. I need to get a few hours in before the kids get here."

"A shower sounds great. Would you like to join me?"

"Not tonight. I'm so exhausted. All I want to do right now is give my bed a big hug."

We headed down the hallway to my bedroom. Travis removed two towels from the linen closet to take a shower. I changed into my cotton pajama top, which barely reached my knees. After saying my prayers, I got in bed and turned on the TV, just in case Travis wanted to watch something when he got out of the shower. Within minutes, I felt myself fading fast. I was in a deep sleep when I felt the mattress wave around and Travis get in bed behind me. His dick poked at me from the back, and as he started to massage my left breast, I used my elbow to nudge him back.

"Not tonight," I repeated in a groggy tone. "I'm tired, okay? I just want to get some sleep."

Travis ignored me. He continued to handle my breast aggressively, and his lips nibbled on my earlobe. "Come on, Nokea. It's been a while. I'm horny as hell. Don't you feel how hard it is?"

I felt it for sure, but I wasn't in the mood tonight. It was rare that I ever declined Travis's offer to make love, so I didn't think it would be a big deal.

"I do feel it, and it feels good. But I'm tired, sweetheart. Just let me get some rest, okay?"

Travis awakened me with his next comment. "I bet if I were Jaylin, this wouldn't be a problem."

His words pissed me off so I hissed back, "You're not Jaylin, and you can take that how you wish. Besides, this doesn't have anything to do with him. I wish you would stop bringing him up. It's becoming very annoying."

Travis grunted and released my breast. He backed away from me, lying on his back with his arm resting across his forehead. I faced him to sort of take back what I'd said. But before I could say anything, he turned his head to look at me.

"Just ten or fifteen minutes," he pleaded. "I just want to feel you if you don't mind."

When I was tired, staying up for ten or fifteen more minutes seemed like a long time. But I surrendered. I lay on my back. Travis lay on top of me. He lifted my pajama top over my head, and within seconds my breasts were being squeezed in his hands. He massaged them together, licking my nipples one at a time. My legs were wide. I could feel his steel expanding between my slit. He reached down to direct his muscle inside of me, and as he proceeded to move, I was bone dry. I couldn't get into the mood, and he could tell right away.

"What's wrong?" he asked. "Are you just going to lie there?"

"Travis, I told you I was tired. I don't have much energy tonight, but if you want to do this, fine."

He released my breasts, and while holding himself up over me, he took swift thrusts inside of me, hoping I would bring forth more juice. Unfortunately, his movements became painful. I squeezed my eyes and pushed back on his hips to slow down his pace.

"Take it easy," I groaned softly while searching into his eyes, which revealed disappointment.

I lifted my head to give him a comforting kiss. As our tongues tangled, Travis kept grinding away. My insides moistened a little, but not enough to excite him or me. He pulled out fast, lowering himself to taste me. My legs were pressed against my chest as his tongue traveled deep within. His slow licks moistened me more, but when he inserted his muscle again, my dryness returned.

"Damn," he shouted and punched air out of the pillow. "What is wrong with you tonight?"

I was so caught off guard that I quickly backed away from him. I reached for the lamp to turn it on. "What's wrong with me?" I said, frustrated. "No, what's wrong with you?"

Just then, my cell phone rang. It was on the nightstand. Travis reached for it before I did.

"Hello," he said then paused. He dropped the phone on the bed next to me. "To answer your question, that's what's wrong with me. Why is he calling here?"

I picked up the phone, putting it up to my ear. "Hello."

"Tell that muthafucka I'm calling because I can," Jaylin said. "Nanny B said you left not too long ago. I know it's late, but I just got back. I wanted to check on you and make sure you're doing okay."

"Just okay, Jaylin, but stop worrying about me so much. I do appreciate your concern, but please do as I asked you to do while we were in St. Louis. Give me some space, okay?"

"I've given you plenty of space, Nokea. I don't know why you think that my concern for you has anything to do with invading your space. If you—"

Travis snatched the phone from my hand, turning it off. "Talk to him on your time, not mine. He is starting to piss me off, and to be honest, Nokea, so are you."

"Apparently so, especially if you feel as if you have to punch pillows and speak to me this way. Why don't you just go home? I'll call you tomorrow after I get me some rest and you sober up."

"Ohhhh, so now you want me to leave. Jaylin must have told you he was coming over, huh? And by the way, I've been doing a lot of thinking lately. Are you sure that baby is mine, not his?"

I'd heard enough for one day. I hurried out of bed and reached for my pajama top to cover up. "Goodbye, Travis. I guess that alcohol is doing quite a number on you tonight, because you're in the mood to argue. I'm not." I marched to my bedroom door and stood in the doorway with my arms crossed.

Travis remained on the bed. "Answer me," he said. "Is it his baby or mine?"

"I'm not going to answer your ridiculous question. You know darn well whose baby it is. All you're trying to do is upset me because you're upset."

"No, honestly, I'm trying to find out the fucking truth. So again, is it his baby or mine?"

I was so disgusted with him that I rolled my eyes and made my way toward the front door. I wanted him out of here now. "Put your clothes on, Travis, and leave. I refuse to do this with you tonight," I yelled loud enough for him to hear me.

Minutes later, he appeared in the hallway with his pants on and his shirt thrown over his shoulder. He took slow, menacing steps forward, and the second he reached the door, he grabbed my arm, using his overpowering strength to shove me away from the door. I stumbled but managed to keep my balance as I staggered toward the couch in the living room. I swung around fast to charge at him but was met with his shaky finger pointed at my face.

"The wrong move will cause me to knock you out cold on this floor. Answer my question, Nokea. His or mine? You're refusing to answer because you know whose baby it is. That's why you haven't shared the good news with anyone."

My breathing halted as I stared into Travis's cold eyes. I wanted to yell at him for acting like this, but I witnessed him slowly but surely becoming unhinged.

"It's your baby for sure," I responded calmly. "I haven't had sex with Jaylin in years. I don't know where all of this is coming from, but can you do me a favor and please go home?"

Travis lowered his finger, but rage was still visible in his eyes. He stepped forward, moving so close to me that I had to step back.

"Years my ass!" Specks of his spit sprayed my face as he yelled. "You've been fucking him, and how dare you disrespect me like you did while we were in St. Louis? You're not going to put this baby on me. Fuck that! The last thing I'm going to do is take care of another man's baby!"

I remained calm, but deep in my mind, all I kept thinking was that this was it for us. It was the end for sure. I didn't even know if I should speak again, but as Travis made his way to the door, I felt relieved. I followed him so I could lock the door after he left. But as soon as he made it to the door, he stopped and swung around.

"Why are you following me?" he asked.

"I just want to lock the door."

His gaze was terrifying. There was pure hatred in his eyes. I saw it up close, and right as we were at the door, he leaned forward, smashing his forehead against mine. The head-butt was so hard that it knocked me against the wall behind me. My brain felt rattled. Painful throbs made my head feel as if it were expanding. My vision became blurred, but I could see him lift his fist. He drove it directly into my midsection.

Spit flew from my mouth. I grabbed my stomach, doubled over, and dropped to my knees. I seriously thought I was dreaming, especially when I saw another fist appear in front of my face. That blow sent me to the floor where I positioned myself in a cradled position, trying to shield my face from his multiple hard blows that kept on coming to the back of my head, at my stomach, and on my legs. Wherever he could strike me, he did.

"See, look what you made me do!" He paused to yell at me. "I tried to be nice to you, woman, but you just had to take me there, didn't you? All I asked was whose baby it was. You had to lie, and this is what I do to bitches who lie to me!"

Travis delivered another punch to the back of my head, causing my mouth to smack the hardwood floor. I instantly tasted blood, and at that point, I realized that I either had to fight back or die. As he started to rant again, I slowly got on my knees. My whole body felt battered. Pain was shooting from everywhere. With my right eye nearly closed and blood raining from my chin down to my neck, I stood in disbelief. Travis stood in front of me. He grabbed my cheeks, forcing me to look at him.

"Tell that bastard I said happy belated birthday. He made me do this to you, and if you're mad at anybody, it damn well better be him."

He released my cheeks. Right as he stepped back to pull his shirt over his head, I reached for a glass vase that was on a table next to me. I lifted it over my head, growling as I pitched it as close to Travis's face as I could. With my arms being so weak, the vase landed on his chest, bouncing off of it as if he were the Incredible Hulk. The smirk on his face said it all.

"I know you can do better than that, can't you?"

He grabbed me by the hair, and that was when I made another attempt to hurt him. I managed to scurry away from his grip. I reached for everything within my sight: glass plates from the table, a cordless phone, a flowerpot, a soda bottle, and I threw it all at him. Nothing stopped him from charging at me with the exception of one of LJ's golf clubs that I batted Travis's face with. The strike caused him to stagger this time, and as he bent over, I struck his back time and time again.

"You fucking bastard!" I yelled as tears poured down my face. My body trembled all over. In the moment, I couldn't feel much pain because I was numb. "Why did you do this, Traaavis! Whyyyyy?"

I was crushed and severely unstable. My hands shook so bad that I couldn't even hold a grip on the golf club anymore when Travis tried to snatch it from me. He tossed it on the couch and reached for my hair again. This time, his grip was super tight as he dragged me down the hallway, pulling me toward the bedroom. I kicked at his legs, causing them to buckle. I scratched at his hands, making them bleed and his flesh to appear. I fought hard, and when I attempted to punch his dick, he grabbed my arms, crossing them tightly over my chest. Gasping for air, I lay on my back in a daze. His knee was pressed into my stomach, delivering so much pain that it felt like I was dying a slow death. Sweat beads were all over his body. He breathed heavily, and since I kept trying to maneuver myself from underneath him, he spat in my face. I spat back, causing him to lash out with a backhand across my face.

"So, you want to play tough, huh? I'll show you which one of us is tough, Nokea. It damn sure isn't you."

Travis lifted me up high, slamming me on the floor then the bed. By now I had no more fight left in me. He dove on top of me, ripping my bloody pajama top away from my body. It was so banged up, sore, and bruised from what I could see. But that didn't matter to Travis. He wanted more, and when his dick entered me, I just . . . just lay there, staring at the ceiling, which looked like it was caving in on me.

My staggering cries and dry vagina angered him even more. "This is fucking ridiculous!" He pulled out of me and walked over to my dresser drawer, yanking it open. He found a picture of Jaylin then reached for lotion that was on top of the dresser. He rushed back to the bed, lying over me again. This time, he squeezed nearly the whole bottle of lotion between my legs and covered his dick with the rest. He put Jaylin's photo in front of me, forcing me to look at it.

"Here you go, Nokea. This is who you want, right? Think about him fucking you instead of me. I'm sure your thoughts of him can get you wet, can't they?"

He slapped Jaylin's photo on my face, holding it there as he inserted himself again. I tried to push him away, but so much pain was rushing through my body that I couldn't do much. All I saw was Jaylin's picture in front of my face. He stared at me, I stared at him. I prayed that Travis's hang-up call would prompt Jaylin to head this way. But after being tortured by Travis for this long, I knew that Jaylin had honored my wishes and had given me my space.

Travis pulled out of me again. He crumpled the picture in his hand and threw it on the floor. "With that look on your face, I can tell you're thinking about him. And since you are, why don't we call him? Let's call to wish him a happy birthday, all right?"

Travis reached for my cell phone, turned it back on, and called Jaylin. I lay there, hoping he would answer, as Travis put on the speakerphone. Unfortunately, Jaylin's voicemail came on. Travis threatened to kill me if I didn't sing with him after the beep.

"Yo, Jaylin!" he yelled into the phone. "Listen up, you punk-ass bitch. Nokea and I want to sing 'Happy Birthday' to you. We've been practicing all night, and I think we're good now." Travis started to sing, but when I didn't, he grabbed my neck and yelled for me to sit up. "Sing," he shouted. "This ho over here tripping, but she probably can't speak because I done tried my best to knock out every last one of her fucking teeth! She still should be able to sing, though, can't you, baby? Sing now or sing while you're six feet under."

I lowered my face into my hands, covering it as I tried to sing along with Travis. My words were near a whisper. "'Ha . . . happy bir . . . birthday to you. Hap . . . py . . .'" I paused then screamed for Jaylin to come help me. Travis hit the END button, and all I remembered after that was another blow to my head.

Morning came, and with my curtains wide open, bright sunrays lit up the bedroom. Travis was kneeling beside the bed, holding my hand as I lay there unable to move. I was numb. I felt like I had died and was in another world. I wished it were a dream, and I kept asking myself what I had done to deserve this. Travis's head was resting on my sore arm. His cries were loud, and snot drizzled from his nose. He apologized over and over again, begging and pleading for me to forgive him.

"Baby, please," he shouted and pounded his fist on the bed. "I . . . I was drunk, and I totally lost control. I never meant to hurt you like this, Nokea. You know this isn't me. I promise you that I will never do anything like this again. I'm going to get help. Today, okay?"

I didn't say, couldn't say, one word. My face was stiff and swollen, as were my lips. From the vision in one eye, I could see dried blood on my face. My body had never experienced this much damage, and with so much wetness and stickiness between my legs, I wasn't sure if I was bleeding. Travis raised his head to look at me. His face was covered with sweat and tears. His eyes were fiery red. His hands trembled as he touched my forehead, gently rubbing my hair.

"Say something to me," he pleaded. "I love you, and I need to hear you say that you love me too. Help me get through this, my love. Please help me. All I need is for you to be there for me and everything will be okay. You, me, and the baby."

His eyes shifted to my stomach. He lowered his shaking hand, felt my stomach, and released a loud, deafening cry that caused him to quiver more.

"You . . . you need a doctor. Let me get you to a doctor, so stay right there and don't move."

Travis stood and stumbled backward while looking at me. Tears ran from the corners of my eyes. My head throbbed so badly. He bent over, placing his lips on mine. I was sure they felt like stone to him because I didn't reciprocate. He gave me two quick pecks then headed to the door. He turned around before exiting.

"You just don't know how sorry I am for this. Please forgive me, okay? I'm going to go get you some help, so wait right here until I get back."

He rushed out of the room, and the second I heard the door close, I struggled to get up. When I lifted my head, I felt nothing but pressure. My body was real stiff, and blood was all over me as well as on the sheets. I didn't know if I had miscarried, but the pain was unbearable. I wasn't sure where my phone was, but as I turned in bed to look for it, I wound up crawling to the floor. I rolled on my back, gazed at the ceiling, and released a thunderous scream to release my hurt and frustrations.

Chapter 17

Jaylin

For whatever reason, I couldn't get a lick of sleep last night. I had too much on my mind pertaining to business and Nokea. I was furious about being hung up on, and just as I got in my car to drive the fuck over there, I changed my mind. I didn't appreciate how funny she had been acting. She was coming off as fake. She had never been like this before, and she had to know how concerned I was about her. There was no way in hell for me not to be concerned about her, especially after all that had happened. I knew how difficult it was for her to lose her father, and I wanted to find out how her mother had been doing, too.

Since Nokea didn't want to talk, I rolled over in bed at six in the morning to call her mother. She was wide awake and was happy to hear my voice.

"I'm doing as well as I'm going to get, Jaylin. I sure do miss my husband, and this old house will never be the same. Nokea wants me to move to Florida with her. I don't know because I'm so attached to this house. If I leave, it'll be like leaving the love of my life behind. I surely don't want to do that, but I also don't want my child to worry so much. I'm deeply concerned about her, Jaylin. She just didn't seem like herself. She and Travis were arguing a lot, and I hate to say this, but there is something about him that rubs me the wrong way."

"Same here, but Nokea loves him. I've noticed a change in her too. When I question her about it, she tells me she's okay."

"I don't care what that child of mine says. The only man she loves is you. Just keep an eye on her for me. If I decide to come there, I'll let the two of you know."

"We'd love to have you here, especially the kids. And this time I think you may be wrong. Nokea doesn't feel the same way about me anymore. I can feel it in my heart, but you know I'm not going to give up on us."

"Please don't. Thanks for calling to check on me, and when you see Nokea, give her a big hug and tell her I said to be nice to you."

I laughed before telling her goodbye and ending the call. My thoughts turned to Nokea again. I wasn't sure if she was heading to work this morning, but I was dying to find out why our call ended so abruptly. I tapped my phone against my hand, and when I got ready to call Nokea, I saw that I had missed a call from her a few hours ago. I immediately called her cell phone, but it went straight to voicemail. I didn't leave a message, but as I hung up to listen to her message, Nanny B buzzed me on the intercom.

"Jaylin, will you come downstairs and open this jar of jelly for me? I may need a hammer if you can't pry it open."

"I'll be there in a minute. Are the kids up yet?"

"Of course. Don't you hear them?"

Actually, I didn't, but I laid my phone on the bed and left my room to go open the jar of jelly. After that task was done, I showered, put on some clothes, and decided to drive by Nokea's house to see what was up. If she wasn't there, I intended to go to her shop where I was positive she would be.

I arrived at Nokea's place almost forty-five minutes later. I was surprised that the door was unlocked, but just in case she and Travis were in the bedroom getting busy, I knocked and waited for someone to come to the door. No one answered, so I pushed on the door and went inside. Instantly, something eerie came over me. Broken glass was all over the floor, a few items were strewn here and there, a golf club was on the couch, and there was a hole in the wall by the door. I could tell there had been some kind of scuffle.

"Nokea!" I shouted as my stomach felt tied in knots. My heartrate started to pick up speed. I rushed down the hallway, and when I got to her bedroom, my heart slammed against my chest. I stopped dead in my tracks, staring at the fresh blood smeared on the floor and on the messy sheets. My thoughts were spinning so fast that I couldn't even think straight. I panicked as I sprinted over to the bed, examining the blood-stained sheets and snatching them off the bed. A crumpled picture of me fell on the floor. I picked it up to look at it. My hands shook as I held it, and as sickening thoughts flooded my mind, I shouted again.

"Nokea! Are you here?"

There was no answer. Feeling myself on the verge of an anxiety attack, I dashed through her condo, calling her name and searching for her.

"Baby, where are you?" I said, busting into the other rooms. I rubbed my aching chest while traveling from one room to the next. "God, please, no, daaaamn, no!"

With clenched fists, I tried to evade my negative thoughts of something horrific happening to her. My thoughts became more realistic when I saw a bloody handprint on the wall in the hallway. I stared at it with tears at the rims of my eyes, which were without a blink. There was no denying that something tragic had happened, and all I could do in the moment was lash out and punch the wall in front of me. A gaping hole appeared, causing a picture on the wall to crash to the floor.

"Damn, baby, daaaamn!" I hollered and spun around in circles with my hands locked behind my head. What knocked me out of the zone I was in were whimpering sounds coming from the closet in her bedroom. I hurried to it, and when I yanked on the door, I gasped to catch my next breath. Nokea was crouched in the corner with a gun in her hand. She aimed it at me. I quickly jumped to the side for fear of being shot.

"It's me," I shouted and was in complete, utter shock by what my eyes had witnessed. "Don't shoot!"

"Jaaaaaylin," she cried out in agony. That was when I heard a loud thud. I knew she had dropped the gun.

I hurried into the closet, filled with so much grief as I examined her face and naked body close up. Seeing her like this was fucking unbelievable. I almost didn't recognize her. The swelling was so severe. Bruises were everywhere on her body, as well as blood. With tears in my eyes, I snatched her into my arms, holding her close to my chest. I didn't know how severe her injuries were, but I knew that I needed to get her to a hospital fast.

"I'm here, baby," I said, rocking her in my tight arms, which calmed her quivering body. "I'm here, and I'm not going anywhere. Ca . . . can you move?"

She didn't respond. I backed away from her, struggling to look at her face, which made more tears slip from my eyes. The lump in my throat was stuck, and as I lifted her from the floor, my legs were almost too weak to carry her. I carried her over to the bed before rushing to a linen closet to get a clean sheet to cover her. After I got the sheet, I covered her battered body, lifting her again. She wrapped her very weak arms around my neck.

"Tell me where it hurts," I said while carrying her as fast as I could down the hall and out the door. "Can you tell me where you're hurting?"

"All over," she mumbled through her cries.

I took the stairs, nearly tumbling down them as I moved so fast. The security guard at the door questioned what was going on, but I breezed past him and didn't bother to respond.

"Jaylin," he shouted after me, "is she okay? Do you need me to call an ambulance?"

An ambulance wouldn't get here fast enough, so I hurried Nokea to my car. I dropped the seat back, strapped her in on the passenger's side, and then got in the car too. I sped away, eager to unleash hell on somebody. This was an out-of-body experience. I kept speaking to myself out loud about this being a dream, about hurting somebody, asking why. So many questions flooded my mind, but I wasn't sure if Nokea was in any condition to answer them. I reached for her hand, squeezing it with mine as she lay next to me with her eyes closed.

"Wake up, baby." I was full of emotions. My devious thoughts were dangerous. "Tell me what happened to you. Who did this to you?"

She whimpered and held her shuddering stomach, which moved in and out as she tried to catch her breath. "I'm tired, Jaylin. Tired of being in all this paaaaain. It hurts so bad I . . . I just want to die right now."

Frustrated, I hit the steering wheel and moved my head from side to side. "Please don't say that. You can't die and you won't! Just chill and tell me exactly what happened. Did Travis do this to you or someone else?"

Nokea sobbed so badly I could barely decipher her words. And with her mouth swollen, I knew it was difficult for her to speak. I squeezed her hand again, letting her know that everything would be okay.

"You don't have to talk right now. Whenever you're ready, all right?"

She removed her hand from my grip and covered her face. Her cries became louder. "Travis hurt me. He hurt the baby too, and I don't want to do this anymore, Jaylin. I just want to go be with my father, because I'm sick of people hurting me. What am I doing to deserve this? I've given every relationship I've been in my all, and . . . and look what keeps happening to me."

Her words caused more tears to fill my eyes. I wanted to pull over to gather myself. Instead, I blinked to clear my eyes and pressed hard on the accelerator so I could get to the hospital sooner. I knew she was speaking about being hurt by men, me in particular. Saying I was sorry just wasn't enough, but I said it anyway.

"We, men, do some real fucked-up shit some-times, and I am so sorry for putting you through what I did. You never deserved any of it, and you will never have to hurt again. I will let no one hurt you again. So you can't go be with your father because you have to stay with me. With me and the kids, okay? So stop talking like that. I love you so much, so you can't be saying things like that, all right?"

Nokea didn't respond. I kept taking my eyes off the road to look at her, and with every glance, I sank to a level I had never been. I kept check-ing her pulse to make sure it was still there. She was so out of it. She kept mumbling, and much of what she said I didn't understand. I did, how-ever, understand that Travis had done this. That angered me to the core of my soul.

"Stay with me, baby." I rubbed my hand up and down her arm. "Talk to me and tell me something good."

My eyes shifted to the rearview mirror so I could check my surroundings. Several cars ham-mered their horns because of the way I swerved in and out of traffic. One lady spewed that I was an ignorant bastard. I couldn't even entertain her foolishness right now. The white parts of my eyes were fiery red and mixed with gray. I looked like a demon. I continued to breeze through traffic like a maniac, and it was a good thing there were no cops around. Regardless, I wasn't about to stop until I reached my destination.

"I can't hear you, sweetheart. Let's talk and tell me something real good."

"I . . . I don't know anything good right now. It hurts, Jaylin. Why is there so much pain?"

"Try not to think about the pain. Think about me and you." I squeezed her hand then brought it to my lips to kiss it. "Us, okay? Can you think about us?"

I glanced at her, and she slowly nodded.

"Good. That's my girl. Hang on because we're almost there."

Nokea's head was slumped to the side. And as my car zoomed down the street, her head shifted from left to right. She mumbled again, but I was so out of it that I didn't understand what she was saying. All I could think about was killing Travis. There was no way in hell that he was going to live to see another day.

We bounced around in my car after I hit a curb that was in front of the hospital. And just as I got ready to drive up to the emergency entrance, an ambulance speeding in the same direction as me sideswiped my Maybach, causing a huge dent on the left side. I didn't give a damn. I hopped out of the car, hurrying to get Nokea out of it. The ambulance driver was out of his vehicle, apologizing and telling me he would help.

"Let me go inside to get her a wheelchair. What happened to her?"

I didn't know what to say, and I didn't have time to wait for a wheelchair. I rushed her inside, telling the first nurse I saw at the counter that I needed some help. Within seconds, a nurse and a doctor charged my way with a gurney. They helped me lay Nokea on it, and when they looked at her face, their faces showed shock.

"What happened?" the doctor asked, feeling for her pulse.

I wasn't sure if Nokea was going to say anything about Travis, but knowing what I was about to do, I had to lie. "She walked in on an intruder who was breaking in. I'm not sure when it happened, but I found her in this condition this morning."

"Who are you?" he asked while touching Nokea's arms and legs to see if anything was broken.

"I'm her ex-husband."

"Have you called the police?"

"I will as soon as I know that she's going to be okay. So please stop asking me questions and see about her."

"Jaylin," Nokea mumbled.

I stood next to her, looking at her with wide, teary eyes. I hated for her to see me like this, but I couldn't help it. She reached for my hand, softly touching it. Her head moved from side to side.

"Don't do it," she said clearly. "Please don't, okay?"

I leaned in to kiss her puffy, cracked lips. That was my reply to her.

She responded by squeezing my hand tighter. "Don't. I love you too, and I need you to please listen to me."

I shut my eyes and backed away from her, knowing that I could not honor her wishes. I felt as if she was now in good hands, and before I left, I asked the doctor for three things: "Take care of her, put her in a private room, and make sure security is at the door."

The doctor said he would do his best, and he informed me again to contact the police. Unfortunately, I would do no such thing. I called Shane, and he answered right away.

"Man, where are you?" he questioned. "I thought we were supposed to meet at your crib this morning. I've called you like ten times already."

"Something urgent came up. I'll be there within the hour. Stay there until I get there."

"Will do. I got some good news for you."

"Unfortunately I don't, but don't go anywhere until I get there."

I ended the call, and as I traveled back to my car, the ambulance driver who had hit it approached me. He looked fearful. I guessed he assumed I was pissed about my car.

"Sir, I take full responsibility for what happened to your car. I need to call the police and file—"

"I don't have time right now. Forget it. It'll get fixed."

"But this is a very expensive car. I'm sure—"

"I said forget it! Now back up before I run you over. Damn!"

The man appeared shocked by my words. He slowly backed up after seeing how unstable I was. I quickly sped off to go to the hospital where Travis worked. I knew that doing something to him would bring about much trouble for me, but seeing Nokea in the condition she was in just did something horrible to me. I couldn't control what I felt inside. Not even the thoughts of my kids could stop me from doing what needed to be done. My guns, however, weren't in this car. One was in another car, and three were locked away in the house. For now, though, my fists had to do. And when the day was over, Travis would be no more.

I arrived at the hospital where Travis was. I knew exactly what floor he worked on. I wasn't even sure if he would be there, but as soon as I stepped off the elevator, I started casing the halls, searching for him with fire burning in my eyes. Several people stopped to ask if I needed directions to somewhere or someone. I just kept it moving and didn't reply. If he was there, I would definitely find him. And I did, nearly ten minutes later.

The motherfucker had the audacity to be standing by one of the nurses' stations, telling a joke. I stood for a moment, listening to his corny ass. The people surrounding him chuckled loudly, and some patted his back. He didn't even see me creeping up from behind. I tapped his shoulder, spun him around, and cracked him right in the face with my fist.

He fell back, knocking over a heart monitor machine and scattering papers on the floor that were on a desk. The people surrounding him scattered like roaches. Some yelled for security, and others simply got the fuck out of the way. The look in my eyes wasn't pretty.

Travis wiped across his bloody mouth. His eyes were bugged, and his face was like stone. I stepped forward, and when I lifted my foot, I tagged his face with the bottom of my shoe. This time his head jerked, and he reached for the counter to try to pull himself up.

"Call security!" a nurse yelled again. "Hurry!"

"Run, Dr. Cooper! Get up!"

I looked at the foolish white woman who was trying to spare him. My sinful gaze, however, caused her to run instead of him. Travis hadn't the strength to stand up, so he fell again and bounced on his ass. He touched his bloody mouth and started to crawl backward on his hands.

I stepped forward again. I didn't have shit to say. He already knew why I was there. A man who did a woman like he'd done Nokea wasn't shit, and he sat there speechless like the scared bitch he was. He tried to rush up and make a run for it, but I pummeled his midsection with punches that made him grunt loudly and gag. He doubled over, dropping to his knees. This time, he lifted his hand, ready to surrender.

"O . . . okay." He tried to catch his breath and spat a gob of blood from his mouth. "I know why yo . . . you're here, but let's go outside to handle this."

I ignored him, and as more people appeared around corners and doors to see what was going on, Travis yelled out to them. "Anybody in here got a damn gun? This man is crazy! I—"

No one entertained his foolish request, and I silenced him when I pushed a metal food cart over, causing it to land on his back. It flattened him, and dishes and food spilled everywhere. Travis growled out in pain as he tried to wiggle himself out from underneath the cart. That was when two other brave doctors rushed over to see if they could help.

"Stop this right now," one doctor nervously barked at me. "Security will be here in a minute, so you need to leave."

I paid his threat no mind. As they lifted the cart, Travis scrambled from underneath it. He backed into a wall near an exit sign that led to the stairs. Sweat dripped from his forehead, and his beady eyes were barely open. He kept squeezing them as if he was in excruciating pain. I stood in front of his pitiful, disgusting ass, eyeing him and listening to him try to defend what he'd done.

"Jaylin, look. Nokea, she . . . she's not the woman you think she is. I'm telling you that she made me do that shit. That bitch made me do it!"

He pounded the floor with his fist and shifted his eyes around, looking at the people he had just confessed to. To me, it didn't matter, because no court of law would ever have an opportunity to hear his case.

Imagining what he'd done to Nokea and listening to his harsh words about her cut me like a knife. I squatted and grabbed his shirt, pulling him closer to me. Still saying nothing to him, I stared into his eyes so he could witness up close and personal the severe grief he had caused me. I winced, and as a smirk formed on that motherfucker's face, I pushed his head back, slamming it against the wall. Three slams later, a deep laceration appeared, causing his blood to paint the wall. Travis's eyes rolled back. He was dizzy as fuck. I could hear more onlookers in the background screaming for help. That was when I opened the door to the stairs, and as I assumed he had done to Nokea, I dragged his ass on the floor, making him screech like a bitch.

"Wait. Wait a minute. I . . . I'll apologize." He managed to break away from my grip but struggled to balance on one knee. A string of blood ran from his mouth, and as he tried to lift his head and speak, the gargling sound coming from his mouth wasn't clear. Then again, yes, it was.

"Yo . . . you must really love that bitch." He spat on the floor again and used his shirt to wipe his mouth. "But I'm telling you she is no good. If I could tell you some of the things she said about you, man, you would have kicked her ass too."

Travis was a sick-ass fool. I responded by grabbing his shirt and tossing him down the concrete stairs. His head bumped the steel rail as he tumbled down one flight. Another gash opened on the side of his head. He lay on the ground, trying to nurture his wound by pressing on it. With tension locked in my body, I moved casually down the stairs with my hands dipped into my pockets.

Finally, I spoke up. "Yeah, I do love that bitch, Travis. Love her so much that I'm willing to kill for her."

Travis swayed back and forth on the ground, displaying much agony as he moaned and squeezed his eyes together. His excuses continued as I stood over him.

"I had too much to drink! Didn't really know what I was doing until it was too late."

My response was a blunt kick to his side that caused him to roll over on his stomach.

"Ahhhhhh, shit!" he grunted and squirmed on the ground. "You don't want to do this, fool!"

"Trust me, yes, I do."

With glee in my eyes, I stomped him with my shoes, which were splattered red from his blood. His blood was on my knuckles as well as on my clothes. I heard security or the police coming from a distance. And figuring that I would eventually be arrested, I kept telling myself, *not here and not like this*. I punted Travis in the spine of his back one last time. He screamed so loud that my eardrum clogged. For a minute, I couldn't hear nothing.

I jogged down several more flights of stairs, jetting to the nearest elevator that took me to the lobby. People scurried away as they saw me, looking as if I had slaughtered somebody. I hurried to the exit door, jumped in my car, and rushed home so I could get my gun and finish Travis off when no one else was around.

Chapter 18

Jaylin

On the drive home, I mistakenly listened to the voicemail message Travis and Nokea left on my phone. It shook me up and had me at a point of no return. I couldn't wait to get home and get the necessary artillery to deal with him. I wanted to catch him alone in his office or at his house and blow his damn brains out. The gun I intended to use was resting comfortably in my hand as I sat behind my desk, telling Shane about all that had happened. He was in disbelief. He sat back in a chair, shaking his head with a tight face. A bandana was tied around his dreads, and he kept cracking his knuckles and rubbing his hands together.

"I can't believe he did that to her," he said. "That is fucked up. What kind of man would do something like that?"

"A man who needs to be six feet under."

I tucked the gun in the back of my jeans and stood to remove my shirt. Travis's blood was all over it, so I went to the closet in my office to get a clean shirt and a new pair of shoes. I threw the shirt over my shoulder and went into the bathroom to wash my hands and wipe my face with a towel.

"Jay," Shane said loud enough for me to hear him, "I know you're not going to listen to me right now, but I have to say this. Killing him is going to swing a whole lot of heat your way. You have to rethink this. Even though I know you're mad, this is not the right answer."

I stuck my head out of the bathroom to reply to him. "Mad? Do I look mad to you? Nah, I'm not mad. I'm fucking furious! There is not one damn word you can say to me right now that is going to stop me from killing him."

"How about Jaylene, LJ, Mackenzie, and Justin? Man, you can't do this. There is too much at stake."

I shrugged while pulling the shirt over my head. I slipped into a cleaner pair of shoes, and then I made my way back over to my desk, laying the gun on top of it. "Maybe so, but what about Nokea? You didn't see her, Shane. You don't know what he really did to her. I . . ."

I paused to swallow the oversized lump in my throat. Visions of her sitting in that closet with the gun in her hand flashed before me. The look on her battered face took my breath away. I couldn't stop thinking about what she must've been going through when he did that to her, and the voicemail message . . . The thoughts of all of it caused me to drop back in my chair. I leaned forward, lowering my head and placing my forehead on the desk. I fought hard to hold back my emotions in front of my best friend, but I couldn't. My hand touched my chest. I squeezed and rubbed it, hoping to calm my racing heart-beat.

"She . . . she's messed up, Shane. He fucked her up, man, real bad." I lifted my head, looking up at Shane, who had tears trapped in his eyes. "She will never be the same. I don't know if she's going to recover from this. He fucking destroyed her!"

Uncontrollable tears streamed down my face. I sobbed to release some of my misery. The only other time I'd felt close to this was when I'd lost my parents, and when Nokea made the decision to divorce me. I'd lost her then and felt as if I'd lost her now. I told Shane just that. My thoughts, however, wouldn't allow me to smack away my tears and be done with it.

I lowered my head on the desk again, rubbing the back of my head and mad at myself for letting a motherfucker like Travis slip into her life. I was so hurt. Too hurt to go back to the hospital and look at her, too hurt to let Travis get away with this, and too hurt to think about what was best for my kids.

"Jay," Shane said, witnessing me lose it, "don't do this to yourself, man. Nokea will recover from this, and how can you say you've lost her? You haven't lost her."

I lifted my head, looking at Shane through my blurred vision. My eyes were narrowed, my lashes dripped tears, and my head was now throbbing. "I say that shit because she said she was tired. She's been through so much, and in every single relationship she's had, she gave it her all, especially with us. I couldn't ask for more from a wife, and all that she gave me just wasn't good enough. I kept fucking with Scorpio, had a child with her, moved her to this fucking city, and basically told Nokea to deal with it!" I pounded my fist on the desk, thinking about how I had fucked up. "How fucking selfish is that, huh? And then I was mad at her for being mad at me."

"You're being too hard on yourself, and I know for a fact you don't regret Justin being born.

You were trying to sort through your feelings for Scorpio. Nothing that you did to Nokea was intentional."

"Stop making damn excuses for me." I wiped my wet face again. "I don't regret Justin, but I didn't think about the level of hurt she must've felt. The truth is if I hadn't fucked up, there would be no Travis. We wouldn't be here today, and she never would have endured a beating like she did. This shit is on me, and instead of using this gun on him, I should be using it on myself for being so gotdamn selfish and blind."

Shane's eyes shifted to the gun. He picked it up and laid it on his lap. "Look, I'm the first person to tell you if and when you're wrong about something. And even though you've made some serious mistakes, I won't allow you to sit there and blame yourself for what Travis did to her. That shit is on him. None of us knew that he was capable of doing something like that, not even her."

Shane was trying to make it all sound good, but I couldn't agree with what he was saying. Reality had set in for me. There was simply no other way for me to look at this. And then I had the audacity to be upset with her for falling out of love with me. For not showing me love, as if she owed me something after all I'd done. I couldn't stop shaking my head. I couldn't stop thinking about my fuckups as well as what Travis had done. It was time to put his ass to rest. If killing him gave Nokea just a little peace of mind, that was enough for me.

"I need to get out of here," I said to Shane and held out my hand. "Give me the gun. I'll check in with you later. Make sure you have your phone handy just in case I need to reach you or have you call Frick for me."

Disappointment was all over Shane's face. "So you're really going to go through with this, huh?"

I glared at him without saying a word. He was starting to irritate me. He knew that when my mind was made up, it was made up period.

"If this is what you want to do," he went on to say, "that's cool. Just keep in mind that Frick can't get you out of everything. The last time you—"

I stood, tired of listening to the bullshit. "Give me the gun and shut the fuck up talking to me. The good doctor is probably still at the hospital or at home. After I finish him off, I'm going to go see Nokea. Remember what I said, all right?"

"I know what you said. Call Frick, but I'm not giving you this gun. Sorry, but you gon' have to fight me for it right here and right now."

I honestly didn't have time for Shane's bull-shit. If I had to beat his ass, so be it. Then again, we didn't have to go out like that. All I did was reach for my phone and let it speak for my actions.

"Flip the script, muthafucka, and listen to this. Instead of it being Nokea's voice, pretend that it's Tiffanie's if you must."

I replayed the voicemail message on my phone: "Yo, Jaylin!" Travis yelled into the phone. "Listen up, you punk-ass bitch. Nokea and I want to sing 'Happy Birthday' to you. We've been practicing all night, and I think we're good now." Travis started to sing but soon paused. There was a tussling noise, and Nokea's cries sounded off in the background. "Sing," he shouted. "This ho over here tripping, but she probably can't speak because I done tried my best to knock out every last one of her fucking teeth! She still should be able to sing, though, can't you, baby? Sing now or sing while you're six feet under." There was another pause, more crying, and then Nokea started to sing. "'Ha . . . happy bir . . . birthday to you. Hap . . . py . . .'" She screamed into the phone, "Jaylin, please come help me! I think he's going to kill meeeee!" The phone went dead after that.

Shane looked at me. His Adam's apple moved in and out as he swallowed hard. He reached out, slapping the gun in my hand. "Blow that mutha-fucka's brains out," he said, "and bring me back a souvenir."

I cut my eyes at him and tucked the gun in my jeans again. As I stepped forward to leave, I heard the doorbell ring. I rushed to pick up the remote to look at the outdoor cameras. Two cops were standing outside.

"I need to go," I said to Shane then tightened a Nike cap on my head. "Tell them I'm not here. Don't tell Nanny B anything. I'll be back. Wait for my call later. I'll deal with the police tomorrow."

I hurried out of my office, going through the back to make my exit. As I walked through the main level, I could see the kids playing in the court area. LJ was trying to show Justin how to shoot hoops, Jaylene was tumbling on a mat, and Mackenzie was sitting on the floor reading a book. Nanny B was next to her while they talked. I smiled even though I hadn't done so all day. Deep down I knew they'd be okay. I also knew that after this was done, there would be consequences I'd have to deal with. My disguise probably wasn't enough to hide my identity, but if recognized by anyone, I would surely deny everything.

I hopped in my SUV that was parked in the back garage. The police never saw me, and after I sped away, I found myself caught up in a traffic jam. It was interesting how something always slowed you down when shit needed to get done. Phone calls usually came too, and when I saw Nanny B's number flash on my phone, I didn't even answer. A few minutes later, she sent me a text, telling me to call her. I wasn't sure if Shane said anything to her. Hopefully, he hadn't.

Either way, I was stuck. Traffic crawled. I kept thinking where Travis would probably be, and I hoped like hell that he would be alone when I got to the hospital. I couldn't stop thinking about what Nokea had endured. I wondered how it all had started. Possibly after my phone call, because there was no question in my mind that he was the one who had hung up on me. His anger had been festering for a long time. He was envious of my relationship with Nokea. The fool didn't even realize how much she really loved him. I was convinced that she really did.

Nearly an hour later, I was still caught in traffic, but cars were moving. This gave me more time to reflect on my life with Nokea. We had our ups and downs, but I kept telling myself that there were more good times than bad. Even she knew that, but I guessed it was kind of hard to look at it that way, considering all that had happened. I just wanted her to be okay. I was eager to get back to the hospital to see how she was doing. By now, hopefully, she'd been cleaned up and was in a bed, resting. I predicted that she would be upset with me for doing this, but I didn't want her to live another day knowing that a man like Travis was still on this earth breathing. If he was alive, she would remain fearful of him coming after her. She wouldn't be right. Her road to recovery was already going to be difficult.

I had to get off the highway to get gas, and I finally made it to the hospital nearly two hours later. But when I arrived, several police cars were parked outside. Many people were standing around. Some people were running, and cars were being directed to another area. The whole scene was chaotic. I wasn't sure what was going on, but I put on my dark shades and checked my gun, which was still tucked behind me. I then got out of the car.

Several crowds of people were standing around. The media was there as well. I was trying to get the scoop, and as I moved in closer, I started hearing people mention that a prominent doctor had been gunned down inside. The media was known for getting it wrong. Maybe they were referring to the incident between Travis and me. Even though it was brutal, no way did it cause this many people to be on the scene. Then again maybe Travis died after falling down the stairs and hitting his head. I wasn't so sure, but I needed more information because the doctor everyone was referring to could have been someone else.

"I need everyone to back up," an officer said. "Move away from the doors, and for the last time, this section of the hospital is closed. If you need to enter, you must go around back where you will be screened before entering and leaving."

I wasn't about to be screened with this gun on me, so I waited around for a little while longer to see if I could find out more. I finally saw a black officer standing alone. After I walked up to him, I inquired about what had happened.

"All we know at this point is they found a doctor in one of the rooms shot up pretty bad. Two more doctors were injured, so we don't know if this was some kind of planned attack against doctors."

"Damn, that's messed up. I know many of the doctors who work here. Have any of the names been released yet?"

"No, not yet. Maybe soon."

I nodded and backed away from the officer, standing around for a little while longer to see if there was any additional news. There wasn't. I would surely catch up with Travis sooner or later, and after I got back in the car, I headed to the other hospital to see Nokea. When I got there, my requests hadn't been honored. I was given her room number, but she was in a room with someone else. There was no security outside the door. I was already on edge, especially when I went into the room and saw her lying on her side. An IV needle was in her arm, her eye was covered with a gauze pad, and her left wrist was wrapped with a beige bandage. An ice pack was beside her, and the eye she could see out of was open. It was red and filled with tears. I stood next to her, bending over to kiss her forehead.

"How are you feeling?" I asked while listening to the other patient's loud-ass TV, which was annoying. So was his laugh.

Nokea moved her head from side to side without speaking.

"Are you still hurting anywhere?"

At first she didn't say anything, but she slowly nodded.

"Did they give you anything for the pain?"

She barely opened her mouth. It was so dry and swollen that her lips stuck together. "No," she whispered. "And I'm thirsty, too. Will you get me some water?"

No pain medicine, no water, no private room, no security, no nothing but a big-ass fucking bill they would send for services not provided. I went into the hallway, stopping the first doctor I saw.

"I need some ice water and pain medicine in that room. I also need a wheelchair so I can wheel my wife the fuck out of here."

He held up one finger. "Okay, sir, I'll be with you in one minute."

I wasn't too fond of doctors right now, so I went off on him. "One minute my ass! How long does she have to wait for some fucking water and pills? All these muthafuckas walking around here and can't nobody help?"

Another doctor stepped forward to assist. "Calm down, sir. I was just getting ready to go in there and check on her. It appears that she's going to be okay, even though she lost a substantial amount of blood. Unfortunately, we were unable to save the baby. It is imperative that we keep an eye on the swelling, especially in her legs. She hasn't been able to tell us what exactly happened to her, but maybe you can shed some light on her situation. This may be a case where we have to get the police involved, especially if it revolves around domestic violence that occurred within the home. Have the two of you had any instances occur like this before?"

I fought hard to stay calm. "Are you implying that I did that to her?"

"I don't know. That's why I'm asking."

"And I'm asking you to get her an ice-cold cup of water, some pain medicine, and a wheelchair."

"Under the circumstances, she can't leave here with you, sir, unless . . ."

I'd had enough of listening to this idiot. Not everybody with a PhD was necessarily bright. I looked around, spotting a wheelchair near the end of the hall. As I rushed to get it, the doctor followed me.

"Sir, considering the condition your wife is in, you can't remove her from here. She is the only one who can sign herself out of here, and I recommend that you don't—"

I swung around to address him. "Get the fuck away from me. I'm not in the mood today, and if you need her signature, you'll get it."

I rolled the wheelchair into Nokea's room, placing it beside the bed. "Let's go home," I said. "I'll make sure you get the proper care, okay? Do you trust me?"

She nodded, and as I carefully removed the IV needle from her arm, the doctor attempted to shove me away. I pushed his ass back, warning him not to touch me again. He held on to the wheelchair to break his fall.

"Back the hell up and get her whatever she needs to sign so we can get the fuck out of here. You got two minutes to get those papers, or they won't get signed."

He stood with his mouth open and still hadn't moved. I carefully lifted Nokea out of the bed and sat her in the wheelchair. I kneeled in front of her, touching the side of her pretty face with my hand.

"You okay?" I asked.

She nodded. "Yes. I just want to go home."

"We're on our way."

I swerved the wheelchair around the doctor and made my way to the elevator. It wasn't long before we arrived at my car. I tried to help her get in. She insisted that she could get in by herself. I watched her take small steps to the passenger's seat before scooting in to sit down. I made sure she buckled herself in before I closed the door.

The ride home was quiet. Nokea's eyes were closed, and her head was leaned back on the headrest. I wanted her to get some rest. It had definitely been a long-ass day. And even though I suspected that her thoughts were all over the place, I didn't want to pry until she was ready to talk.

The second we got home, I helped her out of the car. She wrapped one of her arms around my neck, and I guided her to the front door.

"Where are the kids?" she said softly. "I don't want them to see me like this."

"They won't. Can you make it or do you want me to carry you?"

"I can make it. Just help me, okay?"

I helped Nokea inside, and as we made our way through the great room, we could hear the kids in the kitchen laughing. Nanny B was saying something and being real quiet, Nokea and I got on the elevator instead of taking the stairs. The moment we made it to the second floor, Nanny B came from the kitchen and looked upstairs.

"Jaylin, is that you?"

"Yeah, it's me. I'll be downstairs to get something to eat in a minute."

"Okay. Hurry. The police were here earlier. What's that all about?"

"I'll tell you when I get down there."

She didn't respond, but as soon as I helped Nokea get in bed, my door flew open. Nanny B paused as she looked at Nokea, gasping as she clenched her chest.

"Lord, Jesus, what happened to you?" Her face appeared distorted. She turned to me for answers. "Jaylin, what is going on?"

I wasn't sure if Nokea wanted me to tell Nanny B, so I waited for her to say something. She held out her hand, extending it to Nanny B, who stepped forward to hold it.

"I'll be okay, so don't worry. Jaylin will tell you, but please keep the kids away from this room. I don't want them to see me like this."

Nanny B nodded, and tears filled her eyes. She rubbed Nokea's arm and couldn't stop gazing at her. "Okay, sweetheart. I'm so sorry about whatever happened. Let me know if I can get you anything."

"She needs water and aspirin, but I'll get it," I said. "If you can call Dr. Birch and ask him to come over here, I would appreciate it. Meanwhile, give me about ten minutes. I'll come downstairs and explain what happened. Are the kids almost done eating?"

"Almost. Scorpio came by a few hours ago, and they went shopping with her. They just got back not too long ago."

"Okay. Thanks, and don't forget to call Dr. Birch for me."

Nanny B left the room with a frown on her face. I turned to Nokea, who was lying on the bed with a hospital gown on.

"I have a shirt you can change into. And if you want to take a shower or bath, let me know. I'm going to get your water and aspirin. As soon as Dr. Birch gets here, he'll give you a thorough examination. Is that okay?"

"That's fine, Jaylin. Thank you."

I was glad Nokea was here so I could keep my eyes on her. I had so much to do before the night was over, but the first thing I did was get her situated. I went to the kitchen, and when the kids saw me, they started telling me about a dispute between LJ and Mackenzie.

"Daddy," Mackenzie said, "wasn't Dr. Martin Luther King the one who wrote the 'I Have a Dream' speech? LJ said it was Malcolm X. I keep telling him he's wrong."

"Dead wrong," I said to LJ. "And you should know that, shouldn't you?"

LJ scratched his head. Just like me, he caught an attitude when somebody tried to correct him. "I mistakenly said it was Malcolm X, and then I corrected myself and said it was Martin. Mackenzie just thinks she knows everything, but I got a thousand dollars that says she can't beat me at golf."

Mackenzie responded with snap in her voice. "I do know everything, way more than you do. And if you ever want to play against me at golf, bring it on."

"All right," I said, frustrated with the bickering. "Time to cut it and get ready for bed. By the way, LJ, I'd like to know where you have a thousand dollars to put up for a bet."

"If you got it, I got it," he said with confidence. "That's what you always told me, Dad, plus I've seen my bank account. Trust me, I got it."

"Justin's got it too, Daddy," Jaylene said. "That would be another orange soda. Look!"

She pointed to Justin, who was in front of the refrigerator, turning up a soda can to his lips. I needed to get back to Nokea, so I didn't bother to go there with him tonight. I did, however, get at Nanny B for continuously bringing soda into the house. She ignored my gripes and told me she had contacted Dr. Birch. The earliest he could get here was around ten tonight. I told Nanny B we would talk after I tended to Nokea and after the kids were asleep because I didn't want them to hear us talking.

I returned to the bedroom, seeing that Nokea wasn't in bed. She was in the bathroom, examining her face in the mirror. She had removed the gauze from her eye and the bandage from her wrist. She kept touching the swelling in her face. I felt so bad for her.

"I brought your water and aspirin. Dr. Birch will be here at ten. I'm sure he can give you

something stronger. Until then, why don't you
go lie back down."

"I need to take a shower first. Will you get the
water ready for me and give me a shirt to put
on?"

No questions asked, I did as Nokea had asked.
She kept looking at her face in the mirror, and
as she touched the puffiness in her lips, her eyes
traveled to me. "I look a mess, don't I?" she
whispered. "Why didn't I realize what kind of
man he was?"

"No, you don't look a mess. Don't even think
about Travis right now. Take your shower and
get comfortable until Dr. Birch gets here."

She glanced at the mirror one last time before
removing the gown. As she walked over to the
shower, waterfall faucets rained from six different angles. I held the glass doors open for her,
and she stood in the center, allowing soothing
warm water to pour on her. So much anger was
inside of me as I saw numerous bruises on her
back, hips, butt, and legs. Travis was a damn
animal. The moment Nokea got settled tonight, I
had some unfinished business that needed to be
taken care of. I reached out to hand her a soapy
sponge that I had already lathered with soap.
She didn't take it.

"Would you mind washing me?" she asked.

Knowing that it wouldn't be in my best interest to get naked, the only things I removed were my shoes and socks. I kept my jeans and T-shirt on and joined her in the shower. As she stood with both arms by her side, I proceeded to circle the sponge on her chest and arms. Nokea closed her eyes in thought. I couldn't help but think about how much I missed her being here with me. I squeezed the wet sponge around the nape of her neck, hoping that my gentle movements made her feel good. When she turned around, I washed her back, which had more bruises on it than any other place. Her mountains had bruises too, but they were so perfect that I squatted behind her to tackle them up close. I then made my way down to her legs and feet. When I rubbed between her toes, she lightly snickered.

"That tickles," she said. "You can get to my feet when I sit down. I need to sit because my stomach is cramping real bad."

She moved over to the seat. I kneeled in front of her. I lifted one leg at a time, washing them along with her feet again.

"Your clothes are drenched," she said, raking her fingers through my hair, which had loose, wet curls. Water rained on my face and dripped from my chin. My clothes were melted on my skin. "Why didn't you take your clothes off?"

I hated to admit how hard I was, and I definitely didn't want her to see. "It's best that my clothes stay on, trust me. I'm good just like this."

Nokea smiled and continued to run her fingers through my hair. "Thank you," she said. "I appreciate this. I appreciate everything you've done, but please don't tell me you went after him today. Did you?"

I squeezed the sponge on her leg and looked at her. "You told me not to tell you so I won't. I also don't want to talk about him right now, but eventually, I do want to know the details of what he did to you."

"Trust me when I say that you don't want to know. The sooner I can forget about today, the better."

I wanted her to forget, but I knew it would be a while before that happened. I continued to wash her, and after I was finished, I dried her with a soft, white towel. She was still bleeding from the miscarriage. None of the personal items she needed were at my house, not even a pair of her panties. I lifted my Calvin Klein briefs, asking if she wanted to put them on.

"At least for a few hours until I can go get some of the items you need," I said with a smile.

"I'll manage," she said, sitting on the bed. "The shirt works and this towel underneath me should be fine."

I flicked on the TV before going into the closet to remove my wet clothes. I dried my hair with a towel and then changed into another pair of jeans and a cotton shirt. With the wet clothes in my hand, I left the closet. My steps halted when I saw Nokea staring at the TV in a daze. The volume was up, and the reporter was talking about what had happened at the hospital today. I moved closer to watch the news with Nokea. When a photo of Travis flashed on the screen, our heads turned to each other.

"Jaylin, nooo," she said tearfully. "Please don't tell me you had something to do with this. You're going to be in trouble and the last thing . . ."

She paused to control her emotions. I was shocked by this as well. I knew exactly what I'd done to Travis, and I wasn't responsible for shooting him. Nor did I have anyone do it. I sat on the bed next to Nokea, telling her the truth while holding her in my arms.

"Listen to me, all right? Yes, I went to the hospital and fought Travis today. But after that, I left. I honestly wanted to kill him, Nokea, but apparently, somebody beat me to it. A man like that had to have enemies. You mentioned before that he and his brother didn't get along. Maybe somebody in the hospital saw us fighting and used that as an opportunity to possibly frame me. An officer I spoke to said a few other doctors were injured. It could've been something related to a personal attack on doctors. I don't know yet, but I'm going to the police station with Frick tomorrow to try to clear my name. The police were here earlier, I assume to inquire about the fight I had with him. I promise you that I will get this taken care of, and I hope you know that I wouldn't lie to you about this."

"It's such a coincidence, and I noticed your scarred knuckles," she said. "If you did it, it's not like I'm going to say anything to anyone. I'm just worried because I regret putting you in a situation where you felt you needed to go that far. You didn't have to go to that hospital, Jaylin. The last time you did something like this, the outcome was not in your favor."

"In reality, yes, it was, but that's my opinion, and I disagree with yours. It was necessary for me to go to the hospital and do what I did. I'm glad that muthafucka is dead, and a big shout-out to the person who got to him before I did."

Nokea shook her head as if I'd said something wrong. Her actions angered me, so I backed away from her and stood up.

"Do you have sympathy for his ass even after what he did to you?"

"No, I don't. But I don't condone anyone taking matters into their own hands and murdering people. Vengeance is not yours, and sometimes you just have to be still."

"No, sometimes you just have to beat a muthafucka's ass and leave it at that. I'm not going to argue with you about this. I told you what I did. Fuck his ass, and I hope that son of a bitch rots in hell."

I was so pissed that I had to leave the bedroom. I hated to go there with Nokea, but she was always trying to do and say the right thing. At a time like this, she should've been happy that I beat his ass. She should've given me a pat on the back for looking out for her, yet all I got was head shaking and a "shame on me" for going there. I said it once, and I'd say it again. *May that son of a bitch rot his woman-beating ass in hell!*

While waiting for Dr. Birch to get there, I had planned to go to Nanny B's bedroom and tell her what had happened. I didn't because I was positive that I would hear more preaching from her. I wasn't in the mood for it, so I reached out to Shane to see if he'd gotten in touch with Frick. I also inquired about what the police had said earlier.

"Well, thanks for calling me back," he said. "I've been trying to reach you all evening. The cops said they needed to speak to you with regard to the fight at the hospital. The officer's contact information is on your desk, and you already know where the police station is. I also called Frick. He wasn't happy but said he could be here around two o'clock tomorrow afternoon. So get your story straight and be prepared to let the chips fall where they may."

I told Shane about the breaking news with Travis. He couldn't believe it. "Jay, you know you knocked that fool off. I mean, how coincidental is that?"

"If I killed his ass, I would tell you. I don't know why you think I would lie to you about something like that. It would have been my pleasure to witness him take his last breath."

"Not sure if I believe you, but what I think doesn't matter. If you didn't do it, be sure to get things straight so you don't get accused and find yourself locked up."

I agreed with Shane. My story had to be straight, and by the time I got finished talking to Frick and the police tomorrow, I expected this bullshit with Dr. Travis L. Cooper to be behind me.

Chapter 19

Scorpio

It was interesting how the tables had turned. Now Mario was around here kissing my ass and telling me how sorry he was about everything that had happened. He admitted to his little rendezvous the night before our wedding and confirmed that one of the chicks told him she was pregnant. I wasn't sure if I believed that, but one thing I was sure of was that there were times when I felt like I'd been to hell and back in my relationship with Jaylin. We'd been through a lot. I learned a tremendous amount of things from that relationship, and I had no intention, none whatsoever, to put up with a bunch of shit from another rich man who couldn't control his dick.

Mario had used my defense. That was this had occurred before we were married. Yes, it certainly did, but he was fully aware of the consequences if I ever became so unhappy that I didn't want to be married anymore. I wasn't quite there yet, but if this thing between him and the chick who was supposed to be pregnant by him started to shake things up, I had no intention of being one of those "stand by your man" bitches who often looked like puppets. I would happily seek a divorce, and unfortunately, give Jaylin the half he would probably take me to court to get.

Speaking of Jay Baby, I hadn't heard from him since our encounter at the restaurant. What he'd said to me tugged at my heart. He could have me so angry at him one minute, and the next minute I'd be like putty in his hands. I loved him so much for his honesty. Like he'd said, he could never give me what I truly wanted. If he couldn't, Mario needed to get it right or else.

Whenever I was upset, I went on shopping sprees to help calm my nerves. I'd picked up the kids from Jaylin's house earlier, and we all went to the mall. I spent a fortune on them as well as on myself. When I returned home, I made sure that Mario saw the numerous bags in my hands along with the ones I had to travel back and forth to the car to get. He stood in the workout room with his shirt off, pounding away at a punching bag. I had several bags in my hand, causing him to look at me like I was crazy. I smiled as I placed some of the bags on a weight bench, opening a few to show him what I'd purchased.

"Do you like these?" I displayed a pair of shoes that cost $2,250. I already had the same shoe in another color. "They're cute, aren't they?"

He nodded and flicked his brows. "Real nice, babe, but I already know what you're doing. You're trying to upset me. I don't get upset when you're spending money because that's what you're supposed to do."

"Then you won't be upset when I show you the other house I purchased, will you? I got it just in case things don't work out between us."

That made him punch the bag to release some steam. He then came up to me while cocking his neck from side to side. "You can buy whatever you'd like. But you don't need another house, because everything is going to work out between us. You're going to stay right here with me. So chill, sweetheart, and be happy."

I cut my eyes at him and dropped the shoes back in the bag. "I'm trying, but what's the deal with you and this baby? I want to meet the chick who's supposed to be pregnant by you. When is the last time you saw her?"

He shrugged and punched his gloves together. "I've only seen her twice since we hooked up. The first time she told me she was pregnant, and the second time she demanded money. There is no reason for you to meet her. She's a liar, and her cockamamie plan isn't going to work."

"I still want to meet her. Do what you can to make that happen, because there are always two sides to every story, sometimes three, as in the number of women you had sex with that night. Without a condom, may I add. Just nasty."

This time he cut his eyes at me and reached for my bags. "Let me help you put all of your things in the closet upstairs. I'm sure you have more bags on the bed, too, but you may want to clear it so we can get ready to do other things."

I pursed my lips. "Yes, help me clear the bed, and then you can help me order a new car. I'm really feeling that Bugatti your father has. A white one would help alleviate some of the stress I'm feeling."

Mario laughed. "I don't mind buying you a Bugatti, but you have to do something big for me. I mean so big that I just explode all over the place."

"You mean like you exploded in the woman you have pregnant?"

"No," Mario said, grabbing my waist and pulling me close to him. "Like I want to explode in you as we're making love. Let's clear our minds and make love. It's been a long time. We have to put this petty stuff behind us."

"I agree, but getting another woman pregnant isn't petty. Cutting my hair off wasn't either, and the way you've been treating me must not ever happen again. Got it?"

"Never again, Mrs. Pezzano." He led the way as he carried my bags upstairs. When we got to the bedroom and he saw our bed covered with more packages, all he did was shake his head again.

"You're going to exhaust all of our funds. Then I'm going to make you take every bit of this back for a refund."

"Hey, if you can refund my pussy, then we have a deal. If not, just accept the fact that you have a very high maintenance wife who knows for a fact that broke will never define you."

Mario laughed, and after he helped me put away the items I'd purchased, we took a shower together. We hit the bed around eleven, but around two in the morning, I was awakened by the news. I heard the reporter mention Travis's name. I abruptly sat up, and when I saw Travis's picture on TV, I clamped my hand over my mouth. I couldn't believe he'd been killed. Talk about being shocked, I was. I shoved Mario's shoulder to wake him.

"Baby, wake up," I said. "Look. Do you see this?"

"See what?" he replied in a groggy tone. He squinted while trying to focus on the TV. "Who . . . what is it?"

"Nokea's boyfriend, Travis, the doctor. Somebody went into the hospital and killed him. This is horrible. I know she's probably devastated right now."

Mario acted as if he didn't even care. He tossed the sheet over his head and lay back down. "I assume so, but who cares?" he mumbled. "Your body is so soft and warm. I want to feel it next to me. Turn off the TV, sweetheart, and let's go back to sleep."

I kept my eyes focused on the TV, listening to the details. "I can't believe you're not watching this. Travis was shot multiple times. Two other doctors were shot too. One in the foot, the other in the hand. They survived. This is terrible. I can't wait to call Nokea in the morning."

"Fine," Mario mumbled again. "Call her in the morning. Call Jaylin too, because he's probably the one who killed him."

Mario's words caused me to pause for a minute, giving what he'd said much thought. That could have been a possibility, especially since there had always been friction between the two of them. I started to worry. If Jaylin had done it, he would surely go to jail. Lord knows I didn't want anything like that to happen, and I prayed that he wasn't responsible for this. I kept watching the TV, and when they showed a fuzzy photo of the possible killer, I squinted to see if I could recognize the person. He or she was covered in all black, had a mask over their face, and had gloves on their hands. All I could say was the person had a muscular build and was tall. I didn't know if they were black, white, Asian . . . what race? I couldn't even see the person's eyes. Nothing else jumped out at me. Nonetheless, the person on camera was wanted for questioning.

The following morning I was up early. Mario had already gotten up and left. I showered, ate a quick breakfast, and then drove to Jaylin's house to see what I could find out. On the drive there, I called Nokea, but she didn't answer her phone. I left a message telling her how sorry I was about Travis. She had really been going through it. For this to happen right after losing her father, I knew she was probably losing it. It seemed like things always went from bad to worse. I said a prayer for her right after I parked my car in Jaylin's driveway.

With it being so early, I was surprised to see Shane's truck. Maybe he stayed the night, but when I went to the door, Nanny B let me in. I immediately asked her about Travis. She was just as clueless as I was.

"Chile, I honestly do not know what is going on. Jaylin acts as if he don't have five minutes to talk. He's in his office with Shane. I think they're getting ready to go somewhere."

"Okay. I'll make it quick, and I'll let you know what I find out," I whispered.

I headed to Jaylin's office. The door was open, so I didn't have to knock. He was sitting at his desk, wearing a tan suit and white shirt. Shane was suited up too. His shirt was burgundy, and his suit was black. Apparently, they had an important meeting today. The office was lit up with the scent of masculine cologne, and much seriousness was on their faces. Their heads snapped up as they saw me come through the door.

"Not today, Scorpio," Jaylin said. "Please call later or come back tomorrow."

I got straight to the reason I was there. "I'm glad to see you too, but what happened to Travis? I saw the news last night. Is he really dead? Moreover, are you the one responsible?"

Jaylin opened his drawer to remove something. "Why are you over here asking questions? How many times do I have to tell you you're dead to me?"

I snapped my fingers. "That's right. I keep forgetting." I walked over to the sofa and lay on my back. I closed my eyes and crossed my arms over my chest. "Okay, now you can pretend that I'm speaking to you from the dead. Booooo, Jaylin. What happened to Travis, and did you have anything to doooooo with what happened to him and those other doctors?"

My eyes popped open when Jaylin came over to the sofa, leaning over me. "You play too damn much, and I assure you that this is no laughing matter. No, I did not kill him, but I damn sure wanted to."

I sat up, causing him to back away from me. "You are so handsome when you're angry, but you're right. It isn't a laughing matter. I know Nokea is taking this real hard. I tried calling her, but she didn't answer her phone. You're not happy about that man being dead, are you? That's kind of cold, unless you're lying about killing him or you know who the suspect in all black was on TV."

"I saw the image too," Shane said. "Couldn't make it out, though."

Jaylin shrugged. "Neither could I, but if he's ever caught, I'll be sure to hire a lawyer for him and take care of his legal fees."

I shook my head at Jaylin's coldness. "You need to stop. That's a shame, and I'm going to pray extra hard for you. Now, all jokes aside, where is Nokea? I want to tell her how sorry I am. You may not have liked Travis, but I'm sure it hurts to lose someone you love."

"Losing somebody you love ain't always a bad thing." Jaylin winked at me. "Now, Shane and I have a few things to discuss. We'd really like some privacy."

"Fine then." I stood to leave. "Before I go, I wanted to let you know that Mario and I will be taking the kids to Belize on a family vacation. We need some bonding time if you don't mind."

"Before my kids go anywhere with Mario, he and I need to talk and possibly reconcile our differences. I'm feeling real salty about some shit right now, but I do feel as if he and I need to work some things out pertaining to the kids. I also suggest you ask the kids if they want to go. I can tell you right now that LJ ain't going."

"That's because he's so funny acting like you are. Plus, all he wants to do is send text messages to that girl he has a crush on at his school. I saw some of those text messages. It appears that your son is heading down the same path as you. As for Mario, call and talk to him. He's been in a good mood lately, and I guess I don't have to tell another cheating man why. Right about now, diamonds are indeed a girl's best friend, and I can have anything, anything, I want."

Jaylin and Shane looked at each other. Shane spoke up before he did. "I've always liked your style, Scorpio. And if the man wants to pay for his mistakes, let him."

I reached out to give Shane dap. "See, that's what I'm talking about, Shane. I knew there was a reason why I almost fell in love with you. You're a very smart man, and you're way smarter than your friend over there."

"Well," Jaylin said bluntly, "I always surround myself with people who are much smarter than I am. That's why I'm so successful. You may need to start doing the same. And at least I'm not as dumb as Mario's ass, because cheater or not, those diamonds need to stay at the store. It's going to take more than a trip to Belize to save your marriage, but I'm sure Mario will appreciate your efforts. The kids may have a good time too, but keep in mind that they won't be going anywhere until I speak to Mario."

"Like I said, call him. If you don't get a chance to speak to him in a few days, we're out of here. All of us, Mr. Control."

My business was done, so I left Jaylin's office on a high note. I spoke to Nanny B about Travis being killed, and I also mentioned taking the kids to Belize. I told her it would be an opportunity for her to get a break. She wasn't having that and insisted she wanted to go. I managed to talk her out of going. And by the end of the week, I looked forward to spending time alone with the kids and Mario. Hopefully, his conversation with Jaylin would go over well this time.

Chapter 20

Jaylin

After Scorpio left, I closed the door behind her. The only reason I didn't put up too much of a fuss about the kids going to Belize was because it allowed Nokea to have the space and privacy she needed. I didn't think she'd gotten any sleep last night, but this morning she'd been resting peacefully.

In the meantime, in addition to calling Mario, I had to take care of this mess with the police. Shane and I were trying to piece together the story I would say just to clear my name. Basically, Travis attempted to kill Nokea, I took her to the hospital, went to his job, and we argued. After that, he punched me first, and we started fighting. I left, and the rest was history. I didn't know who had killed him, nor did I know why he was killed. That was as close to the truth as it could get, with the exception of Travis putting his hands on me first. There were plenty of witnesses who would say I was at the hospital to accomplish one mission. That was to beat his ass, and I was the aggressor, not him. It would be my word against theirs. And with Travis being a dead man, he definitely couldn't tell his side.

I glanced at my watch. "What time is Frick supposed to be here again? I hope his ass don't be late."

"He said two," Shane said. "You want to go grab something to eat real quick and tell him to meet us at the police station?"

"Naw, I'm not really hungry. I just want to stay here until he comes. Besides, I don't want to be away from Nokea for too long. She jumped a few times in her sleep last night. I'm real worried about her. If only you could see what he did to her. I'm sick to my fucking stomach."

"I don't want to see. I'm sure it's bad. I told Tiffanie about it last night. She was in tears. I can't imagine a man doing that to a woman. What made him that mad where he felt like he had to do something like that?"

"He was upset about how close we were. And I don't care who Nokea and I are in relationships with, when certain situations happen in our lives, we always find our way back to each other.

There's a level of comfort that is needed during those times. The only way to heal is if we have each other. As for her condition, Dr. Birch said she'll be okay. He wrote her a prescription for pain and swelling. Said he'd be back in a couple of days to check on her. I just hope she comes out of this okay. Travis was a monster. There was something so devious in his eyes when I saw him. He got a kick out of that shit for sure."

With one hand in my pocket, I walked over to the window and looked outside. "It was something I should have noticed, and something I can't help but wonder if Nokea knew was there. Maybe she ignored the signs because she was so adamant about making things work. I mean, had he hit her before? Did she hate me so much that she was willing to accept whatever he dished out? She had to feel something negative about him. I can't believe that out of nowhere he just snapped and did that to her."

"I can believe he snapped. We all can snap, just like that." Shane snapped his fingers. "Even the kindest person can do it, and when certain things trouble you, and you find yourself in a situation where you have to protect the people you care about, your mind starts racing. Before you know it, you've done something that you may have done before but you told yourself you'd never do again. I won't say much else, but I can promise you this: Travis wasn't laughing in his final moments. I'm sure he expressed his regrets to the killer before he pulled the trigger."

I slowly turned my head, looking at Shane, who stared at me with a blank expression on his face. Mine was scrunched. I was in a state of shock at what he'd said. "Are . . . are you saying to me what I think you're saying?"

"What I'm saying to you is there are certain things that a best friend should never know. Every man has secrets, and pertaining to murder, sometimes silence is golden."

I stood as if cement had been poured over me. I continued to examine him. I had no words right now. My mind traveled back to yesterday. I started thinking about some of the things he'd said. There was nothing that led me to believe he was thinking about doing what I set out to do. Then there was the delay in traffic. He had every opportunity to get to the hospital before me if he'd taken a different route. And who in the hell would suspect Shane? I was the obvious one, not him.

I wanted to hit him with many more questions about this, especially about why the other two doctors were shot. Maybe to throw people off, but whatever the reason was, Shane was right.

Silence was golden. This was one secret that would go no further. I owed him my mother-fucking life.

Everything wrapped up around six o'clock that evening. All the police said was an investigation was ongoing, and they would be in touch if anything came up. I refused to let Shane go to the police station with me. Frick and I were the only ones there. For the most part, I was satisfied with how things had turned out. Frick wasn't happy, but after I wrote his ass a fat check, he got on the plane with a wide smile on his face. I returned home. The second I entered the house, Nanny B snatched me into her bedroom. She was highly upset with me.

"Listen to me, you high-yellow Negro. I will not be ignored by you. I talked to Nokea, and how dare you not tell me what Travis did to her?" I had rarely ever seen Nanny B cry. To see tears rolling down her face wasn't a good feeling. "Why did Travis do that to her, Jaylin? And what in the hell did you do to him? Please don't tell me you killed him. Please, Jaylin, don't tell me you did something like that. If you did, Lord have mercy on us all."

I gave Nanny B a hug to calm her. "I didn't kill him, but I had every intention to. I don't know what caused him to snap like that, but it doesn't matter because he shouldn't have done that to her. Nokea isn't saying much, but when she's ready, I'm sure she'll talk more about it. I left the police station earlier, and hopefully, I've cleared my name. I have no idea who killed Travis. There's an investigation going on. I didn't pay anyone to do it, and that is the truth."

Nanny B squeezed me tighter. I hated to lie to her, but there were certain things that even she didn't need to know. She backed away from me, wiping her wet face.

"Since Scorpio is taking the kids to Belize, I'm going back to St. Louis to spend some time with Gloria and my sister. While you're here, see about Nokea. She really needs you. Don't make her feel guilty about being with Travis, and try to be more understanding. You've been so crabby, and you need to stop fussing about things that don't even matter, like soda. I'm grown, and you will not tell me what I can and can't give my babies. That's all there is to it, and like it or not, your gripes go in one ear, out the other."

"Look, I'm the nicest man you know. I'm a pretty damn good father, too. But if you continue to go against my wishes, you will get cussed out.

You can ignore me all you want. There will come a time when I may have to utilize my belt. Not on Justin but on you for not listening."

She threw her hand back at me and laughed. "You will need more than a belt to deal with me. Now g'on upstairs to see about Nokea. I think she's still up. She just got finished eating a little something. Did you eat anything yet?"

I told Nanny B I would eat later, and then I went to my bedroom. The doors to the balcony were wide open. Nokea was sitting outside, gazing at the ocean. I stood in the doorway, leaning against it.

"Peaceful, isn't it?" I asked.

"Very much so. I forgot how beautiful the view is out here."

"I'm surprised that you forgot, especially since we spent so many days and nights out here."

"For many reasons I forced myself to forget."

"You'll have plenty of time to tell me what those reasons are. And then I have so much that I need to tell you. For now, I'm going to get out of these clothes, get something to eat, then come back and chill with you if that's okay."

"That's fine. Before you go eat, I want to apologize for getting angry at you about Travis. I know that seeing me like this is difficult for you, and I know how you prefer to deal with things on your own terms. That's just who you are, and so many years later it makes no sense for me to gripe about the way you react to certain things."

"I agree, but we'll talk more later. Can I bring you anything when I come back?"

"Maybe some popcorn and a deck of cards. I also need my cell phone so I can check my messages. It's at my place, but I don't want to go back there again."

"I'll go by there tomorrow and get it. And you don't have to go back there unless you want to."

Nokea sat silent. I went to my closet, changed clothes, and while in my office I got down on two seasoned pork chops Nanny B had made. I talked to Shane for about thirty minutes, following up on how things had gone at the police station. Frick also called to tell me that my stop at the gas station saved my ass. The cameras showed I was there at almost the same time Travis was killed by the person in the video. The clerk also vouched for me. I told Shane about that, and I also told him I needed to take a short break from business. He understood why, and he didn't elaborate on Travis's killing or the video, because smart people involved in shit like that didn't go around bragging about it or discussing it.

"Go all in, my brotha," he advised. "See about Nokea and focus on nothing but her. I'll handle things in your absence as I have done plenty of times before. Besides, I tend to make more money when you take a back seat."

I had to laugh. "Shane, don't fool yourself. If it weren't for me, you would still be in business with Felicia, catching pure, deep hell. If not that, you'd be somewhere on an island, still professing your love for Scorpio and broke as hell."

This time he laughed. "Yeah, you did save me. I don't mind giving credit when it's due. But I do mind how long this conversation is going on. Tiffanie and I are going dancing tonight. She signed us up for salsa classes that have been kind of fun. I think we may be ready for *Dancing with the Stars* soon."

"That would not be good, and on that note, I'll holla tomorrow. Be sure to tell Tiffanie not to let you break a leg."

We ended the call with laughter. It felt good to laugh. I couldn't help but think about what Nanny B had said earlier, what many people close to me had been saying all along. I needed to release some of my anger inside, stop being so serious all the time, and laugh a little. It was good for my soul. Hopefully, I would be able to do just that now that Nokea and I were in a position to do us again.

By the time I returned to the bedroom, she was back in bed. Her back was against the head-board, which touched the ceiling. A magazine was on her lap, and unfortunately, it was a pornographic magazine that had been in my drawer for a long time.

"I got bored," she said, shrugging her shoulders. "But I didn't think you still had this kind of stuff lying around. Why not utilize the internet? There's plenty on the net for you to see, isn't there?"

After putting the popcorn and cards on the nightstand, I lay sideways across the bottom of the bed. "If you really must know why that magazine was in my drawer, I'll tell you. Your curious, precious son had it. I removed it from his room."

Nokea rejected my explanation. "Don't you dare lie on him like that. If it was in his room, where did he get it from?"

"It had been in a drawer in my office for a long time. LJ be going through my things. I guess he found it."

"If that's the case, you really need to have a talk with your son. He shouldn't be looking at stuff like this. Lord knows it's too soon for all of that."

I reached for the magazine, taking it from Nokea's hand. "You shouldn't be looking at stuff like that either, and just so you know, we had a looong talk about that already. Some kids are more curious than others, but I guarantee you that he won't be doing any of the things I was already doing at his age."

"I hope not. I don't even want to imagine it." She held out her hand. "Now give me back the magazine. I told you I was bored."

"If you're bored then let's go do something. Tell me what you want to do, and we'll do it."

"I'm still a bit weak, so I can't do much walking yet. But I did start on something interesting today." Nokea opened the drawer, pulling out a piece of paper and pen. "I started working on my bucket list. Came up with several things I want to do before I get too old or before I leave this earth."

I wasn't sure what made her create such a list, especially since she was nowhere near old. I also didn't want to think about her leaving here, but I was interested in what was on her list. "What are some of the things you came up with?"

"A few of them include you, too, so I'll let you read it."

She gave the piece of paper to me. I studied it. The first thing I saw was a big fat no. "'Bungee jump with Jaylin, go skiing, build a tree-house with the kids, climb to the top of a mountain with Jaylin, get a tattoo, run a marathon, meet the Obamas, jump from a helicopter, go to an NBA game, and enter a hot dog–eating contest.'" My eyes shifted to Nokea. "You can't be serious."

She snatched the paper from my hand. "I'm very serious. I have a lot more to add to my list. That's only the beginning."

"Well, leave me out of it because I won't be doing any of that shit. The only thing I will help you do is build the kids a treehouse. That's it."

"You're no fun, Jaylin. I guess I'll have to tackle those things by myself then."

"It's your list and you should."

We both laughed. After Nokea put her list back in the drawer, we got comfortable in bed and started watching a movie. I was all into it before she interrupted me.

"I'm so angry at myself for falling in love with a man like Travis," she said. "My poor judgment really hurt me a lot. I feel like such a fool for not knowing what he was capable of doing."

"Well, it's not like men like him go around with signs on their foreheads saying, 'I'm a woman beater.' But I can't help but wonder if you saw any signs from him that would've let you know what was up."

"Not really, Jaylin. He raised his voice every now and then, but for the most part, Travis was kind, sweet, and very charming. He started drinking heavy about a year ago, and then he'd bring you up and accuse me of still being with you. My father's funeral seemed to trigger something in him. That was when I noticed a big change in him. It was like he was a different man. I was so shocked by what he did to me. It's obvious that he had issues I didn't know existed."

"Yeah, people don't just turn that way overnight. I bet if you had a heart-to-heart conversation with his mother, she could probably tell you an earful about her son."

"Probably so. She's a nice woman. I didn't care too much for his brother, but I'm sure they're suffering right now. I guess they're probably wondering where I'm at, but I don't have anything to say to them. I just want to move on and be done with it."

"Sounds like a plan. Hopefully, the police will get to the bottom of what happened. They'll be able to give his family the answers they're looking for."

Nokea nodded and released a deep breath. She reached for the aspirin and water on the nightstand. After she downed the aspirin, she moved closer to me, laying her head on my chest.

Before she went to sleep, there was something that I needed to know.

"Can I ask you something?" I asked.

"Sure."

"Will you be honest?"

"Always."

"Did you fall out of love with me?"

Nokea hesitated to answer. She lifted her head to look at me. The sight of her bruised eye tore me up, as did her reply.

"Yes, I did. I was so upset with you after our divorce, and even though we continued to see each other, I was dying inside. I just didn't feel the same anymore. When I met Travis, it was so easy for me to forget about us."

I figured that was the case, but to finally hear her say it didn't make me feel good. I planted a kiss over her eye and told her to get some rest. She laid her head on my chest again, and within minutes she had fallen asleep. I, however, was wide awake. I couldn't help but think about the long road ahead of us. There was no telling how long it would be before Nokea fell back in love with me again. I damn sure had my work cut out for me. This time there would be no fuckups.

Chapter 21

Nokea

A couple of weeks had passed, and I was starting to feel better. The kids were on vacation with Scorpio, and Nanny B was back in St. Louis with my mother. In no way did I tell her what had happened. When she inquired about Travis, I told her we had gone our separate ways. I didn't even tell her about him being killed. That was still a big mystery to me, and as I watched the video of the killer numerous times to make sure it wasn't Jaylin, I believed that he wasn't the one. I kept thinking about who could've done it, but then I'd gotten to a point where it started not to matter. I was sad about the whole thing. I couldn't believe it had come to this. I was just thankful to be alive.

Since everyone was away enjoying themselves, Jaylin and I were alone at his house. The swelling in my face and legs had gone down. My eye was open, and the bruises had started to fade. I still felt slightly weak, but Dr. Birch recommended some vitamins, which gave me plenty of energy. Jaylin and I took slow walks on the beach nearly every morning. We worked out in the workout room and swam in the pool. This morning, we were playing basketball. I was no good at it, and the only shots I made were when he lifted me on his shoulders so I could shoot at a high level. I threw the ball at the rim, and it rolled right in.

"I told you I could beat you," I cheered with my arms in the air.

He squatted to lower me from his neck. "If that's how you want to see it, cool. But if you ask me, you cheated."

"I don't cheat, Mr. Rogers. I won that game fair and square. But now that we're done with basketball, I'm ready to move on to bigger and better things on my bucket list. Are you ready to go bungee jumping with me today?"

Jaylin picked up the basketball, tucking it underneath his arm. "Listen, I have some rope somewhere around here, and I'm sure we can find a high enough place to jump from, like the second floor. I'll be happy to do that with you, but jumping off cliffs and from planes ain't exactly my thing."

"I know, and that's what'll make it so much fun. Besides, jumping from the second floor is more dangerous. There's no way to secure the rope. We could seriously hurt ourselves."

"No, we could seriously hurt ourselves bungee jumping. I'm not ready to die yet, so count me out. Now if you would like to do it, I'll go to watch you."

"Okay, fine then. I'll go, and you can watch."

Jaylin agreed. If he thought I was going to tackle this alone, he was crazy. I would beg him to do it with me. Deep down I had a feeling he would change his mind.

After breakfast, I made reservations, and we left. Jaylin had to stop by Shane's house to drop off a package. When we got there, Shane was outside washing his convertible. His shirt was off, his dreads were pulled back, and his Nike shorts matched his shoes. He smiled as he saw Jaylin's car pull in the driveway. Excited to see me, he came up to the car and bent over to kiss my cheek.

"What's up, beautiful?" he said. "I'm glad you're feeling better."

"I'm almost there, Shane, and thanks for the compliment."

"No, don't let her fool you," Jaylin said. "She's all the way there. If she weren't, she wouldn't be talking about going bungee jumping right now. You get invited to salsa classes while I get invited to go risk my life."

"Bungee jumping?" Shane questioned. "Hell no."

I cut my eyes at both of them. "You two are such big wimps. The dip is only eighty or ninety feet, and these people are professionals. They're going to make sure we're strapped in correctly."

"Excuse me," Jaylin said, correcting me. "You keep saying we. I'm not doing this, Nokea. I promise you that I'm not, so please don't get your hopes up, baby, because it ain't happening."

"I'm afraid it wouldn't be happening with me either," Shane said. "Not in this lifetime."

Jaylin tossed Shane a package, and he caught it. "That should finalize everything," Jaylin said. "Look it over and holla if you need me to do anything else."

Shane nodded. "Will do. And have fun today. Call me later just to let me know you're still alive."

He laughed as Jaylin backed out of the driveway. I waved, and as I took a double look at Shane, a quick thought about the man in the video came to mind. I quickly washed those thoughts away. Jaylin would be capable of doing something like that, but surely not Shane.

Before Jaylin got on the highway, I asked him to stop by my condo. I said I didn't want to go back there, but since he was with me, I thought it would be an appropriate time.

"Are you sure?" he asked. "Why don't you wait a while longer?"

"No, I haven't been there, and I still have my belongings there. I just want to see what it feels like to be there again."

Jaylin seemed reluctant to take me there. I didn't know why until we got there and I stepped inside. Basically, mostly everything in the place had been cleared out. The living room furniture was gone, kitchen cabinets were cleared, pictures were removed from the walls, which all had been painted white instead of the tan color I'd had them painted. The whole place was spotless. My bed was still there, but there were no sheets on the bed. The carpet had been cleaned as well as the bathrooms. My closet and the kids' closets were empty. I turned to Jaylin. He stood with a peculiar look on his face.

"Where are my things, Jaylin? Did you do this?"

"You said you didn't want to come back here, so I put most of your things in storage and had the place cleaned. I didn't want to leave it as is, and I didn't want you to walk back in here and see the way it was left."

I released a deep breath as my mind traveled back to that horrific day. I began to tell Jaylin everything that had happened, including when Travis raped me and slapped my face with his picture. How he'd spit on me, called me names, and then cried and apologized for what he'd done. I became emotional while speaking about it. That was when Jaylin wrapped me in his arms, holding me tight.

"It's over with, baby. He can't hurt you anymore, and going forward I will always protect you. I was seconds away from coming here that night after being hung up on. I was in my car and everything. I regret listening to you when you told me you needed space. When everyone kept telling me to back off and be still, I just didn't want to because I will always feel as if we need each other."

I surely needed him now. His arms around me felt tranquilizing. I also needed him later, and as I stood on the bungee jumping tower, preparing myself to jump, I begged Jaylin to jump with me.

"You just said we needed each other. Now you're going to stand there and allow me to do this all by myself?" I whined and pouted.

"I sure am. I'll be praying for you the second you jump."

I reached out, holding his hand with mine. "Please, Jaylin. Do it for me. It's only ninety feet. If we die, at least we'll go to heaven together."

He stood with a stern look on his face. "No, Nokea. I'm not doing that. This is crazy, and if you die, I'll see you in heaven when I get there."

The man who had put on my harness laughed and explained how safe it actually was. Jaylin still wasn't sold.

"Give me a hug before you jump," he said.

I gave him a hug then bravely turned around, keeping my eyes focused straight ahead. Seconds later, Jaylin gave in.

"Damn," he said with a frown on his face. "Give me a harness, shit. I can't believe you got me doing this. You knew I wasn't going to let you do this alone."

I predicted that much, but I almost wasn't sure. Either way, the man helped Jaylin slip on a body harness, and we were ready to go all in. As we faced each other in a tight embrace, the man secured the cord and our harnesses together.

"Look on the bright side," I said, feeling Jaylin's heart palpitating against mine. "If the cord breaks, at least we both can swim."

"Nokea, don't play with me right now. I'm seconds away from changing my mind. If we don't survive this, there is going to be a lot of chaos between us happening in heaven."

The man asked us to turn our heads so he could take a picture. I smiled, Jaylin didn't. I kissed him on the cheek, causing him to display a smirk. The man counted down. Our bodies were pressed together real tight. He pushed us off the ledge. I couldn't tell who screamed the loudest.

"Shiiiiiiiit, fuuuuuuck, hellllll nooooo!"

"Ohhhhhh, myyyyyyyyy God! Neverrrrr again!"

My stomach felt as if it left my body and dropped into the water. My neck had been jerked around, and my body was aching all over. But as we dangled from our feet, swaying from side to side, we couldn't help but laugh.

"You are out of your mind," Jaylin said. "That bucket list of yours is a wrap!"

The way I felt, I agreed for now. This was a bit much, and I was so glad when it was over and we were back on our feet. Jaylin rushed me to the car just in case I had more bright ideas. Actually, I did, but I didn't tell him until we got in the car. My body was still aching, but I pretended as if everything was intact.

"Now that we got that out of the way, are we going skiing or what?" I asked.

"The only thing I'm doing is going home to tend to my sore muscles. My head hurts, and the way my body jerked, I'm not feeling that shit."

Truthfully neither was I, but it was fun. Plus we had the cutest picture ever for memories.

When we returned to Jaylin's house, I called Scorpio to check on the kids. She was surprised to hear my voice. I hadn't spoken to her since the incident with Travis had happened.

"I tried to reach out to you several times," she said. "I'm so sorry for your loss. I'm glad the kids are with me and Mario just so you can take some time for yourself and relax."

I didn't want anyone to know what Travis had done, so I thanked Scorpio for the condolences and left it at that. I also talked to the kids. They all insisted they were having a good time. Jaylin spoke to them as well, and after his conversation wrapped up with them, I called St. Louis to check on my mother. She didn't answer, so I left a message for her to return my call.

Jaylin was already upstairs, but when I went to the bedroom, he was lying across the bed, holding his back, moaning and groaning as if he were in excruciating pain.

"I must admit that I'm a little sore too, but you can't be serious," I said.

"I am very serious. I think I threw my back out or something."

I walked over to the bed and sat next to him. "What part of your back hurts?"

"Right here." He removed his shirt and pressed his lower back. "All down in here."

I started to massage his back and really dove in with my rubs when he rolled on his stomach.

"Ahhhh," he said, relieved. "That feels soooo good. Right there, baby, right in that spot."

I pursed my lips, predicting where this was going, especially when he turned on his back.

"Harder," he groaned and held his stomach. "Right there, but press harder."

I used both of my hands to press harder on his tight abs.

"Yeah, that's it. Now, go just a little bit lower. Right where the hump is."

I snatched my hands back as if I had touched a hot stove. "Jaylin, I'm not messing with that, so you can forget it. You can't lie there and tell me your penis hurts."

"Shit, it does hurt. I think I lost a few inches when that damn cord yanked us up. At least look at it to make sure all of it is still there."

"I think it'll be perfectly fine, especially after I go run you some bathwater so you can chill. Meanwhile, I'm going to take some aspirin and see if I can find us something good to watch on TV."

"Yeah, go get my water together and make it real hot. I'm going to cook us a little something, and then we can chill in the theater room to watch a movie. How about that?"

"Sounds even better to me."

I prepared Jaylin's bathwater, and after he was settled in, I went to another bathroom to shower. I still had effects from the miscarriage, and after bungee jumping my body didn't approve. I was sore all over, but I wouldn't dare tell Jaylin. He would talk bad about me. I had to pretend that I was actually the brave one.

After my shower, I put on a robe and returned to the bedroom. Jaylin was in the tub for quite a while, and then he headed to the kitchen to start on dinner. I wasn't sure what he was going to cook, but nearly an hour later, as I was watching TV, he came into the bedroom, carrying a tray in his hand. I wasn't exactly sure what was on the tray because his near-perfect, muscle-packed, naked frame had my attention. An apron was around his waist. That was pretty much it.

"I hope you're in the mood for breakfast," he said, kicking the door with his foot to close it. "Because all I know how to do is scramble eggs, fry some bacon, and put jelly on toast. I thought about some baked chicken or something, but I feared it wouldn't be juicy enough. With breakfast, I couldn't go wrong."

"No, you couldn't, but stay right there while I snap a quick photo of the naked chef. I'll put it in my scrapbook. Maybe on Instagram."

Jaylin stepped forward, and when I tried to take the picture, he removed my cell phone from my hand. "Pictures like that can turn up anywhere. Let's not go there."

He laid my phone on the nightstand, and after he put the tray on the bed, he walked over to the light switch to dim the lights. I quickly picked up my phone, snapping a picture of his nice ass, which was toned, tight, and just right. He turned around, shaking his head.

"Would you stop?"

"No, I will not," I said, taking another picture. "I like the apron, but it is really messing things up. I can't see anything, and my Instagram followers are going to want to see more than an apron."

"I'm sure you'll still get thousands of likes, maybe even millions. But don't put my picture on Instagram or Facebook."

I didn't respond. We enjoyed breakfast, and after our plates were clean, we headed to the theater room to watch a comedy movie. Less than fifteen minutes in, Jaylin had fallen asleep. His head was sideways on my lap, his rippled abs moved in and out as he breathed, and his apron was now gone. I used my phone to snap another picture. I didn't post that one on Instagram, but the one with him in the apron I surely did. My followers loved every bit of it. Likes were calculating fast. I chuckled a bit from posting the picture as well as at how much this busy day had worn him out. I was certainly looking forward to our amazing ski trip that, as of yet, he didn't know was already planned.

Chapter 22

Nokea

A week later, it was time for round two. After Jaylin and I attended an NBA basketball game with Shane and Tiffanie, we hit the ski slopes in Colorado. This was truly going to be a challenge because none of us knew how to ski. Nonetheless, we settled in at a cozy, 2,000-square-foot condo that had breathtaking views of the snowy mountains, ski slopes, and trees. The room had a king-sized feather bed and a luxurious bathroom with a stainless-steel Jacuzzi tub. The vaulted ceilings, tall glass windows, and wooden columns decked out the place. I took many pictures for my scrapbook. It was all about collecting more memories.

Tiffanie and Shane had their own condo. Jaylin was putting wood into the stone fireplace in ours. It wasn't long before the sitting area started to heat up. I was excited about our trip, because Jaylin had no idea what I had in store for us. He and Shane thought we were all going skiing today. But Tiffanie had plans to tell Shane that she was pregnant again, and I had dinner prepared so Jaylin and I could do away with the "End Celebration" he'd had and replace it with a "Celebration of Love."

In order for things to go as planned, I had to keep him busy. We left the condo around noon, and instead of skiing, we went shopping. He purchased nearly everything he touched. Then again, so did I. So many bags were gathered in our hands we could barely open the door to the condo.

"Reach into my pocket and get the key," Jaylin said, turning sideways.

"Does it look like I can reach into your pockets to get anything? My hands are full."

"Full with unnecessary stuff that you don't even need. And for the record, I won't be caught dead in that sweater you purchased for me. Who in the hell wears a sweater with a reindeer on it?"

"It's not any ol' reindeer, Jaylin. It's Rudolph the Red-Nosed Reindeer. It was too cute, and I couldn't resist. Now be quiet, put those crappy boots you purchased on the floor, and get the key."

Jaylin dropped two bags on the floor and removed the key from his pocket. When he unlocked the door, he picked up the bags and went inside. I followed him. The condo was dark, but right in front of the fireplace was a table for two with flaming candles on top. A bottle of wine was chilling on ice, and two plates were each covered with a plastic cloche. Jaylin looked at the cozy setup then turned to me.

"What's up with this?" he asked.

"I thought it would be nice if we could have a little love celebration. There's so much that I want to say to you, and I couldn't think of a better way to do it. So go put all of our bags in the bedroom. I'll be waiting for you when you come back."

There was a smirk on Jaylin's face. He happily took our bags to the bedroom, and when he returned, I was standing by the table, tightening the bow on his present, which was already wrapped. I released the bow and pulled the chair back for him.

"Have a seat," I said. "And don't say a word until I'm done."

He sat in the chair, watching my every move. I lifted his cloche, displaying his food on the plate.

"You like your steak medium rare with mushrooms, onions, and cracked pepper on top," I said. "Your baked potato with a hint of salt, no butter. Salad with a vinaigrette dressing and sliced pecans. Drink is Rémy, but we're drinking champagne tonight. Dessert you can't have because you didn't have any for me. Enjoy." I moved to the chair across from him and lifted the cloche over my food. "As for me, I have a chili dog and fries. Nothing special, just wanted to make sure you were good. Are you?"

"That all depends on who cooked this steak. I know Nanny B didn't cook it, and from the looks of it, I'm not so sure. As for me being good, yes, I am. I haven't felt this good in a long time."

Pleased to hear him say that, I took a seat as well. I laid a napkin across my lap then proceeded to tell him what was on my mind. "I haven't felt this good in a long time either, and I want to thank you so much for being there for me once again. You reminded me why I have loved you almost my entire life, and I'm deeply sorry for making you feel as if you didn't matter to me anymore."

Jaylin looked down with a bit of sadness displayed on his face. "You don't have to apologize to me. I'm the one who messed—"

"No, please. Listen and hear me out, okay?"

He lifted his head and nodded.

"I do owe you an apology, only because I purposely wanted you to feel the pain I felt after our divorce. I wanted you to move on and go be with someone else, but had you done that I would've been devastated. So thanks for never losing faith in us. Thank you for knowing and believing that we would one day be here again. Thank you for always helping me stay on my feet, and thank you so much for not falling out of love with me. I'm so ashamed of myself for falling for a man like Travis. I ran from you, thinking, hoping, and praying for a perfect man who didn't exist. In my mind, I made Travis who I wanted him to be. I ignored certain things, and I wound up paying a price for doing so. Now I'm ready to put all of that behind me. I can't really say what the future holds for us, but I do know that it's something good. In the meantime, please allow me time to process everything. I need just a little more time, and I hope you understand why."

Jaylin swallowed hard and cleared his throat. "Baby, take all the time you need. I'm in no rush over here, but my food is getting cold. You do expect me to eat this, don't you?"

I couldn't help but laugh. "Of course I do. Eat all of it, and if you want more, extras are in the fridge."

"Good. And in addition to what you said, thank you too. You saved my life, and I'm not ashamed to say that a life without you isn't worth living at all. Travis is no more, okay? I don't ever want you to feel guilty, ashamed, or foolish for loving him. I want this to be the last time we discuss him, because in doing so he still wins." Jaylin was ready to move on from this conversation. He lifted the neatly wrapped box on the table and shook it. "What's in here? I hope not another one of those sweaters."

"Nope. If you want to know what's in there, you'll have to open it and see."

He ripped the box open, only to find another box that he had to open and another one. When he got to the tiny box, he opened it and saw his wedding ring.

"You can go ahead and put that back on," I said. "It looked nice on your finger, and I have a feeling that you're going to need it in the near future."

He looked at the ring then laid it on the table. "Most likely I will need it, but not like I need a big ol' kiss and hug and booty rub, all of that good stuff, from you right now."

I opened my arms. "Don't sit there then. Come over here and get it."

He got up from the table and so did I. As we embraced each other, Jaylin lowered his hand and squeezed my ass.

"Say, uh, when you said you needed a little more time, were you talking about sex too?" he asked.

I nodded and smiled. "Yes, I was, and I hope you're willing to—"

He silenced me with a kiss. It was a short kiss with a powerful impact. "I hear you, baby," he said. "And I truly meant what I said about taking your time."

We released each other, and ready to tackle his food, he returned to the chair. We chatted more while eating, laughing, and drinking. I couldn't believe when Jaylin complimented the food, though. That was until the entire steak was gone. He griped about the toughness of the steak and said he needed to go brush his teeth.

"After I brush I'm going to take a bath. I know you don't want to join me, but feel free to clean up this mess so I don't have to."

"You can be sure that I will, so go ahead and take your bath. I'll be right on the sofa, chilling and catching up on a book I've been dying to read."

Jaylin headed to the bathroom, and so did I. I washed my hands while he brushed his teeth. After brushing, he stood by the Jacuzzi tub, which was deep and square. It had waterfall faucets on two sides, which released crystal clear water that bubbled from the jets. Jaylin liked his water too hot for me, and as he filled the tub high with water, steam started to fill the bathroom. He removed his clothes, stepping his naked body right in.

"Ahhhhhh. Crank up the music, close the doors, and leave me in peace," he said. "And prepare yourself for a snow fight tomorrow."

"I'm looking forward to it. Maybe then we'll actually learn how to ski."

I left the bathroom and returned to the sitting area. The fire was still burning, and the blaring sound in the background of Miles Davis's horn set the mood. As I started to clean up, I couldn't stop thinking about the man I loved. Jaylin was one in a million for sure. I was so lucky to have him, but I struggled a little with how to move forward. If anyone knew that tomorrow was never promised it was me. I mean, why wait when I had a chance right now to go all in? What was I waiting for? Perfection that I would never get from any man? I wasn't perfect myself, nowhere near it.

After having a tug-of-war with myself, I finished tidying the room then removed my clothes. I relaxed on the chaise section of the sofa, which took up most of the room in the sitting area. Feeling comfortable in my silky skin, I lay back and waited for Jaylin to exit the bathroom. But nearly forty minutes later, he was still in the tub. I wondered what was keeping him, so I tiptoed back to the bathroom to see what had caused the delay. I stepped through the double doors, smiling at the sight of him. He was slumped in the tub, sound asleep. The Jacuzzi jets were still going and tiny bubbles boiled inside of the tub. His head was tilted to the side, his hair was curly and wet, and his tanned body glistened. I stood for a moment in the cloudy, steam-filled room with my arms crossed, thinking about all we'd been through. It was a lot, and every time either of us had slipped away from each other, it always, always resorted to this.

I quietly moved closer to the tub. My mind was consumed with so much enthusiasm for our future. Thinking more about it, I bent over, placing my lips on Jaylin's. His lips were wet and soft to the touch. I thought my kiss would wake him, but with his eyes still closed, he shifted his head to the other side and swallowed. I pressed my lips against his again, this time slipping my tongue between his lips. His eyelids fluttered, and seeing me close to his face, his beautiful gray eyes focused. I rubbed my nose against his.

"Wake up," I said softly. "Do you mind if I join you?"

"The water is still kind of hot because of the heater." He sat up a bit, causing the bubbling water to wave around. "But don't let that stop you."

I eased into the semi-hot water, straddling Jaylin in front. His eyes scanned down my body, and as I lowered myself to sit on top of him, I felt his steel grow immensely.

"Are you sure you're ready for this?" he said. "I'll wait if you're not ready yet."

I showed him how ready I was when I wrapped my arms around his neck and leaned in to kiss him. Our lips smacked, and our tongues slow danced. It felt so good to taste his tongue again. I savored every moment of the sweetness. His hands softly caressed the small of my back. I massaged mine all over his broad shoulders and chest. As the kiss intensified, he backed away from it, bringing my firm breast to his mouth. I sucked in a deep breath, closing my eyes from the feel of him massaging my breasts together and teasing my erect nipples with the tip of his curled tongue. My head dropped back, and the arch in my back was high. My eyes rolled back as I tried to calm the electrifying feeling that was already taking over my body. My nipples couldn't take much more, and when he lowered his tongue to turn circles in my navel, I was slightly relieved.

"Stand up," he whispered. "Because if I enter you now, this will be over in a few minutes."

With his muscle aimed high, I took him at his word. I stood with water raining down on me. Jaylin held a gaze as if he were in a trance again. He signaled what he was about to do by tapping his lips with his fingers. He leaned in, face first, targeting my goods. My leg was lifted, and he placed it on top of the tub. With my pearl peeking through my shaved slit, he took action. My legs instantly weakened, but I ran my fingers through his hair, pulling it at times to stay strong. His twirling tongue worked magic, and with his hands gradually massaging my butt cheeks, there wasn't enough water in this tub to put out the fire I felt building by the minute.

"You're about to get it," I whined and straightened my spine so I wouldn't falter from his swift licks tearing me up.

He backed away from my dripping insides, which moistened his trimmed goatee. I traced it with my manicured fingernail, thinking how much I had missed this. Yes, I missed this more than he would ever know. As he brushed soft kisses on my inner thighs, my legs weakened more. "Hold on," he said between pecks. "Don't give it all to me yet."

His request was difficult to honor, especially with the way his hands roamed all over my body, squeezing me here and there. And when he turned me around so my backside could face him, I had already been schooled on what was coming next. Jaylin parted my cheeks, and to be sure he had access to my hotspots, I bent over, latching my hands on the tub for support. I fully endorsed the way his tongue journeyed through my hole, painting my walls and tickling my spot that made my heartrate pick up speed. My toes curled underwater. My eyes grew wide, and my mouth began to fill with saliva. In a matter of minutes, I rewarded him with creamy fluids that filled his mouth. My body melted right before his eyes. I found myself back in the tub, facing him again with more steam surrounding us. There was silence as we stared at each other, but no words needed to be spoken when our eyes said it all. This was pure love. It felt like love, and I regretted that I had turned my back on true love. I was sure that Jaylin had many regrets too, but we were about to correct our mistakes and live a life that both of us truly deserved.

As I sat comfortably on his lap, his muscle tapped at my door. My folds opened. His steel came in quickly, tearing down my walls and causing me to rise up to the tip of his thick head.

With my hands gripped on each side of the tub again, I glided my goodness up and down, polishing his steel with more cream, giving it a shine. My legs rested along his chest while my feet poured slightly over his strong shoulders. He kissed my feet and lightly rubbed my legs as I kept sucking him in inch by inch. Our eyes remained fixed on each other, but minutes later his eyes lowered to take a glimpse at what was stirring between my legs. He appeared hypnotized, and to calm the intensity of what he was obviously feeling, he slowly shut his eyes. This time his head dropped back. I felt his thick meat pulsating inside of me.

"Nooookea," he moaned and clenched his fingers into my hips. "Do you have any idea whatsoever how much I love you?"

His head straightened, and his eyes opened as he looked at me, awaiting a response. I continued to ride him at a tranquilizing speed but paused just for a minute to respond to his question.

"I know. But you'd better know, trust, and believe that I love you more."

That must've been like music to Jaylin's ears. A smile appeared on his face, and instead of allowing me to have sexual control, he immediately took over. With my goodness still comforting his muscle, his thrusts lifted me up high from the water. He pushed. I pushed back. He pushed again. I returned the favor. Eventually, I stayed up because the feel of his lengthy pipe slipping in and out of me, tickling my spot, garnered a reaction from me. I delicately touched my pearl and widened my mouth to speak out.

"I . . . I can't stop raaaaining," I shouted with tightened fists.

"Rain, baby, rain all over me."

My fluids flowed on him and in the tub. Jaylin kept the rhythmic strokes coming, and the last punch that he delivered caused me to squeeze my eyes and dip my hand in the tub to splash water on myself. I needed to cool down, and so did he. He wrapped his arms around my waist, lifting me out of the tub so there was now no water between us. As he sat his solid frame on top of the tub, I straddled his lap with my legs clamped around him. We kissed feverishly. Our hands roamed everywhere, and his steel slipped right back in.

I braced myself as he stood to get a solid grip on me. And as he stepped away from the tub, his hold on me was tight. My legs were open, and my arms were around his neck. Using much strength, he pulled me slightly back then brought me forth to feel his muscle, which was harder, thicker, and bigger than I had ever felt it before. He carried me while making passionate love to me at the same time. With each step toward the sitting area, where a more romantic setting awaited us, I was on cloud nine.

Jaylin laid me back on the sofa right in front of the fireplace. The crackling sound of the sizzling fire, the strawberry scent of the candles, and his irresistible sexiness drew me right into the moment. My flat stomach trembled as he lay over me, delicately kissing my lips, nipples, and coochie, which was ready for more action. Our eyes locked together again. This time mine were filled with tears. I reached up, rubbing the side of his handsome face. My thoughts turned to how I intended to keep this fire burning. Instead of creating more years filled with drama, it was time to make our years together really count for something.

As Jaylin entered me, I threw one leg over the sofa to widen my legs and satisfy my throbbing pelvis. My hands were clenched on his ass. I forcefully pushed it in so I could suck in every inch of what he was feeding me. With each pleasurable thrust, I could feel his veins gliding against my walls. His muscle dug deeper and deeper to the depths of my soul. My mouth cracked wide open. I loved every bit of the way he made the sweet syrup between my legs flow. I was so hungry for more of him, and as our lips hugged we held an unbreakable gaze into each other's eyes. It was more than love. Black and beautiful love. I was a woman in love with my soul mate, who was never going to leave my side again.

"Are you ready to do this?" he whispered and tapped a spot that set off an explosion.

All I could do was slowly nod. Our euphoric moans echoed loudly, and that was when I started having flashbacks of our time together. Right before my very eyes were reflections of us. As children playing together. As teenagers, walking the halls at school together, laughing, holding hands. As young adults, trying to figure out life and having discussions about our future. Thinking about our wedding day made tears fall from my eyes. I grunted louder, and as I passionately kissed Jaylin, soaking his lips with mine, more tears came when I thought about the day Jaylene was born. Jaylin was so emotional as he witnessed her come into this world. She was the only child he'd seen, but the reason why that was didn't even matter anymore. There was too much good in this relationship to focus on the bad. Too much good like now, the way he flipped my body, placing me on my stomach as I kneeled in front of the chaise. Jaylin kneeled behind me, planting gentle kisses down my spine and delivering smooth moves that made my goodness expand and drip juices all over him.

"I feel you, baby," he whispered as if he had read my mind. "We have so much to be thankful for, don't we? And it's a damn shame what you do to me."

No, it was what he was doing to me that made me push back and increase my pace. That was a hint for him to continue. As he did, I couldn't help but think that if Travis had ended my life that day, this moment would not have come. Jaylin and I had wasted too much time already. There was no more time left trying to figure out why men cheat or why they did this or that. No more time for heated arguments that always brought about pain and tears, no more disputes over kids and money, and no more disrespect that left too many relationships in disarray. It was time to live the best life we could as a couple, and to no surprise, by showering me with these amazing memories for the past several weeks, Jaylin had made me fall in love with him all over again. I knew he could do it, simply because he had the endurance to do anything he put his mind to. That included making real changes for the woman he loved. I was delighted that he had done so for me.

Chapter 23

Scorpio

We were having a fabulous time in Belize, but there was always some unnecessary drama that managed to slip through the cracks. Mario's trick kept calling his cell phone, and instead of turning it off, he kept arguing with her over the baby he claimed wasn't his. I had my doubts, but I wasn't naïve either. If by chance the child was his, it would be his first biological child. That could turn into a little problem for me, so I had to make sure I got ahead of this situation and find out the truth before he did.

While he was out kayak fishing with the kids, I stayed in the cabana to make a call. We were on a private island where fewer than twenty other people joined us. Some had kids, too, so our kids played with theirs. The kids didn't want to go home anytime soon, so our vacation had been extended for a few more weeks. Of course, when

I called Jaylin, he griped about it. But the pleasant conversation between him and Mario had been a good one.

Jaylin told me that he didn't want things to go sour between me and Mario like they had with Travis and Nokea. I didn't know things had gotten bad between them before he was killed. He also told me Nokea was at his house with him. I wondered what that was all about. I figured he had been a shoulder for her to cry on, and now that Travis was clearly out of the picture, Jaylin obviously had made his move.

I pushed that thought to the back of my mind. I didn't have time to think about him and Nokea. Miss Camila was already keeping me busy, and I waited for her to answer the phone. I'd already gathered some information about her, and when I saw several pictures of her, I had to admit that Mario had very good taste in women. She'd been in several beauty pageants but was never a winner. And there were plenty of other photos of her when I Googled her name. She'd dated numerous well-known athletes, and it was apparent that she had a thing for rich men. I didn't knock her for that, but for the time being the only rich man she couldn't have was mine.

"Hello," she said, attempting to sound sexy.

"Camila?"

"Yes, who is this?"

"This is Scorpio Pezzano, Mario's wife. He made me aware of a little incident that happened between the two of you. I would like to know more details about the sudden pregnancy."

The last thing I wanted to be was rude and disrespectful to her. Women always made the mistake of doing that, but all that was going to do was prevent me from getting the information I needed from her. I wanted her to think I was truly concerned about her unfortunate situation. In reality, I was only looking out for me.

"I'm not sure how detailed I can get other than to tell you I'm pregnant with Mario's child. I found this out three weeks after we had sex. I told him right away, but he has doubts about the baby being his."

"Well, considering that sex between the two of you only happened one time, that very well may be hard for him to believe. I'm not saying that it isn't his child. What I'm saying is time will surely tell, and proof will be required."

"I have no problem with that. I told Mario I would do anything to prove that this child is his. He'll soon know the truth. By the way, one time is all it takes. And no offense, but he was pretty excited that night if you know what I mean."

I cringed at her words. I could only imagine what had happened that night. "I'm sure he was

excited, and I'm very disappointed that he felt a
need to go there with you and two other women
the night before our wedding. It was a very stupid mistake that could wind up being costly."

"Normally, I wouldn't do anything like that, but
I had waaaay too much to drink that night. His
father invited me and my friends to come, and
before I knew it, one thing just led to another."

I should have known that his conniving father
had something to do with this. That man was
going to be a real pain in the ass, especially if
this child turned out to be Mario's.

"I definitely know how that can be. Sometimes
things happen, and then you find yourself in
situations like that." I choked on my words. Only
tramps found themselves in situations like that.
"What I would like to do is keep in touch. Mario
says you've been demanding money from him
and making threats about telling me. You don't
have to do that because I'm well aware of what's
going on. I want my husband to do the right
thing if the child is his. So keep my number and
feel free to call me anytime. As soon as Mario
and I get back from vacation, let's do lunch,
okay? Meanwhile, please allow us to enjoy our
vacation in peace. Our children are here with us,
and the interruptions are a little annoying."

There was a long silence before she responded.
"Well, I'm not trying to annoy anyone. I just want

to make sure he takes care of his responsibilities. And I didn't threaten him about money. What I told him was his child will need to be well taken care of. I will have it no other way."

I rolled my eyes. Mario surely had me in a situation that I didn't want to be in, but for the time being, I would deal with it.

"As I said before, I understand how you feel. You won't have any problems with him stepping up to do what is necessary. If you want peace and solutions going forward, I suggest you speak to me. Mario isn't real happy about all of this right now. All you're going to get from him is disrespect. So again, let's talk when I get back from vacation. Okay?"

"That's fine. See you soon, I hope."

The call ended there, leaving me in deep thought. I had been that other woman before, had been that little thorn in the side, and had been that bitch who many people simply wanted to go away. In this case, however, Mario nor Camila would win. I'd make sure of that.

We returned home nearly two weeks later. I was still riding high from our vacation. The kids were with Jaylin and Nokea. She had officially moved back in with him. I couldn't say that I was surprised, because I wasn't. I always expected the two of them would get back together, and whether Travis was dead or alive, it would have eventually happened. In no way did it pain me anymore to say this, but I was happy for them. My feelings for Jaylin would always remain, but when you know where a man's heart is, it's best to let go and stop yours from breaking into a thousand pieces. I didn't want any more heartbreak. That was why it was so important for me to expeditiously deal with this situation with Mario and move on from it if I had to.

I had reached out to Camila again and was on my way to a restaurant to meet with her. Even though I'd seen her picture, thoughts of what she looked like in person consumed my mind, and I wondered if she had ever seen me. I was sure to make myself look flawless today, and displaying much self-assurance I walked into the restaurant with my head held high. Like always, approval was granted by the men who watched me as I made my way to the table where Camila sat. My hips swayed from side to side. Even she couldn't keep her eyes off me. She greeted me with a fake smile. I shot her one in return. The first thing I thought was that she was cute, but in no way was she as gorgeous as me.

"Hello, Scorpio," she said, extending her hand to mine. "Thanks for inviting me to come here."

"No problem." I shook her hand, but when my eyes dropped to her belly, which clearly showed she was pregnant, I eased my hand away. "Nice to meet you. Sit down and let's talk."

Camila took a seat, and within a few seconds, she started giving me the scoop. "I'm surprised you didn't bring Mario with you. I've spoken to him since the two of you have been back from vacation, but I didn't tell him we were meeting. Did you?"

I was surprised to hear she had spoken to him, but my expression showed that it didn't bother me. "I'm glad the two of you had another chance to talk. I expect for you to keep him informed about the baby, and you should, especially if he's the father."

"He is the father," she confirmed. "We didn't necessarily talk about the baby. We spoke about something else."

See, I hated to play games with silly women. She was beating around the bush, hoping that I would sit here and beg her for information. That wasn't going to happen. She was dealing with a pro at this. The sooner she realized it, the better off she would be.

"I'm not concerned about the details of your conversation with Mario, and as I said when we talked before, my concern revolves around your child. The baby will determine how I intend to move forward in my marriage. If it is his child, I have plans that will make me a very happy woman, possibly you too."

The smile on her face grew wide. She was beaming even more. I could already sense that getting me out of the picture was her goal. She reached into her purse, pulling out a small recorder.

"I know you said you're not concerned about what Mario and I discussed, but just so you know that I'm not the one pursuing and bugging him all the time, I wanted you to hear this."

She hit the play button, and we both sat silently, listening to Mario speak. "Hey, babe," he said. "I'm home now, so when you want to talk, let's talk. I can come over there, or you can meet me somewhere private. I've been missing you a lot, and we need to talk about what to do when my child is born. I can't make you any promises because I do love my wife. But I'm finding myself thinking more about us, too."

Camila clicked the stop button and looked at me across the table, probably searching for tears. What she saw was me blushing and thinking about my exit plan. Unfortunately, I had to wait until the baby was born. That way, I could pretend to be the distraught wife who was damaged beyond repair and whose husband had truly wronged her. I expected for Mario to give me more ammunition, and stupid Camila would provide me with all the evidence I needed to build my case against him.

"If you don't mind," I said, holding out my hand, "can I have that recorder? I won't share it with Mario, but I need it for closure in the near future."

She didn't hesitate to give it to me. She wanted me out of the picture soon. This time, I didn't mind giving up my spot in the bedroom. I started to see what kind of man my husband truly was, so she could happily go live in hell with him. Until everything was finalized, I'd keep my spot warm for her.

"Thanks for giving this to me." I tossed the recorder in my purse. "And any time you want to let me know what Mario is doing behind my back, please call me. I can't stay for lunch, because my housekeeper sent me an important message about the kids. I am, however, glad we had a chance to meet, and this time lunch is on me."

I gave Camila twenty bucks to take care of her meal. She kept checking me out, staring as if something was wrong.

"Are you okay?" I asked.

"I . . . I'm fine. You're just so pretty. I didn't think you would look like this. Mario should be ashamed of himself for betraying a woman like you."

I looked at her, thinking about what an idiot she was. Mario would run all over this fool for sure. "I'm more than just a pretty woman. Simply gorgeous would classify me much better. My pussy tastes pretty good, too, and I'm a lot brighter than you may think. But none of that matters when it comes to men like Mario. It doesn't matter to most men, so I advise you to wise up soon, because that baby in your stomach will not stop him from dragging you through the gutter." I bent over, whispering close to her ear. "Remember this though: when a cheating, no-good motherfucker go low, you go high, real high, and know that the sky is your limit."

I had no other advice to offer her. Hopefully, she understood. I waved with my fingers as I left the restaurant and headed home to play the good wife role for my husband. The second I walked through the door, I saw him chilling by the pool. He was pouring himself a drink. I asked him to pour me one too.

"Vodka and cranberry juice would be nice," I said, squinting as I glanced at the bright sun. "What a beautiful day it is, isn't it?"

"Indeed it is. Why don't you go put on your bikini and swim with me? Then we can have dinner and go dancing at Rizzo's."

I threw my arms around Mario, giving him a juicy kiss. "That sounds great, and since I'm in a good mood, why don't we throw in a little car shopping, too? I also want to get Mackenzie something special for her birthday. You don't mind if we go look for her something, do you?" *Hey, gotta look out for the kids, too,* I thought as Mario handed me the glass of vodka.

"Of course I don't mind. Just hurry up and go change."

I sipped from the glass then placed it on top of the bar. While prancing away from Mario, I damn near danced my way inside. He had no idea what was about to come. I would choose money over marriage for sure, and for the first time in my life, I would have the wealth my heart had always desired. No, I wasn't a gold digger. Referring to me as one would be incorrect. What I was and always had been was a woman who made decisions that I thought were best for me and my kids, who sometimes utilized my goodness to get what I wanted, and who refused to allow wealthy and broke-ass men to have their cake and eat it, too, without giving up something in return. There was a reason I often required a man with money, and this was it. And if more women thought like I did, they could be on top of the world too instead of dealing with slick men who often left a trail of broken hearts. Jaylin had done enough to wake my ass up, and at this point, Camila's baby couldn't get here fast enough.

Chapter 24

Jaylin

Nokea and I returned home to energetic kids and a nanny who was delighted to see us. The only person missing was Nokea's mother, but in due time we expected her to make a move this way. Meanwhile, I had my baby officially back at home with me. She wasn't going anywhere this time, and it was left up to me to make sure I handled my business and treated her like the queen she truly was. I too reflected on our relationship quite often. Why did Black Love have to be so difficult? Too many mistakes had been made, but I was glad we were able to finally understand why this journey had been chosen for us. Timing was everything, too, and the man so many women wanted me to be during a certain period in my life, I couldn't be. Change for everyone comes at different times, and realistically speaking, age isn't always the number-one factor that brings about change. I just had to get real with myself, finally take responsibility for all that I'd done, and I realized that I never, ever wanted to lose Nokea again. She was and always had been my biggest blessing. Believe it or not, I had been hers too. And as we sat on the beach, watching the kids play volleyball, she admitted it.

"Did I tell you how thankful I am for you today?" she asked.

"Nope, but what exactly are you thankful for?"

With her white bikini on, she stood and started massaging my shoulders. A floppy straw hat was on her head, and a smile was etched across her face. "I'm thankful that you're going to help me accomplish one more little task on my bucket list."

I cocked my stiff neck from side to side. "No, Nokea, I'm done. I promise you I am done with your bucket list, with the exception of building the kids a treehouse."

"Awwww," she whined. "It was only one more little thing. At least you should find out what it is before you shut me down."

"I don't care what it is. I'm sure it has something to do with me jumping from somewhere, risking my life, or getting run over by a train."

She laughed. "Come on, Jaylin. I wouldn't ask you to tie yourself to a train track, so stop being ridiculous."

"Then what is it?"

"Are you sure you want to know?"

"I really don't. I'm pretending like I care just to stay on your good side."

She laughed again and released her hands from my shoulders. She then gave me a piece of paper, telling me to open it. The title read, "Bucket List Finale." Underneath it, she had written, "Become Mrs. Jaylin Jerome Rogers again. Legally!"

This time, I laughed and tossed the paper back to her. "Nope. You can't have my name again. Not after the way you broke my heart when you divorced me. In case you forgot, I cried and everything."

"Poor baby," she said, giggling. "I'm so sorry, but you, uh, did make me go there."

"Maybe so, but why do you want my name again? What benefit is it to you, legally?"

She started massaging my shoulders again. "Please. Do you have to ask? Being Mrs. Rogers again will enable me to inherit your good fortune should something unfortunate happen to you. It will allow me to compete with Scorpio, and if she can have it all like she does, why can't I?"

I turned my head sideways to look at her. "You need to come up with a better reason than that. I'm not feeling your answer."

"Okay. Maybe you'll feel this. Being your wife would be an honor. I would be sooo happy, and no one could tell me anything because I would be married to the sexiest, most intelligent, super loving, richest, romantic, God-fearing, and hand-somest man I know."

I smiled and nodded. "Keep it coming, baby. Make the case for why you want to be Mrs. Rogers."

She made the case by lightly smacking me on my head. "Forget it," she said. "Don't worry about it. I'm good as is."

I pulled her into my arms and laid her across my lap. I kissed her at least a thousand times before telling her the pleasure would be all mine. I offered her real change this time, and two days later she was legally given my name again.

Nearly a year after that, Scorpio divorced Mario and found her happily ever after with Mr. Money. It was the one thing, the only thing, she loved more than me and Mario put together. Kudos to her for learning some valuable lessons from our relationship and for making me even richer than I already was.

I finally got my happily ever after too, and perfect or predictable ending or not, we deserved to be happy. I wasn't so sure if we would ever reach this point in our lives, and in no way would I ever allow this story to fully depict the true pain I experienced from losing the woman I loved. Nokea, however, came through for me. We never knew that our love story would wind up being this interesting, but it is my hope that the message from *Naughty* came across loud and clear. What you dish out will come right back to you, and change can only happen when one is ready. Relationships aren't always easy. Shit can get real messy at times. But whenever you find love, be patient with it, enjoy it, and more than anything, respect it.